WHISPERS
ON
MAIN STREET

MARIE
O'CONNOR

POOLBEG
CRIMSON

Published 2024 by Crimson

an imprint of Poolbeg Press Ltd.

123 Grange Hill, Baldoyle,

Dublin 13, Ireland

Email: poolbeg@poolbeg.com

ISBN 978-1-78199-6966

www.poolbeg.com

ABOUT THE AUTHOR

Having worked as a digital editor in television and as a window dresser for a leading high-street retailer, being creative on a daily basis was literally part of Marie O'Connor's job. Marie possesses a natural joie de vivre and sense of adventure which she has always reflected in her writing. Having grown up in the countryside in the west of Ireland, she spent several years living in Dublin but is presently living and working in Galway City.

ACKNOWLEDGEMENTS

Thank you to my publisher Paula Campbell and my editor Gaye Shortland, at Poolbeg, for their continued enthusiasm, advice and guidance, bringing only the very best out in this story.

DEDICATION

To my late beloved father.
Thank you for all the tales of yore.
See, Dad, I was listening.

CHAPTER 1

The Travelling Shop

December 1961

Ignatius Wheatley sold everything. Ropes for pulling calves. String for pulling teeth. Gloves for pulling weeds and more importantly he had a great sense of humour for pulling people's legs and participated wholeheartedly in all of the above, if needed.

Ignatius, or 'Nate' as he was known locally, was in the grocery business which was a mobile one. Five days a week he travelled across the length and breadth of central Mayo in his quirky, purple truck which was uniquely adorned on each side by a yellow dragon motif. From it he sold groceries at the homesteads of his long-served customers. Most of Nate's customers were women, and the elderly who could not drive. Even though in 1961 motorcars were becoming more common, they were seized by the men of the house who drove them to work. In these situations, the travelling shop was a blessing. The nearest shop in these rural country villages could be several miles away and, while walking or cycling to them, one could endure bad weather and wet, muddy roads. Even a small provision can become cumbersome and a nuisance when carrying it for a few miles and it could be a physical struggle to carry heavier goods home. The basics like paraffin oil, a bag of flour or potatoes, washing powder, hairy bacon and a small turnip could pull the arms of the most agile while walking for a lengthy period of time.

Saturdays, Nate drove nowhere. He made sure the truck was maintained with oil, water and fuel. He did an inventory on his goods and stocked up on the items that were running low. He went into the town of Castlebar and paid some of his suppliers, while getting more provisions if needed. Then, every Saturday evening he had a big dinner as prepared by his wife, Babs, and a bath as prepared by his wife, Babs. Fresh-looking for fifty, he brylcreemed his strawberry-blond hair and pulled on his tweed jacket with the leather elbow patches. Always inclined to be rotund, his sedentary occupation didn't help his circumference but all in all his big frame carried him well. After sprucing himself up, he would walk into Slattery's bar in a blaze of glory in his own local small town, Ballantur. Everyone there enjoyed being in his company. He had all the news from around the place and if you wanted to know anything Nate was the one to ask and he glowed in that capacity.

"God, you're a great man for the news, Nate!"

"You're better than any newspaper!"

"Radio 1 couldn't keep up with you!"

"Well, I never knew that!"

"Ah, stop, will you – you're joking!"

This was the type of reverence he received and he revelled in the uniqueness of his position. He believed himself to be important, a necessity to the locals in the trade of news and information. Rarely would he concede to calling it gossip – which it was, truthfully. He never questioned the reliability of the source of his information and was disingenuously prone to adding a few white lies to it if he felt the tale needed to be fattened up a bit.

He was a newshound for all personal and professional developments around the place. On the subject of births, he would know if it was a boy or a girl, what side of the family it was the cut of and whether it was "a butterfly" or "a bruiser". On funerals, even if there was an attendance of a thousand people, Nate was the one who would comment on who wasn't there and why they should have been there. On jobs, he knew who got one and more importantly who got it for them and lent his opinion on the person "not being cut out for it at all", "a dead pair of hands on him", and "sure the father never showed him how to work – he wouldn't move muck from a hobby horse".

A lot of his customers would gather together at a crossroads central to their respective townlands. While Nate had no difficulty driving to their individual houses for their own comfort and ease, sometimes they preferred the central location as it provided a social gathering for the ladies, who looked forward to meeting the other womenfolk and it was a welcome communal break from surly husbands, feral children and overbearing, elderly in-laws.

Now, it is universally accepted that women love to gossip. And it was through no fault of their own that these local ladies indulged in what was exercised throughout the country, with their husbands gone to work in towns or labouring in fields. For a lot of the time these ladies were on their own and this might be the extent of their social outings. The minimal rural group who might live in the heart of a village with a pub, school, shop, church and village hall were lucky. An annual sports day, market or a '25 Drive' card game even though they might have little interest in it, was alluring for some shared company and enjoyment. There is never an ill wind that doesn't blow in the right direction for someone. A funeral could provide an outing with a very rewarding chat and refreshments afterwards. Even a day in the bog, hayfield or the arrival of a trashing machine could deliver a meeting of minds. Every opportunity had to be capitalised on. Telephones were few and far between and usually the owner of such a technical advantage could somehow unfortunately become the target of a grudge. Letters were still the main form of communication and the postman, like Nate, provided more than a basic delivery service. He provided a human contact, vital to so many in these isolated areas.

Nate's contribution to the relaying of news and information was considerable. He might be the only person many of these country folk saw on a weekly basis. Therefore their need and desire to offload and receive news was absorbing. Sometimes they gave Nate a nugget of news and they marvelled at how much the story would have developed and grown by the time Nate returned the following week. They would be proud of their creation. So much so that one could easily believe they conjured these tales up just for sheer entertainment and devilment. Nate was equally guilty for indulging them. He could have selective hearing for intentional naivety just so he could misinterpret what he was hearing to spice it up and give it legs before communicating it further. This practice was a prime example of Chinese Whispers – where a sentence is spoken, passed on, added to and has the potential of returning nothing like it originally started out.

When the men returned home from work in the evenings the women would be dying to share the "news". And be it sad, curious, strange or funny, sometimes it made more of an emotional impact on them than anything they had experienced all day at their mundane work. Not that the men were not capable of furnishing their own gossip and transmitting it but, with their minds focused on their work, there was little time to be conjuring up stories and passing them on. The women, on the other hand, were naturally more susceptible to frivolous and trivial details and had a wonderful capacity to dissect them anally while at the same time inflate them completely out of proportion.

But, aside from all of that, Nate's primary service was providing much-needed food and provisions to these customers who had no means of acquiring them themselves. Nate's decent and caring side was evident when, without question or nosiness, if a customer wanted to pass a genuine message to someone on Nate's run he would do it for them willingly.

The exchanges between Nate and his customers always played out in the same way. Subdued to juicy.

"How'ya, Nate."

"How'ya, Pa."

"How are things?"

"Not too bad."

"Awful weather."

"Ah, you wouldn't put an iron gate out in it."

"Any news?"

"Not a bit."

"Will you give me two pounds of bacon – how are you anyway?"

"Good now, can't complain."

"And a head of cabbage. Anything strange with you anyhow?"

"No, not really, all is quiet."

"I'll take six eggs off you too."

"How's your new neighbour up there, Pa?"

"The German lady? Oh, you won't get much news out of her, she keeps to herself. She's after getting a Pomeranian but I suppose he'll keep her company. And a packet of Rich Tea biscuits."

"Have you seen him?"

"Not much. Just knocking around the house with her – oh, a half pound of cheese too."

"Is that all, Pa?"

"That's all, Nate."

And then later:

"Hello, Mrs Devaney."

"Hello, Nate."

"How are you?"

"I'm grand, thanks."

"Awful weather."

"Ah, you wouldn't put a Russian soldier out in it."

"Any news with you?"

"Devil a bit – can I have a pound of rashers and a pound of sausages and a ring of black pudding? Any news with yourself?"

"Not much now."

"I need a bag of flour and a pound of butter. How is Pa Leonard keeping? Any news with him?"

"He's good. He told me the German lady, Mrs. Huber, has a lodger."

"Really?"

"Yeah, he's a Pomeranian."

"God! Where is he from?"

"I don't know. Pomerania, I suppose."

Meanwhile, in the town of Castlebar an interrogation of another sort was going on.

"Yes, Mam ... I know ... I'll do the best I can ... don't be giving out to me ... I'd love to be home for Christmas too ... I'm starting a new job, Mam. I'm the last person to get time off. Oh, come on, there'll be other gardaí working in that station for years and they'll get first preference, not me. Oh God, Mam, I have to go! My bus is coming."

Caitlín Kennedy dropped the receiver, dashed out of the phone box and ran to catch the bus to Ballantur.

Twenty minutes later she arrived there on a murky, drizzly afternoon. After getting directions, ironically from a German lady walking her dog, she walked the short distance to the small cottage she was renting on the outskirts of the town. The one-storey cottage was impressive on the outside, neatly kept and very well painted in whitewash with a red timber door and red window frames. Smoke billowed from the chimney where someone had lit a fire to welcome her. She could smell the turf and it reminded her of home. She put her hand in her pocket to take out the key which the owner had previously posted to her, but her heart sank when she couldn't feel it. Oh Jesus, she thought, where the hell is it? Then instantly in her mind's eye she could see it on the ledge in the phone box in Castlebar. She had taken it out of her pocket when she was looking for change and was foostering with it in her hand while being distracted by her mother's lament.

She looked around the front of the cottage and noticed that a top window pane was pulled open. She convinced herself she could fit through it. Turning her navy suitcase on its side, she used it as leverage to push herself up on the windowsill and grasp the inner frame. On the count of three, she heaved herself through it and found herself stuck halfway in and halfway out. She then realised what a ill-conceived notion this had been. She couldn't balance herself enough to push herself back out, nor could she use anything on the inside to pull herself in without falling headfirst on the hard, flagstone floor. Her stomach muscles were aching from supporting her dangling body each side of the window. Oh God, what am I am going to do now, she asked herself, panicking.

"*Stop it right there!*" came a male voice from outside.

Oh fuck, she thought in shame, acutely aware her skirt was blown up around her waist with the wind and she could feel the cold air on her exposed legs and backside.

"*Don't move, you are under arrest!*" said the male voice which was very near her now.

"*I can't move! I'm stuck!*"

She was more relieved than embarrassed now to have assistance because the searing pain in her stomach was more than she could bear. She resigned herself to accepting any sort of help, regardless of the price of the exposure.

The gentleman who berated her walked up to the front door and went inside. She could hear its creaking frame being pushed open. Then he, in a Garda uniform, was standing in front of her.

"OK," he said calmly. "Give me your two hands and I'll pull you in slowly."

Caitlín said nothing but complied. The garda caught her two hands and pulled her down towards him. She landed forcefully against him and they locked eyeball to eyeball. She knew her face was crimson.

"Oh thank you! I am so sorry. I got stuck. I couldn't get in, or out," she said.

"Save it, you are still under arrest for breaking and entering into these premises."

"I wasn't breaking in! I had a key, but I left the flipping thing in a phone box in Castlebar!"

"But, sure, the door was open. Why did you need a key?"

"Well, I didn't know it was open! Why did the owner send me a key if I didn't need it?" Caitlín was becoming frustrated at the situation as it unfolded before her.

"A likely story! Come on, you're coming to the station."

"*What?* Are you charging me?"

"Well, if the crime fits, as they say," he said, ushering her out the door.

"Hang on, let me explain, you won't believe this but –"

"Plenty of time to explain when we get to the station."

"Right, well, if that's the way you want it, that's fine with me!" snapped Caitlín, secretly satisfied that this was going to end a lot better for her than for him.

Following a short and silent journey in the Garda car to the station, the garda marched Caitlín inside. All the staff stopped what they were doing immediately, sensing the tension.

"Well, what have you brought us, Garda Tully?" enquired Sergeant Lamb who was in charge of the station.

"Caught red-handed this one was, trying to break into Lowes' cottage through the front window in broad daylight!"

Sergeant Lamb fixed his gaze on Caitlín. "So, let's hear it. How are you going to justify your actions, young lady?" he asked smugly.

"I was in a phone box in Castlebar when suddenly my bus arrived. I dashed out and left my key to the cottage beside my change at the phone. I am renting Lowes' cottage because I start my new job here in the town tomorrow. My name is Caitlín Kennedy. *Garda* Caitlín Kennedy."

"*Ha, ha, ha!*" laughed Sergeant Lamb. "Well, the circus has come to town! We have one clown making a false arrest and another breaking the law. Kennedy! Be here tomorrow morning at nine sharp. Oh, and come in the door, not the window!"

All the staff in the room burst out laughing.

When Sergeant Lamb had left, Garda Tully approached Caitlín.

"Why didn't you say something?" he said crossly. "You made us both look like idiots."

"I tried to tell you but you wouldn't listen to me. Forget it." She walked out the door.

Finding a local shop on her way back, she bought a few essentials like tea, milk, bread and jam. But she didn't feel that hungry anymore. Her appetite had died, like the fire in the cottage which she left abandoned.

She didn't sleep very well that night and she had torrents in her stomach from anxiety when she woke the next morning.

She needn't have worried, though, as all her apprehension about what kind of welcome she would receive today at that station was instantly squashed the minute she arrived.

The station was a hive of its limited activity. A Superintendent and two colleagues were already in situ, having just arrived from Headquarters in Dublin. Caitlin didn't know if this visit was scheduled or not.

"Ah, Garda Kennedy!" exclaimed Sergeant Lamb. "Let me introduce you to Superintendent Ruane. Superintendent, we are indeed delighted and honoured that Bangharda Caitlín Kennedy, one of the first women gardaí recruited in the country, has been assigned to us at our station here in Ballantur."

The Superintendent smiled and nodded in her direction.

God, Lamb has changed his tune, the prick, thought Caitlín to herself.

"Now," continued Sergeant Lamb, "we've got a tip-off that an illegal alcohol production in our community is currently in operation, so I am dispatching Garda Tully and Garda Kennedy to investigate this immediately. It's an obvious grab so I expect both of you to be back here again in jig time, with both evidence and culprits apprehended."

"Good morning," Caitlín said as she joined Seán Tully in the car.

"Morning," he replied quietly.

"I think we should start over," said Caitlín.

"OK, but let's do that later. We really need to deliver this one, especially with the Head Honcho down from Dublin. If you think Lamb was a short fuse yesterday, he'll turn into a bloody lion today if we don't close this down."

The location of the purported illegal activity was at the homestead of Waxy Carolan, a man of questionable character. A steep hill descended down to his yard so Garda Tully turned the engine off and let the car roll down so Waxy and his accomplices would not hear them arriving. An old rundown house and a couple of old stone sheds, just about propping up orange galvanised roofs and broken doors, occupied the enclosure. A trail of steam was emanating from a hole in the barn adjacent to the house.

The two gardaí gently closed over their car doors and took very slow, steady footsteps in the direction of the barn door.

In unison they looked and nodded at each other before suddenly shoving the door ajar in one swift heave.

Mouths hit the dirty floor inside as Waxy and his two assistants, near the still, stood stunned by this sudden incursion.

"You're under arrest for the illegal production of unauthorised alcohol with the intent to sell for monetary gain," said Caitlín firmly, impressing Garda Tully with her no-nonsense direct approach.

"*Ah ha, ha, ha!*" responded Waxy in a scolding laugh. "Well, look who it is! Tweedledum and Tweedledee. How did ye manage this on your own? Did a British spy, a fortune teller or divine intervention bring you here?"

"You are under arrest, Waxy," said Tully. "Now start dismantling this equipment immediately because we are confiscating it."

"*Con-va-skate*? Now what does that mean?" enquired Waxy mockingly.

"You know well what it means – we're taking this as evidence and any more of it you have," said Caitlín.

Waxy stared at the ground for a moment, mentally weighing up his options.

Caitlín watched him. He definitely had a bad-boy swagger about him. He wore a full-length coat on his tall frame which created a denbonair look. His peaked cap nearly covered his wispy hair but most of all he possessed what every woman envied – long eyelashes!

Slowly he lit a cigarette and then, with the help of his two friends, started to dismantle the still, pipe and tank, spilling its contents onto the ground outside. Then, stepping aside, they watched the gardaí place everything in the boot of their car.

"Waxy, if you have any more of this equipment, or a set-up in a location other than in this barn, now is time to tell us about it," said Tully.

Caitlín was standing close to Waxy and could sense his defeat.

"I'll ask you again," said Tully. "You're already in serious trouble here and if it transpires that you did not disclose all of your illicit operations at this point in time you will face further charges."

Waxy looked at this two friends and then admitted that he had more equipment in another shed. "It's up that boreen," he said, pointing, "but you won't be able to drive up there – it's too overgrown."

"No bother at all, Waxy," said Tully, picking up the handles of a squeaky wheelbarrow in the yard. "You lead the way."

"Wait here, you two! Don't even think about going anywhere," Caitlín warned the two accomplices.

Tully and Caitlín started to follow Waxy up the unkempt lane.

Ten minutes later the two gardaí and Waxy re-emerged from the bushy overgrowth of the boreen. Tully was out of breath from pushing rusty old machinery that had not been used in a really long time. Caitlin had ruined her new uniform, carrying more of the same.

"I'm telling you honestly it's not worth taking that stuff – it hasn't been used in years," pleaded Waxy. "Look at the rust on it! It would kill a camel if he drank out of it, never mind a human."

"People could be dying already with the unregulated stuff you're making," said Tully.

"No, he's right. Leave that rubbish there, Tully – we won't fit any more in the car anyway," said Caitlín. "Right, get in the back seat, you lot – we're going to the station where you'll all be formally charged."

Tully and Caitlín sat into the car, smiled at each other in satisfaction and sped off.

Sergeant Lamb, Superintendent Ruane and other staff members had already stepped outside on hearing the car approach. Caitlín couldn't stop smiling when she saw them.

"Well, Superintendent," said Sergeant Lamb, "we've had a very productive morning here in our sleepy little town, although it could be that everyone is sleeping off the hangovers they've been getting from this rural menace." He nodded in the direction of the three dishevelled suspects who were now standing at the wall.

"Right," he continued, "open the boot, Kennedy, and let's see the fruits of your labour."

But the fruits of their labour withered like the blood running from their faces.

In fact, the fruits had vanished altogether. There was absolutely nothing in the boot except a small bottle of poitín with a note on it saying '*You might need a drop of this*'.

"What the hell is going on?" enquired the Superintendent. "Where is the big haul you've been telling me about all morning?"

"*You bloody scumbags!*" shouted Caitlín at the three accused. "The other shed was nothing but a decoy, Waxy! Your two mates opened the boot and took everything out while you had us on a wild goose chase up that boreen!"

"Don't know what you're talking about, Garda. All I know is that you two arrived on my property, arrested me and my two friends with no evidence of anything to charge us with."

"But we saw it with our own eyes!" retorted Tully.

"I don't know about that, Garda. I think you two have been indulging in harmful illegal alcohol yourselves. You'd want to be careful – apart from the delusions, that stuff could kill you, you know!"

"*You slimly so and so!*" said Caitlín, lunging at Waxy out of humiliation and anger, but she was restrained by Tully.

"Oh Jesus, and now assault by a garda on a civilian! Did you see that, Superintendent? You must be very proud of her!" said Waxy, laying it on.

"Take the suspects inside," instructed the Superintendent.

Once they were led away, he turned around to the stunned gardaí.

"Proud? Proud? I have never been so ashamed and disappointed by my representatives. What a bloody shambles! The task was very straightforward to execute. They could have been caught red-handed. Case closed. But ye couldn't even manage that!"

"But they *were* caught red-handed!" pleaded Caitlín.

"The only thing you should be, Garda Kennedy, is red-faced after this fiasco today. You will be reprimanded for this. Paperwork, I think, will be your forte in this station. Now, excuse me, gentlemen, but I have a big bloody journey back to Dublin to write a big long bloody report on the incompetence of this station."

After the Superintendent's car sped away, Tully pulled Caitlín by the arm. "Don't worry, Caitlín, we won't let Waxy get away with this."

The rest of the day at the station was a long one. Caitlín and Tully were brought into the Sergeant's office and got the faces eaten off them, he was so furious.

Caitlín returned to her desk and placed her cap on it. She wanted to go home and crawl into the bed. Under the bed. What a start to the day, what a start to her new job! Sheer humiliation and all she wanted to do *was* her job.

"*Caitlín!*" called Tully. "*Caitlín!*"

"What?"

"Sergeant Lamb wants to see you again."

"For what?"

"I don't know."

Great – is one roasting not enough to get on one day? She started to get nervous and that sick feeling came back into her stomach.

When she turned around, Sergeant Lamb was standing at reception.

"Now, Kennedy," he began, "I have a new assignment for you. Do you think you are ready for it? I mean, so soon after your debacle this morning?"

"Yes, of course, Sergeant," she said eagerly.

"It's a tough one, a bit sticky – I'm not sure if you're up to it," he continued, screwing up his face in a mocking manner.

"I am, sir."

"Right. Go down the town and fetch myself and the lads a few iced buns from the shop for the tea, like a good girl. Tully will give you a bit of change from the kitty."

As her mouth dropped open, they all sniggered at her expense.

Pig, I hope he chokes on it, she thought to herself.

Caitlín got the buns and even a sample slice of Christmas cake from Cassie Quirke, the owner of one of the two grocery shops in the town, a formidable single lady who was a magnet for gossip and all the news. She always wore a functional housecoat over her jumper, skirt and ankle boots but endeavoured to glam herself up a bit with a sliver of red lipstick. She told Caitlín if she liked the cake to get her order in as soon as possible because they'd sell out very fast. She didn't. She bought a packet of cigarettes instead.

She sat outside on the wall, eating her own bun. She couldn't bear to go back to the station again so soon. Then she decided to have a cigarette too. She hadn't smoked in ages but today she felt so tense, she needed something.

A very vulnerable-looking man came around the corner of the wall.

"Hello," said Caitlín.

The man just walked by her and sat on the steps of the cross in the square. Charming, she thought, so much for being friendly.

What Caitlín didn't know was that the man who passed her by was known locally as "Mutey", an uninspired name for sure as the poor man was mute. He had lived in the town all his life. His immediate family had all moved away so he led a minimal existence. He had never received much of an education because of his disability so he was raised to make his own way in life. He grew all his own potatoes and vegetables like most of his neighbours, but he had the added bonus of being a good fisherman too, be it on lakes or rivers. He had a modest income from giving his vegetables, hen eggs and fish to Nate who sold them on to his customers on his behalf. He also set up a stall on market day in the town. He was a quiet and shy man but was dear to the local community who knew that there was no harm in him and pitied the disability which left him with a lifelong cross to bear.

Caitlín's observation of the silent man was interrupted by a familiar voice. Waxy's. She heard it as he came out of Quirke's shop door. He didn't see her. He and his cronies from earlier sat on the wall at the other side of the shop. She was out of his sight and she began to wonder what kind of a man he was.

On paper Waxy Carolan and Mutey were cut from the same cloth but sewn into very different costumes. Both men came from homes of poverty. Waxy had a sister. His father emigrated to England and in the beginning, when the children were small, he came home when he could to see them but as the years went on he rarely came home at all, to the point of no return. So Waxy went through his formative years without a father figure. He had no one to show him how to do anything. He was a poor student with no aptitude for learning or reading books and left school early. He relied on neighbours to give him some manual labour until their compassion ran out due to his poor timekeeping and laissez-faire attitude. Since his mother passed away and his sister married he had been on his own and left to his own devices to fend for himself. As a result, producing illegal alcohol was just one of many illicit operations he had undertaken. He allegedly had at one point transported and sold contraband cigarettes and rumour had it he also smuggled guns across the country into Northern Ireland.

But despite his and Mutey's mutual circumstances, there was a big difference between the two men. Mutey had decided that, despite the hand of cards he had been dealt, he was going to live a life as normal and productive as God willing he could. Waxy decided to take revenge on his unfair position in life and let all his anger and hate consume him and that continued to lead him along a troublesome and unremorseful path.

Under Caitlín's current observation Waxy finished eating an apple he had bought in the shop. The local postman, Sammy Joyce, was cycling up the street. Then, suddenly and for no reason other than Waxy being Waxy, he flung the butt of the apple at Mutey who was sitting peacefully on the steps.

"*Hey!*" shouted the postman who'd had to duck to get out of the line of fire.

"*Mutey!*" called out Waxy. "*Ya dumb fuck!*"

The apple had hit Mutey on the head, knocking his woollen hat off. Waxy and his cronies thought this was hilarious.

Sammy Joyce dropped his bike, walked over to Waxy, grabbed him by the collar of his coat and pulled down him off the wall.

"Oh, you're the bastard, you are!" said Sammy. "Can you not leave the poor man alone? What has he ever done to you? It's not the first time you've picked on him, you scumbag!"

Caitlín ran to separate them.

Poor Mutey took off, afraid of the trouble he might be causing.

"OK, that's enough!" Caitlín said as she tried to insert herself between the two confrontational men. "Waxy, you are under arrest!"

"For what? This ass just attacked me!"

"You provoked him by nearly knocking him off his bicycle and, more seriously, you assaulted that poor man sitting there."

"Are you joking me? Mutey? I just threw an apple-butt at him. It was only a bit of craic."

Caitlín stood firm and said nothing. Waxy picked his tweed peaked cap up off the ground and dusted it off.

"You just have it in for me now, lady. Two arrests in one day. Well, let's see you make a balls of this one too."

"Shut up, Waxy – you're nothing more than a bully." Caitlín put a pair of handcuffs on him.

"Are you alright, sir?" she enquired of the postman.

"I'm grand and my name is Sammy Joyce, miss."

"Well, *Sammy Joyce*, if I go down for this you'll be one sorry man!" threatened Waxy.

Caitlín looked across the square as she pushed Waxy up the road towards the station. There was no sign of Mutey.

"Is this déjà vu from this morning?" asked Sergeant Lamb when Caitlín bumped Waxy in through the front door.

"I've arrested him for assaulting a man on the head with an apple."

"So now you've arrested one man for hitting another man on the head with a piece of fruit. Oh my God, Kennedy, how on earth did we manage before you came here? With us being terrorised by such heinous crimes?" said Sergeant Lamb. "Tully, sort this out, will you?"

"Sergeant, there's more to it than that!" Caitlín protested.

"Kennedy," said Sergeant Lamb quietly and slowly, "where are my buns?"

"Oh no! I left them on the wall when the fight broke out. Sorry. I can go back and get them!" Oh God, can this day really get any worse, she thought.

"Kennedy, go home. I do not want to see sight of you again until the night shift tomorrow night."

"But I am not on the night-shift roster yet, sir."

"Excuse me?"

"Oh, OK, sorry, Sergeant, I understand. I'll report for duty then."

CHAPTER 2

Murder Delivery

Billy Brisco was a performer who toured the country with his band. He was very popular and had a very good reputation. Frequently his songs would be played on RTÉ Radio 1. It was little surprise then that Slattery's pub in Ballantur was a full house when he played there on a Sunday night in the run-up to Christmas.

Slattery's pub was an average establishment for its location and time. It was also part of a guesthouse run by the Slattery family themselves. The viability of the B&B had slackened off, naturally, over the winter season but the pub was busy all year round. "A foot of counter is better than an acre of land," so they say, and indeed every bit of the counter was gold dust on this occasion. It was covered in pints of porter, gin and tonics, hot whiskeys, sweet sherries, dry sherries and minerals for the Pioneers. The walls were adorned with enamel pictures advertising Guinness or cigarettes such as Sweet Afton, Players or tipped Carroll's No.1. Empty bags of Tayto lay strewn on the formica-covered tables the customers had gathered around, sitting on the corduroy stools. An open fire was lit in the hearth which welcomed the attendees in from the cold but it was competing with the body heat that was radiating from the jovial crowd.

Knowing that the band could draw the locals and indeed strangers from out of town, the customers had made an extra effort with their appearance. There was no mistaking the pungent smell of carbolic soap or if you were posh you might have used Palmolive. In some cases these were overwhelmed by a good splash of Old Spice or Brut on the gentlemen while the ladies indulged in Shalimar or Yardley perfumes. Luckily tight trousers were fashionable for both genders and they were advantageous against the cold weather, especially for the women. The miniskirts were demoted until the spring.

Babs gave up waiting for Nate and headed off to Slattery's without him. Unfortunately, while Billy Brisco was warming up his vocal cords, Nate was warming up his hands, feet and every other bit of himself after being exposed to a water leak in the house of one of his neighbours. There had been a few hard nights of frost in a row now and it was beginning to take its toll on some of the houses, one of which belonged to the Foleys. A pipe burst in their bathroom and the water was flooding all over the ground floor of their house. Nate could tell the man of the house was making useless attempts trying to fix it so he felt he had no choice but to offer his assistance. After some time they managed to bring the leak under control and swept the water out the front door with a brush.

Ironically, despite the exposure to all that water, Nate never felt more like a pint and even though it was late now he decided to go for one. Arriving home, he removed his shoes like he always did before entering the house and changed as quickly as he could before a brisk walk down the town to the pub. He knew that Dennis Slattery would be in no hurry to abide by the law tonight and would give his very merry customers all the time in the world to enjoy themselves.

Sergeant Lamb had other ideas, though, and he was all too aware that such a well-known musician would draw a big audience to Slattery's. Nate saw him and the new bangharda coming towards him on the street and they met coincidently right outside the pub.

"Good evening, Sergeant Lamb."

"Good night to you, Nate. May I introduce you to our newest member of the force, Garda Caitlín Kennedy."

Nate and Caitlín shook hands and exchanged pleasantries. They could hardly hear one another as their voices were overridden by the raucous celebration coming from inside the pub.

"Well, it looks like these people have no homes to go to at all," said Caitlín laughingly.

"Jesus, is that the time it is? I didn't realise they had stopped serving," said Nate, pretending to check his watch.

"By the sound of things I don't believe they have," said Sergeant Lamb as he attempted to shove the front door open. It was locked.

He knocked on the door and the three of them waited for a response but clearly this intrusion was not registering at all, such was all the laughing and talking that continued to go on inside.

"Right!" said Sergeant Lamb and raising both his fists up parallel to the wooden door he started pounding on it like Tarzan. *"This is the Garda Síochána! I order you to cease serving alcohol and open this door at once!"*

The banter inside began to subside.

"Shhh, shhh, shhh!" was all that could be heard, followed by audible whispering.

Then the scraping of chairs, stools and tables could be heard and a quiet shuffling of feet. Then silence.

Again Sergeant Lamb pounded on the door, demanding entry immediately.

Moments later a bolt on the inside could be heard being slowly undone and then the sheepish half head of Dennis Slattery, the proprietor, emerged behind the half-open door.

"*Open up, Dennis! What the hell is going on in there?*"

Dennis had no choice but to step aside and let Sergeant Lamb, Caitlín and a cheeky Nate inside. They all walked straight into the lounge and halted in bafflement. The abandonment of the *Mary Celeste* could not have been choreographed better than this. There was no one to be seen anywhere. Drinks were still half-full, crisp packets open but not eaten and the most blatant giveaway of all were the abandoned cigarettes still smouldering in overflowing ashtrays where frantic efforts had been exercised to quench them.

"Where is everyone, Dennis?" asked Sergeant Lamb impatiently.

"They've all gone."

"I can see that but *evi-dent-ly* they have just left and have not gone far. I could choke on the cigarette smoke in here. Maybe it's time you finally gave me a grand tour of this guesthouse of yours. Kennedy, go around to the back door and nab anyone trying to get out that way."

Caitlín exited, to do as instructed.

Poor Dennis knew the game was up. He would be heavily fined for this. Any money he would profit over the Christmas period would be absorbed to compensate for this misdemeanour. Feck Sergeant Lamb anyway, he thought. Why couldn't he just turn a blind eye for one night instead of spoiling it for everyone? Any revellers caught would be prosecuted too for drinking in a licenced premises after hours. And when he thought about all the nights Sergeant Lamb "off duty" enjoyed himself well into the night in the lounge, it made him so mad. What a hypocrite, what a bollix!

Nate quietly followed behind them as they moved into the hall which led to the stairs up to the guestroom quarters. It appeared they had forgotten he was still there or didn't care. Either way he was laughing to himself and thought this was great craic. He wondered who was up there, who'd get caught?

Another locked exterior door on the right-hand side of the hall had a full-length curtain hanging on it to exclude the draughts. Sergeant Lamb walked over and looked down.

"Nice curtains, Dennis – tell me, when did they start selling them with shoes?"

And, sure enough, following his gaze a pair of feet was visible sticking out at the bottom. Sergeant Lamb withdrew his truncheon and used it to pull across the red velour curtain. There, with his head bowed, was Frank Carey.

Caitlín rejoined them, explaining how, on her late approach to the back door, she could just about make out a few shadows escaping into the dark night.

Sergeant Lamb grunted.

"Get your book out, Garda Kennedy," he said. "I think you're going to have a lot of writing to do tonight."

After taking Frank's name and address, they climbed the stairs, Nate following. They opened the first guestroom door. Ruairi Nealon and Jimmy Fleming were sitting on the bed. Mike Bolger was standing at an open window.

"Don't even think about it, Mikey. Do you want to break your bloody neck? Book them, Kennedy."

The next door revealed Elise and Pa Leonard with a very drunk Darby O'Donnell propping himself up by the dressing table. The third room turned up two other drunks but the innovative pair had hidden under the bed and were in knots laughing when Sergeant Lamb started pulling them out by the legs.

Nate continued to stand in the corridor, witnessing all of this unfold. This is unreal, he thought, laughing to himself.

Garda Kennedy took the lead with the next door.

"Ah no," said Dennis. "That's not a room – it's only a hot-press."

She opened it anyway and, boy, it was a 'hot-press' alright – there was a couple in it participating in a very passionate embrace in the dark.

"Well, what have we got here?" asked Sergeant Lamb, perplexed at how they physically fitted in there in the first place with shelves on one side and the water tank on the other. "I think they'll be requesting to book a room, Dennis. Come out here, the pair of ye!"

The couple stepped out, heads hanging.

"*Babs!*" cried Nate, who could not believe his eyes. "*What are you doing?*" His stare darted between her and the significant other who turned out to be the postman, Sammy Joyce.

The bystanders were shocked.

Babs didn't answer Nate. She couldn't even look him at him.

"Well, I can't charge ye with infidelity but ye're both going down for drinking in a public house after hours," Sergeant Lamb said, smirking.

"*Oh, he's going down alright,*" said Nate, lunging at Sammy. "*You dirty bastard, get your hands off my wife!*" He locked his own hands around Sammy's neck and they both fell to the floor in a struggle.

"Pull him off, Kennedy!" said Sergeant Lamb as he grabbed Nate's arm.

They both pulled him back up.

"*I'll kill you, I'll fucking kill you!*"

"That's enough, Nate, or I'll charge you with assault. Get out of here and take your troublemaker missus with you."

Nate dusted himself down, fixed his tie and straightened his hair. He stuck his neck out like an agitated rooster brewing for a fight but instead he turned and ran down the stairs.

"Good man, Nate!" said an onlooker. It was unclear whether the expression was commending peace or encouraging him.

Babs squashed her coat under her arm, said nothing to anyone, including Sammy, and fled down the stairs too.

"Jesus, Mary and Joseph, did you ever see the like?" said Pa Leonard.

All the bystanders sniggered among themselves because no one knew what to say, at the same time knowing this wasn't funny.

"Alright, that's enough," said Sergeant Lamb. "You'd swear you all had no work to be getting up for in the morning. Go on. Go home."

He shuffled all of them down the stairs. He didn't want to take any more names – he was reasonable enough to leave it at that.

Caitlín turned to Sammy who was standing beside her.

"Are you alright, Mr. Joyce?"

"I'm fine."

"You know you can charge Nate with assault if you wish – we're all witnesses."

"No, Garda Kennedy, I think I've caused Nate enough trouble."

"I've only met you twice so far, Mr. Joyce, and on both occasions you have been involved in an altercation. You don't make life easy for yourself, do you?"

"No, but I was only trying to make life easier for someone else."

Caitlín felt herself raise an eyebrow involuntarily.

Nate was already at home when Babs arrived there. He had the jacket and tie pulled off and the top button of his shirt opened. He had poured himself a generous glass of whiskey and was pacing up and down the floor.

God, he's so mad, thought Babs as she approached him to face the music.

"What the hell are you playing at? With that playboy above all people? Sure he spends all his time romancing Mrs. Huber. Did you know that? *Did you?*"

She didn't know that. "Nate, I'm sorry. I'm –"

"*Sorry? Sorry?* I have never been more humiliated in all my life! Bad enough to be playing away behind my back but to get caught red-handed, so publically, in Slattery's! In a bloody hot-press! For Christ's sake, what are people going to think?"

"But that's the problem, Nate – you only ever think about what people think about *you*. You never think about *me* at all!"

"Ah, give me a break!" he replied. He grabbed his coat and headed out into the freezing, dark night.

Babs sat in the armchair beside the fire which was dying – and that was exactly how she felt about the state of her marriage right now.

It was still dark at a quarter to eight in the morning at the Garda Station. Caitlin looked at the clock. Fifteen minutes to go and her first night shift would be is over. *Alleluia!* But surprisingly she felt fine.

Sergeant Lamb had bidden her farewell after the pub fiasco the night before and had instructed her to write up all the illegal drinking charges and start processing them. She did exactly as she was told and flew through the workload, thanks to the peace and quietness of an empty station. In fact, after the paperwork was done she put her head down and nodded off for a few hours. Now she had the kettle on to make a cup of tea to kill the last few minutes before the literal changing of the guard.

She had just pulled the custard-cream biscuits out of the tin box when a loud banging began on the front door. When she opened it, she saw a distressed Pa Leonard standing there.

"*Come quick! It's Sammy Joyce! I think he's dead!*"

Caitlín jumped into the Garda car with Pa.

Just then Seán Tully drove in and got out of his car, ready to start his shift.

"*Quick, get in here!*" Caitlín shouted at him. "*It's an emergency!*"

Tully jumped into the back seat. "Go easy, Caitlín, the road is like a bottle," he said.

After a moderately cautious drive, they arrived at the scene on the outskirts of the town.

There, ahead of them on the left-hand side of the road, by a gate leading into a field, was a motionless body face down – a bicycle lying beside it.

Caitlín's heart was beating out of her chest as she got out of the car.

Watching her steps, she walked slowly and gently forward. She bent down and checked the victim's pulse. With her fingers on his neck, she looked at what she could see of the man's face. It was indeed Sammy Joyce, the man she had separated from Waxy Carolan and the same man she had separated from Nate Wheatley the night before. There was no pulse to be found or a breath of life coming from his chest or nose. Nothing. The body was turning cold.

"Seán ..." Caitlín drew him a little further along the road, out of the earshot of Pa Leonard who was leaning against the car.

"Is it Sammy Joyce?"

"Yeah, it is. Looks like a hit and run. Look at the tyre-mark on the body. Poor guy, he's horribly crushed. We need to cordon off this area as soon as possible."

"I'll go back to the station, Caitlín, and call it in. Lamb should be in by now. Stay here and don't let anyone near the body."

"Yeah, I know. We need to close off this road."

They walked back to Pa.

"Pa, which end of this road is busier?" Caitlín asked.

"This road isn't busy at all but it joins the top road heading back into town and there are lot of houses on that road."

"OK – I need you to stand at the top of this road and don't let anyone down here until we get more gardaí on the scene."

"Right, sure, no problem. Is he dead?"

"I'm afraid he is."

"Someone drove over him?"

"Pa, we can't say anything further. This is a Garda investigation now and we are not at liberty to say anything at this point in time. Please go to the end of the road and we will relieve you as soon as we can. We may ask you to come into the station later for questioning but don't worry about that now. Thanks, Pa." Caitlín turned away, cutting him off before he started asking anything else. She didn't know what they were dealing with yet.

She stood and observed the scene. The weather alone was lending a naturally cold and dark ambience to it. It was still below freezing. The sparse grass in the middle of the road was stiff and white. The water-filled potholes had been frozen until something had driven over them and smashed the ice. She looked up and down the road. A relatively long stretch of it was straight with no bends. It was a narrow road with only room for one vehicle at a time. However, there were definite lay-bys at gates and homesteads that gave ample room for road-users to pass each other. Despite the seasonable deterioration of the natural vegetation, the hedges were still thick with a few trees overhanging along the way. This, of course, provided shade which prolonged the frost on the road.

She considered the direction the victim had been taking. It looked like Sammy was commencing his rounds, leaving the town and heading to the first village – Friar's Hill. She presumed he was hit by a vehicle that was travelling in the same direction. Scanning the road, she looked for a broken headlamp or some type of debris that might have been displaced during the impact. She walked nearer to the body. The road had evident tyre-tracks of a vehicle entering and exiting the little lay-by at the gate in a swerving motion. They were broad, probably those of a truck. Part of the hedge had been flattened at the right-hand side of the gate by the weight of the vehicle. She examined the grass more closely and it appeared that the heat of the vehicle had melted the ice, indicating that the vehicle had become momentarily stationary. She could vaguely make out more than one set of shoeprints – one set her own. The others could be Sammy's own, and perhaps Pa Leonard's? One blurred set was imprinted from the other side of the road approaching the body and perhaps retreating. Or did the driver get out to see what he had done and then drove off?

She suspected Sammy must have been walking in the centre of the road on the green bit in the middle, probably for a better grip while holding the bike on his left-hand side. You couldn't cycle on this icy surface. When he heard the vehicle approaching he would have walked into the lay-by at the gate to let it pass. The bike had fallen away from him and was now lying by the gate. It did not appear to have been damaged at all, with its carrier bag still intact. She got closer to Sammy. She didn't know if she should but she shoved her hand down inside the back of his coat and jacket. His inner body was still warm. Blood had trickled from his nose. Most of his injuries would be internal. The most distressing thing was the mark of the wheel that was ingrained across his back, its black, wet and oily track easy to see on Sammy's navy knee-length coat. She looked at his emotionless face. His hat had been thrown ahead to his left. She saw his smoke-stained fingers.

Caitlín's concentration was broken by the sound of cars approaching. She straightened herself up and saw Sergeant Lamb, Garda Tully and off-duty Garda Martin getting out of one car, while a more important-looking garda with a walking stick, accompanied by three other officers, dismounted from another.

Sergeant Lamb beckoned her towards them, making her feel a bit intimidated by their strong manly presence.

"Garda Kennedy, this is Superintendent Patrick Jordan from Castlebar. His men are here to assist and will cordon off the area."

"Good morning, sir."

"Ah, a new bangharda! Can you tell me what we have been presented with here this morning?"

"Yes, sir." Caitlín calmed herself and took a deep breath, despite being surrounded by seven men subconsciously attacking her composure.

"Identification confirmed as Sammy Joyce. Mid to late forties. Male. Occupation, local postman – on duty. He appears to have received a fatal impact to the back of his body. The body is still insulating heat so exact time of murder to be confirmed but I would estimate within the last couple of hours. Weather conditions are evident of a hard night's frost, leaving the road surface very icy, creating hazardous driving conditions. Indications would suggest the victim was hit from behind by a vehicle moving at speed. He fell where he is. His bicycle which I presume he was pushing is at scene undamaged. There is a clear imprint of a tyre on the back of the body. It is a wide mark which suggests it was not a car, or a van, but a truck. There are also footprints on the road which suggest that perhaps the driver stopped, walked to the body and then returned to his vehicle and drove off. However, they could be those of Mr. Leonard, the man who found him. Or possibly the victim's own. Until and if we hear further, sir, it appears to be a fatal hit and run. Whether it was deliberate or not at this stage is unclear."

"Very good. What's your name again, Garda?"

"Caitlín Kennedy."

"Next of kin need to be notified, Garda Kennedy. Was he married?"

"I don't believe so, sir."

"Is there a reason to believe it was deliberate?"

"Mr. Joyce had been involved in two physical altercations, one as recent as late last night. The first was a scuffle in the town square where he took on a local troublemaker for abusing a deaf man. In the latter, last night, he was assaulted and his life was threatened by a man who caught him fraternising with his wife. Whether either of these altercations led to this is hard to say at this stage without further investigation. However, the tyre-tracks showing how the vehicle swerved towards the victim might indicate that it was deliberate rather than a skid."

"The State Pathologist and forensics in Dublin have been rung but if this ice is nationwide they will be a while getting here. So what do you plan to do next?"

She felt the Superintendent was testing her.

"A full-scale examination and search of the scene and surrounding area," she said. "Door-to-door enquiries with a particular interest on the sightings of any trucks in the area. We need to question the people who threatened him to see if we can establish a motive. Oh yeah ..." She was startled at remembering something else all of a sudden. "May I borrow your walking stick, sir?"

Obviously perplexed by her request, the Superintendent handed it to her.

Caitlín walked back to the body, treading very carefully. She reached over it with the stick pointing in the direction of the bike. With the aid of her new extension she was able to lift up the flap of the self-contained waterproof carrier basket attached to the front of the bike but the hope she was clinging to dissipated.

"It's gone!" she called back. "The bag of post and parcels, all of it, it's gone!"

The whole team were taken aback.

"The hit and run was deliberate so," said Tully. "It means there are endless motives now from a wide circle of people who perhaps desperately needed to see one letter before anyone else did and they were prepared to murder someone for it."

"Or," said Caitlín, "they stole the inner bag to make it look like that, and make us think like that, but all along their target was Sammy Joyce."

"Plenty of time for the theories, Garda Kennedy," said the Superintendent. "We need to find that bag. I'll get my men scouring the surrounding area and fields straight away."

"We'll crack on with the door-to-door enquiries and go about notifying the next of kin," said Sergeant Lamb.

"I'll set up an incident room at the station," said Caitlín.

"Good work, Garda Kennedy. Keep me updated on all developments," said the Superintendent as he turned away.

Caitlín was satisfied with her on-the-spot presentation even if that feeling was a bit selfish, considering the circumstances.

Sergeant Lamb, on the other hand, felt resentful at the lack of attention the Superintendent had paid to him. He was tempted to ask Caitlín more about the incident room but decided it was in his best interests to stay nothing and be a spectator. Truthfully, he had never been involved or conducted a murder investigation in all of his career or anything similarly untoward, but of course he was not going to admit that now. He realised he was twenty years behind Caitlín in knowledge of technical procedures, coming out of training college as she was, so perhaps it would be sensible for him to let her build the foundations of the enquiries and see how far she could bring it on. Besides, there were plenty of tasks for everyone and there was no doubt this had brought a new sense of protection towards the community that this small team of guardians was so fond of.

Lamb sent Caitlín to the door of Nate Wheatley's home as he sat and watched from the car.

Caitlín asked Babs about Nate's commercial route for the day. She casually asked her what time he had set off, trying to keep any hint of suspicion to a minimum. Babs was curious, naturally, but Caitlín told her that they only required information from him, without revealing any other circumstances. Babs accepted this and told Caitlín where she presumed Nate would be at this time. Caitlin thanked Babs for her assistance, knowing well that Babs would be taken in for questioning herself later.

CHAPTER 3

Investigation

Nate was at the crossroads of Drumancnoc and Gortamor. The two back doors of the truck were pulled back and Nate was sitting inside on an upturned galvanised bucket waiting for his customers to arrive. He was a bit earlier than usual this morning because he had set out earlier. He sat with his head in his hands, trying to banish the memories of the night before from his mind. What would people be saying? What would he tell them? He knew the scandal would not have been circulated yet but by the end of the day the gossip would have travelled faster than he would. God, how much he hated Babs right now! That stupid woman, what was the matter with her? She had ruined him despite all he had done for her, the comfortable life he provided for her. He hadn't even known there was anything wrong. What more did she want? All the questions he had never asked her.

A disturbance of gravel pulled him from his misery and, looking up, he saw Mike Treacy walking towards him for his shopping. Nate decided to behave as normally as possible and just get through the day.

By the time Sergeant Lamb and Caitlín had tracked Nate down to his present location three more locals had arrived to his shop. Both of them got out of the car and beckoned Nate down from his stall. Practising attempted discretion out of earshot at the side of the truck, overlooked by one of its dragons, they instructed Nate that he was required to attend at the station immediately in relation to a road-traffic accident.

Nate was confused because he had presumed that they wanted to talk to him about the incident in the pub the night before. He tried to ask them what it was about but a firm "*Now*" from Sergeant Lamb convinced him that this was serious and he should just do as he was told. As no one present was capable of driving a truck, Nate was told to follow them in it to the station.

The bystanders were speechless and watched the gardaí and Nate drive away without realising they hadn't even finished their shopping yet.

On the slow journey back on the potholed road net curtains were twitching on the windows of the village, the residents getting a feeling that there was something not quite right about today.

"Ignatius Wheatly, you are being arrested on suspicion of the murder of Sammy Joyce," said Sergeant Lamb.

"You're arresting me for *what*? What happened to Sammy Joyce? Whatever it was, I had nothing to do with it!"

Despite Nate's confusion and protests he was led into a cell where the door was firmly closed behind him. He was shocked not only by the allegation, but the unbelievable news that Sammy was dead.

"I'll prepare a line of questioning," said Sergeant Lamb. "Detective Brendan Cullen will be joining us from Castlebar. Tully, Kennedy, notify the next of kin immediately – not nice but you need to know how to handle this kind of thing. Just deliver the facts, keep it simple. Offer your condolences and any assistance, if required. Don't get personal or emotional and don't start speculating or answering questions you are not in a position to answer. Is that clear?"

"Yes, sir. So who are the next of kin?" asked Tully.

"I don't know." Lamb shrugged, looking around the room. "Anyone?" No one replied.

"Well, he must have brothers, sisters, parents?" continued Lamb. "He must have someone? You know what's so frustrating? Time and time again the irony is that even though we are custodians of our communities we don't originally come from the locality, therefore very often our knowledge of the life lines of the inhabitants is limited."

"Pa Leonard?" suggested Tully.

"Is he a relative?" asked Lamb.

"No, but as an elderly member of the parish he might know who Sammy is related to."

Caitlín and Tully jumped in the car and drove to Pa Leonard's house.

Pa came out to meet them because his crazy barking dogs meant they were not going in.

"Jesus, did Nate do it?" asked Pa immediately. He had seen the Garda car and Nate's truck passing by earlier.

And then Mike Treacy stepped out of Pa's doorway along with Elise Leonard so they knew that Pa was up to speed with developments.

"We are following a line of enquiry, Pa, that's all," said Caitlín. "We are here to ask you if you know whether Sammy had any family nearby?"

Pa thought for a moment and looked back at his wife and Mike Treacy who didn't look like they knew anything.

"He was an only child and his parents died a long time ago. There could be aunts or uncles but they don't live around here," he said.

"Damn, what will we do now?" Caitlín quietly asked Tully.

"There's only one person who would know," said Pa. "The man you have locked up. Nate is the only one around here who knows everything about everyone."

"Thanks, Pa," said Caitlín. "We'll ask Nate."

They hopped back into the car.

"Nate is hardly going to withhold any information about this if it helps him," she said to Tully.

Back at the station they headed straight for the kitchen and made tea.

Caitlín hadn't eaten anything substantial since the night before. As she reached for the Custard Creams, Sergeant Lamb marched in behind them.

"Well, how did ye get on? Did ye locate his relatives?"

"All Pa knew was that he was an only child and his parents are dead," Tully said. "He said the best man to ask is the one we have behind bars right now."

"Nate? Well, needs must. OK. Go and ask him then, both of you. I'm reluctant to get this investigation under way until the next of kin have been notified – it's not appropriate otherwise. Give me that cup of tea, Kennedy, no point in it going to waste."

Caitlín and Tully pulled up a chair each when Nate had been led into the interview room to meet them. He was shaken and white-faced.

"Nate, we apologise for the delay," said Caitlín, "but we cannot proceed properly with the investigation until the next of kin have been informed as I'm sure you can understand. Unfortunately we are having difficulty identifying Sammy's immediate family and we were wondering if you know anything about them?"

"Sure, yes," replied Nate, eager to sort this out as soon as possible. "He has a cousin in Claremorris and he's an only child too, funnily enough. But they're not talking to one another. Well, I mean their mothers who were sisters didn't talk to one another and sadly that divide continued into the next generation."

"What happened?" asked Tully.

"Sammy's mother was one of three girls – no brothers. They were Larkins – Frances, Margaret and Teresa."

"Sounds like three nuns," said Tully with a laugh.

"Oh, they were far from nuns!" said Nate. "A man by the name of Henry Coyle, I think he was called, started courting Frances and it was all looking very promising until Frances brought Henry home to meet her family and didn't Henry set his eyes and heart on Teresa instead. So to make a long story painful, he dumped poor Frances and starting taking Teresa out instead. Frances was heartbroken. I remember my father telling me about the two women having an awful row on the main street in Ballantur. Headscarves were pulled off, hair pulled out, and the pair of them were wrestling on the ground until they were pulled apart. And apart they remained – they never spoke to one another again. Teresa and Henry went on to get married, had a son called Ralph and lived in Claremorris. Of course, Frances didn't go to the wedding but the other sister, Margaret, did and damn it didn't Frances fall out with *her* over that and didn't speak to her again either. Margaret got fed up with the pair of them and went to America. She got married there alright to a guy who owned an air-conditioning company but they had no kids – he's dead now, I think. Anyway, when their parents died Frances was the only one left at home and she inherited the place. Their parents died relatively close to one another and I heard my father saying they weren't dead a wet week when Frances took up with Gerry Joyce, a neighbour only down the road from her, and married him. Land boundaries were levelled to join their holdings together. They appeared to be happy and had one son, Sammy."

"Wow, families, eh?" said Tully. "Who told you all that?"

"I heard my father on about it and then myself and Sammy were in England around the same time and we used to meet up for a pint sometimes in the Irish Centre in London and he told me about it. It was sad, you know, how it affected the next generation too."

"Did the two cousins ever meet?" asked Caitlín.

"Hardly ever as kids, although they did attend the funerals of each other's parents."

"Do you know anything about this cousin, Ralph Coyle?"

"Not much."

"Do you know where he lives?"

"I do. As you're heading into Claremorris town there is a road down to your left to the football pitch. I don't know the name of it but you can't miss the house. There's a big rose garden in front of it. I know the wife better." Nate blushed. "I mean, she's a great gardener and she's won loads of prizes for her roses at the Claremorris Show, Ballinrobe show, Ballina show, shows all over the country. She's also won prizes for making jam, brown bread, apple tarts, you name it. Ralph is a lucky man!"

"Right. Thank you for your help, Nate," said Caitlín and she and Tully left to deliver the bad news to Ralph Coyle.

—— *ell* ——

"*What is that stench?*" gasped Caitlín as they pulled up outside Ralph Coyle's house.

"Well, it's not me," said Tully, smirking as he got out of the car. "It's just farmyard manure."

"Are you sure?" It was familiar to Caitlín but she couldn't put her finger on what it was.

"Imagine a country girl like yourself not recognising the sweet smell of manure!" teased Tully.

"I'm not a country girl, I'm a townie from Ennis."

"*Ha*, I'd hardly call Ennis an urban metropolis."

"*Shh!*" Caitlín hit Tully on the arm to bring him into decorum as they approached the front door.

They knocked once and a woman holding a red-check tea towel opened the door.

A powerful waft of cinnamon and ginger knocked the two gardaí nearly senseless. Clearly Mrs. Coyle was making her Christmas cakes.

"Hello, you must be Mrs. Coyle?" said Caitlín.

"I am."

"Is Mr. Coyle at home?"

"He is."

"Can we speak to him, please?"

"You can." She turned and hurried back into the house, returning immediately with Ralph.

"Mr. Coyle, I'm Garda Tully and this is Garda Kennedy. We are from Ballantur Garda Station. Can you confirm if you are a blood relative to a Mr. Sammy Joyce?"

"I am, yes, he's my cousin."

"I'm sorry to inform you that Mr. Joyce was involved in a serious road traffic accident this morning and tragically died at the scene."

"Oh, God bless us!" cried Mrs. Coyle, covering her mouth with the tea towel.

"A criminal investigation is under way as it appears to be a hit and run that occurred as he was out on his postal delivery. At this point in time we are unable to establish if it was an accident due to the weather conditions or if foul play was committed."

Mr. and Mrs. Coyle stood speechless.

"A pathologist and forensics team have come down from Dublin to examine the scene and a post mortem is currently being carried out on the body."

"Would you say you are the next of kin, Ralph?" said Caitlín.

"Yes, I suppose I am. He doesn't have anyone else."

"OK," she said. "If you contact the station tomorrow we can update you further about claiming the body and making funeral arrangements, and we can also update you as to how the investigation is proceeding,"

"Mr. Coyle, Mrs. Coyle, on behalf of the station may we extend our condolences on your loss," said Tully, shaking both their hands.

Caitlín did the same and then she and Tully walked silently down the drive.

The Coyles hadn't been at all close to Sammy but Sergeant Lamb was right: it was not a nice part of the job and one would never get used to doing it, but unfortunately it was something that would occur from time to time and it was their responsibility to deliver that kind of news in the most factual but sensitive way they could.

When they got back to the station Caitlín returned to the kitchen in an attempt to make another cup of tea while Tully updated Sergeant Lamb about notifying the next of kin.

"Right, Kennedy, grab your biro, you're taking notes. It's time to question Nate," said Lamb.

Nate was sitting in the interview room when Caitlín walked in. She set down her tea, biscuits and notebook on the table that divided them.

"Oh fair play to you, I'm starving," said Nate, pulling the tea and biscuits towards him.

Caitlín said nothing as he started to consume them.

Sergeant Lamb had come into the room followed by the detective from Castlebar Garda Station.

Lamb began by introducing the unfamiliar face as Detective Brendan Cullen, who would lead the interview.

"State your name for the record."

"Nate, Ignatius Wheatley."

"I believe you have been cautioned and you understand that you have been arrested on the suspicion of murder of one Samuel Joyce."

"Yes, but I didn't do it."

Detective Cullen didn't blink at his response. "I have been briefed on your whereabouts last night and indeed your actions. After witnessing an unfortunate situation between your wife Mrs. Barbara Wheatley and Mr. Joyce, you physically attacked the deceased and threatened to kill him."

"Yeah, but I didn't kill him. I was fit to kill him. I had just caught him kissing my wife in a hot-press and I know I let my temper get the better of me but I swear I did not kill him."

"Did you know your wife was conducting an affair with Mr. Joyce?"

"An affair? I'd hardly call it that. No, I didn't know."

"Where did you go when you left Slattery's pub?"

"I went straight home."

"What did you do then?"

"I don't know – I sat down for a while and then Babs came home but I was still so mad I went out for a walk – but it was freezing so I sat into the truck and stayed there for the night."

"All night?"

"Until the morning. I went back into the house, had a wash and made some breakfast."

"What did you have to eat?"

Nate was a bit surprised at the question but answered it. "I made tea, ate brown bread and a bit of left-over cold chicken."

"Thank you, Mr. Wheatley, that's all for now."

"Can I go?"

"Not yet. Your truck is being forensically examined and searched."

"What? You can't be serious! You have the wrong man for this, Frank. You have to believe me."

They all left the room, with Caitlín realising that she hadn't known Sergeant Lamb's first name was Frank. She finally got to sit down and starting yawning at her desk.

Tully brought her a cup of tea and a ham-and-cheese roll from the shop.

"Here, get that down you, looks like you could do with it. Need to keep the energy up for round three. Pa Leonard is on his way in for questioning and the others are currently trying to track down Waxy Carolan."

"It's been such a full-on morning," said Caitlín. "My head is spinning. I met Nate for the first time last night at the pub raid. I felt really sorry for him after catching his wife like that. He was *soooooo* angry though."

"I don't know him that well either. I'm only here a few years myself. But you know as well as I do that crimes of passion can be the most heartless. Oh, Pa must be here, Cullen is on the move. I'll take this one, you have a break."

"Thanks, Tully. What's Detective Cullen like?"

"He's grand. He's been out here a few times. Did an art heist with us before. He said the only thing he knew about art was to appreciate it and that was the most important thing. He said he likes it because you expect a lot of it and it expects nothing of you. He transferred from Dublin to Castlebar after that. He must like our fresh air over here. I don't know if he's a very laid-back kind of guy or just couldn't give a shit. Better than some jumped-up jack who thinks he's Sherlock Holmes."

Caitlín thought he sounded very interesting but said nothing.

———ℓℓℓ———

"Can you state your name for the record, please?" said Detective Cullen who was again leading the line of questioning, joined in the room by Sergeant Lamb and Garda Tully.

"Pa ... Patrick Leonard."

"You appear to have been first on the scene?"

Pa blinked back, not sure if this was a question.

"What time did you come across the accident?"

"About half past seven this morning."

"What were you doing? Where were you going?"

"I have an outhouse down the road from the house, where I keep half a dozen turkeys – well, five now because they took one for the raffle last night. It's getting close to Christmas so I was going to kill the others and start plucking and preparing them for my customers. It's a time-consuming job so I wanted to get started as early as I could."

"Can you describe the scene of the incident when you came upon it, Mr. Leonard?"

"It was dark and very icy so I was concentrating on my footing. I had nearly walked on top of poor Sammy before I figured out what I was looking at." Pa paused. "He was just lying there face down, blood coming from his nose, his body crushed. The bike was lying beside him and you ... well, you could see the marks of the car that swerved over him and on to the hedge and out again."

"What did you do then?"

"I knelt down and shook him. I called his name but he said nothing so that is when I ran to the station and raised the alarm."

Detective Cullen looked at Tully and quietly said, "This witness has unknowingly tampered with the scene. Take his fingerprints so we can identify his presence there."

"Yes, sir."

"Are you wearing the same shoes you were wearing at the scene?" Cullen asked.

"No, I had my wellies on."

"That's OK, Patrick. Garda Tully here will take you home and take prints off your wellingtons. Now, did you see or hear anything else strange this morning?"

"No, nothing."

"Are you sure – because it seems the accident had happened shortly before you came on it. Did you hear anything passing along the road around that time? Or see any lights?"

"I didn't," Pa replied, feeling bad that he hadn't more to tell them.

"Patrick, I believe you have lived in this community all your life. Would you know if Sammy Joyce led a peaceful existence or were you aware of any enemies or feuds he had? Was he known for brawling or causing breaches of the peace?"

"No, I always remember him being a nice happy-go-lucky fellow. The Lord have mercy on him. No harm in him, he was well liked."

"Would you be knowledgeable about the relationship between him and a Mr. Ignatius Wheatley?"

"Nate? Do you think he killed him?"

"We are only following a line of enquiry, Mr. Leonard, especially after Mr. Wheatley threatened Sammy in the pub last night which I believe you too witnessed."

"Ah yeah, an awful business but I don't believe Nate would kill anyone over it. They were friends for years. They were in England at the same time and everything until Nate suddenly went to America."

"So Nate spent time in the United States too?"

"Yeah, fled overnight, they say. I heard he got into trouble in England."

"What kind of trouble?"

"Ah, there was an accident on a boat and a young woman drowned."

"What else do you know about this accident?" said Cullen and looked at Lamb in some concern.

"That's all I know."

"Who told you about it?" Sergeant Lamb asked.

"It was Sammy who told me when he came back home that year at Christmas, without Nate."

"And what exactly did he tell you?"

"Not much, to be honest – I think out of loyalty to Nate. He just said Nate was at some social event on a boat and there was some kind of mishap and someone died. I don't recall exactly how Sammy phrased it but he kind of alluded to Nate being compromised in the investigation that followed and that's what made him go to America."

"Right, Mr. Leonard," said Detective Cullen. "Thank you for your time. We appreciate that this has been a shock for you and, if there is anything we can do, or if there is anything else you can remember which could be helpful, please contact us immediately."

"I will."

Tully led Pa out of the room.

Detective Cullen turned to Lamb.

"Did you know about this accident in England?"

"No, I didn't."

"We're going to have to extend Nate Wheatley's detention. Looks like we have more questions to ask him now," said Cullen.

"Yeah, it looks like Nate is a bit accident-prone alright and today's may not be the first one he's caused," agreed Sergeant Lamb.

Caitlín was sitting her desk. This was becoming a very long day. She was trying to do her paperwork but her mind was speeding faster than she could write. There were so many things she was afraid she was going to forget and her focus was already on the next thing – the incident room. She initiated it so she would have to set it up. But her fluster was stalled when she looked up and saw Garda Martin coming into the station, pulling Waxy Carolan after him.

Oh, here we go again, Caitlín said to herself, grabbing her notebook and heading into the interview room after Detective Cullen and Sergeant Lamb.

"Ah, Mr. Carolan! We meet again. What's it been, three years?" said Detective Cullen. "You didn't stay out of trouble for long. State your name for the record, please."

"Waxy Carolan."

"Your real name."

"Edward," he said quietly, scrunching his cap between his hands.

Caitlín smirked to herself, wondering how such a scumbag could have such a sensible name.

"You have been brought in for questioning in relation to a hit and run in which Mr. Sammy Joyce tragically lost his life this morning."

"And I suppose I'm going to be blamed for that too."

"We're not blaming anyone, Mr. Carolan, but you publicly and physically threatened Mr. Joyce yesterday afternoon which was witnessed by a member of the Force sitting in this room and that is very serious," said Cullen sternly.

"Ah yes, we had a little get-together alright, isn't that right, missy?" Waxy replied, winking at Caitlín.

He disgusted her, despite the fact a minute earlier she was thinking how wastefully good-looking he was.

"Mr. Carolan, can you confirm your whereabouts last night and this morning?" continued Cullen.

"Well, over a hundred people saw me in Slattery's pub last night if you would like to confirm that with all of them. Then myself, Billy McLaughlin and Tom Leahy went back to my house and were playing cards till the early hours of the morning which meant that while Sammy Joyce was having the life squeezed out of him, myself and my mates had fallen asleep at my kitchen table. I don't have a truck, for the record."

"How do you know a truck was involved?"

"Sure everyone knows. It's the talk of the talk of the town. Say hello to Nate for me."

They continued to question Waxy about the incident, his alibi, as well as his relationship to and knowledge of Sammy Joyce.

Caitlín concluded that Waxy was a thick ignorant man who was incapable of having a reasonable conversation with anyone. It frustrated all of them that his alibi was not penetrable because they knew his cronies would back him up regardless of the truth.

They had to let Waxy go.

ell

Caitlín went back to her desk and yawned slowly. Her head was spinning from the interviews while at the same time she was trying to refocus on what to do next.

"Kennedy!" shouted Sergeant Lamb. "That's enough for one day. Go home! I want you back on days tomorrow to continue on with this investigation."

He didn't have to tell her twice.

She bought some groceries on the way home. Quirke's shop had put up some Christmas decorations and piled high tins of biscuits and boxes of sweets on the counter. She bought some Christmas cards to bring some normality back into her surreal day.

Sometimes you didn't know how hungry you were until you start eating and when she got back at the cottage she ate a tin of corned beef, bread, sweet cake and biscuits and drank two mugs of tea. Finally, she filled the hot-water bottle and climbed into bed, taking the box of Christmas cards and a biro with her. She selected a snowy landscape to send to her mother. She closed her eyes to think about what she was going to write but then ... zzzzzz ...

ell

Meanwhile down in Slattery's pub the rumour-mill was cranking up.

"Oh, it's a crying shame what happened to the poor postman," said a customer, starting the ball rolling.

"And look who they locked up for it! Neither of those men would hurt a fly. They were friends, for God's sake!"

"Yeah, but they weren't friends after Nate caught Sammy with Babs in the hot-press! I heard Nate was fit to be tied. He was ready to kill him there and then."

"Ah yeah, but that was just a reaction – he wouldn't actually kill him over it."

"They've known each other for most of their lives. They were in England and everything together. No, they have the wrong man."

"Now if you ask me, Sammy had a much bigger enemy than Nate."

"Who's that then?"

"Who do you think? Waxy Carolan, of course."

"Ah, that's rubbish! What did Sammy ever do to Waxy?"

"You have a short memory, sir. Don't you remember what happened last September when we had the storm? Sammy nearly killed Waxy. They had a big fight, remember? Pa Leonard's granddaughter nearly died that day. Sammy had a right go at Waxy over it."

"Ah, there's more to that than meets the eye, if you ask me. Some were saying it was Sammy who tipped the gardaí off that time about the robbery up at the Big House."

"I didn't hear about the storm or the robbery – what did you hear?"

CHAPTER 4

Bootleg Barbie

September 1961

Saturday was market day in the square in Ballantur. It was always very busy because of the variety of stuff on sale and it was efficiently seasonal. In the line of livestock, cattle and sheep were sold, the deal sealed with a spit on the hand and a firm handshake. The price was often haggled by the increasingly inebriated dealers and buyers during their fluctuating negotiations as they dipped in and out of their office, which was better known as Slattery's pub. Hens and ducks were for sale too with gaggles of geese and rafters of turkeys at Christmas time. This occasion was post-harvest so endless pots of jam and preserves were available. Fruit in its natural form was on offer, such as apples, blackcurrants and gooseberries while an annual supply of potatoes, cabbage and carrots were in abundance.

Mutey ran the greengrocer stand, most of it his own produce and if he'd had a successful fishing trip the evening before he sold what he'd caught. A cake stand proved to be very popular, its mouth-watering smell luring customers to buy fruit cakes, apple tarts, scones, brown soda bread and whole white loaves. Another favourite stall was run by a lady from Pakistan who brought great colour with her many rolls of fabrics in chiffon, cotton, linen, polyester, wool and silk. The local ladies were all skilled at making clothes but nowadays it was becoming more of a hobby than a necessity. They flicked through the boxes of patterns while having a good old natter with their friends.

Mutey was driving a tractor and carefully trying to unload a barrel of water at the back of the square. The town was on a water scheme but its Committee was still campaigning for the County Council to install a tap in the square. In the meantime they had the laborious task of hauling water from an old well situated in a field at the back of the street. A bone of contention was not just the hassle of it but the responsibility of covering it over again by whoever used it last. This was causing all sorts of concern.

Waxy Carolan also had a 'seasonal' stall. Seasonal as in he sold whatever he could get his hands on at the time. It was always an eclectic arrangement, ranging from tools, spades, shovels, forks, yard brushes and wellington boots. Unintentionally, but humorously, these agricultural products were lined up in front of a table that displayed cards of soap and Old Spice aftershave. Then your eye could be drawn to the domestic items such as enamel teapots, tin kettles and saucepans, delph and cutlery. He usually had a few toys on display as it was always some child's birthday and, on this particular day, September 2nd, it was little Molly Leonard's.

Molly and her brother Tadhg spent a lot of time with their grandparents, Pa and Elise Leonard, because their mother Grace was sick. She had been diagnosed with cancer two years before. They lived in Castlebar but, with the children's father an absent figure, they spent a lot of time in the care of Pa and Elsie in Ballantur while she was receiving treatment and recovering from the after-effects.

Today, Elsie had taken Molly to the market with her and together they browsed through the various stalls. It was all very uninteresting for

Molly except for the few token toys Waxy had on display. She and her grandmother stopped to look at them.

"Molly, would you like one of these?" she asked, holding up a baby doll.

"No, thanks."

"But you like dolls! Let me get this one for you for your birthday."

An obliged purchase, always easy money, thought Waxy to himself. "Are you sure you wouldn't like one, love?"

"No, thanks, I don't like them."

"I thought all little girls like dolls?" said Waxy, trying to sound surprised.

"Ah, I know, she wants a particular doll, Waxy," said Elsie. "You probably never heard of them. They're called 'Barbie' dolls. She's seen them with her cousins in Dublin so now she wants one too. They look like adults. I don't see anything cuddly about them at all."

"What age are you, darling?" asked Waxy.

"I'm eight today."

"Well, there you go, Mrs. Leonard! She's a big girl now. She doesn't want to play with baby dolls anymore – she wants a doll so she can do her hair and change her outfits."

"So you *have* heard of them," said Elsie with a laugh.

"Of course I have. They're expensive but I might be able to get my hands on one for you," he said, smiling at Molly who was smiling back at him.

"No, thanks," said Elsie. "They're too dear – we'll get something else." Not only was the price bothering Elsie but she knew if Waxy came up with the goods she would be uncomfortable at the thought of the unreliable source they probably came from – off the back of the proverbial lorry, no doubt. Molly, have another look there, pet, and see if there's anything else you would like." With that, Elsie went to look at the stand with all the fabrics and started chatting to the other ladies who had gathered there.

Molly was disappointed. She could hear the usual enquiries about her mother and the usual replies about her getting more treatment in hospital in Dublin.

"You have your mind set on what the heart wants," said Waxy, engaging Molly's attention again. He looked sideways to see if Mrs. Leonard was out of earshot and, satisfied that she was, he leaned forward towards the little girl. "I could get a Barbie for you," he said quietly.

Molly smiled and her eyes lit up.

"The next time I'm meeting my supplier I'll ask him to get one. It will cost you though. How would you be able to pay for it?"

"I have my Communion money," she answered innocently.

This was Waxy version of taking candy from a baby. He was unscrupulous about it.

"OK, if you come back here – say in two weeks' time – with three pounds, I'll have one for you."

"They don't cost as much as that!" Molly replied, vexed at him.

Waxy laughed at her tenacity. "Fine, let's say two pounds so, because I have to make a profit on it, you know. But this is our secret, little girl – no need to tell your grandparents or we'll be both in trouble. Do you understand?"

Molly nodded silently because she heard her grandmother returning to her.

"So, miss, did you pick out something?"

"There's nothing here I like today."

"I see," replied Elsie, disappointed that she couldn't buy Molly something to mark her special day.

Molly sensed her regret and said, "It's OK, Granny. I'll be eight for a whole year so there's no rush."

They laughed at her wise pertinence.

When they turned to leave, Waxy watched Molly straighten the crutch under her oxter. She had been affected by polio and it had developed an unfortunate inward curve in her left leg, preventing her from walking properly.

It's not holding her back, thought Waxy to himself. Give her another few years and she'll be a right force.

What Waxy or anyone else didn't know at this stage was that on the West Coast of Africa another youthful energy was strengthening in the form of a storm and no one could imagine what force it was capable of bringing.

—ele—

By September 15th that storm had been upgraded to a hurricane because since its formation it had gained both power and strength over the Western Azores. Its unfavourable characteristics were proving to be frustratingly evasive and unpredictable to track. It had already caused a lot of destruction in its ever-changing path.

It was only in the early hours of September 16th that the weather forecasters picked it up again to announce its imminent arrival to Ireland. Now known as 'Hurricane Debbie', as if giving it a name would make it any more hospitable, this announcement meant that a huge responsibility fell on the emergency services to prepare for such a big threat in a small window of time. The national radio station did continuous reporting, tracking Debbie's location, and announced constant warnings to the public to prepare themselves and their property for what was coming.

A weather event like this was not very common in Ireland and it took a lot of convincing to persuade people about the immediate seriousness of it. Ballantur was no exception and while the conditions were blustery and gusty some people were still going about their normal activities on the Saturday morning it arrived.

The market opened in the town. A lot of the vendors sensibly did not turn up but for those who did it was becoming a struggle to keep the tents and stalls steady, not to mention the smaller lighter goods on display. They all chatted about the storm among themselves but were naive about its potential.

It was a marketing disaster for Waxy Carolan's latest line. He had a big glass tank of goldfish for sale on display.

Mutey, who was selling some produce to Sammy Joyce at one stage, nodded in Waxy's direction. They couldn't help laughing as they watched him top up the tank with water he had fetched from the well.

"They won't live long in that bog water," said Sammy. "That's if they make it home at all today."

Those who had taken heed of the warnings made sure they got plenty bread and milk in, candles and rosary beads being other necessities. Outside they put away anything that might fly away, like buckets, bags and pot plants. They tied down their stacks of hay. Ropes were flung over flapping galvanised roofs and tied to blocks or rocks at the ends. Clothes were stripped off the washing lines.

Some came knocking on Nate's door for further provisions as Quirke's had sold out of flash-lamps, paraffin oil and batteries. Nate was only too happy to oblige. Didn't they say it was an ill wind that doesn't blow in the right direction for someone?

Sergeant Lamb on the other hand was furious. How stupid could some people be? He summoned Tully and both of them headed down to the market to officially close it down and send both the customers and vendors home immediately. They were relieved to see that the market was nearly empty and that most of the customers had the good sense to stay away.

He had to raise his voice over the howling wind. *"Lads, you have to go home! We are ordered to shut this market down by the emergency services! The storm is on its way and it's meant to be a bad one! So pack up and get out of here!"*

The sellers did as they were told. Nothing like a bit of authority coming from a uniform to add a bit of gravitas. Sergeant Lamb and Tully helped disassemble the stalls while Sammy Joyce helped Mutey with his. Waxy was last to get his stuff packed away and, as Mutey departed, he indicated to Waxy to check that the well was covered before he left.

"Yeah, no problem," said Waxy, chasing a cardboard box across the square.

When all appeared in hand, Sergeant Lamb and Tully set out to return to the station. They didn't notice the small figure approaching Waxy's stall behind them.

Hell or high water, it was little Molly Leonard. She stood behind the open door of Waxy's van. When he closed it and saw her standing there like an apparition he was shocked.

"Jesus Christ, Molly! You frightened the shit out of me! What do you want?"

"My Barbie doll."

"Ah God, yes, I have one but I've just finished packing up the van. I don't know where it is now."

"But you *promised*."

"We're all being sent home before the storm and you should do the same," he said, trying to get rid of her but she was not budging. "I tell you what – if the storm is not too bad later on, say around four o'clock, come up to the house and I'll give it to you then, alright?"

"OK, so."

"Molly! What the hell are you doing over there?" Pa Leonard shouted at her. *"Come back here! Quirke's are out of batteries – we'll have to go to Nate Wheatley's house!"*

Molly was very disappointed as she gripped the crunched-up money in her pocket, but she was determined not to give up yet. She had spent the last two weeks dreaming about Barbie. She had made a doll's house out of a big cardboard box. She had even cut up some of her own clothes and sewed miniature outfits together in anticipation of dressing her new doll. She had borrowed her brother's toy truck to pretend it was Barbie's car just like her cousins except they had a real doll's house and a convertible toy car – but that didn't matter right now.

As the afternoon rolled on so did Hurricane Debbie. The force of the wind increased significantly and people were prepared to sit it out, hoping it would pass over without threat despite the worrying forecasts. Pa Leonard and Elise still managed to have their daily forty winks after eating their stodgy dinner which acted as a natural sedative.

Down the hall in the bedroom, Molly was acting more like a stimulant, goading her older ten-year-old brother to go with her to Waxy's house.

"You're just a scaredy cat!"

"I'm not, Molly. I'm not going out in that weather – are you mad?"

"Come on, we won't be long."

"No. Go on your own. Why do you want me to go with you anyway?"

"Because I don't know where he lives."

"I am not going out in that storm just so you can get a stupid doll. I mean, what's it in for me?"

"A pound."

Tadgh was silent. He was tempted.

"Ah, I don't know, Molls – we'll get into fierce trouble."

"We'll be back before they wake up. They'll be conked out for ages. *Please, Tadgh. Please!*"

"Right. Come on so," he said without giving it another thought – he knew, if he did, he would lose his nerve.

They pulled on their coats and headed outside quietly.

Ominous swirling black clouds in the sky were ignored by the children. However, Tadgh was always conscious of his sister's disability and knew walking would take ages, so he jumped on the bike and told Molly to sit on the carrier.

"What about my crutch?"

"Leave it there. You won't need it."

And, like the hand of God on their backs, the wind pushed them as they accelerated down the road at full speed.

"*Weeeeeee!*" shouted Tadgh, exhilarated by the power of the wind.

Leaves and small branches decorated the road before them but on they went.

The wind was howling around Waxy's house. It made it look very creepy, thought Tadgh as he propped the bike against the wall and followed Molly up to the front door.

She was relieved to see Waxy's van parked outside. She knocked on the door as loudly as her small hand would allow.

Waxy struggled to open the door and keep it steady as the wind seemed to want to whip inside and engulf his house like a demonic spirit.

"Jesus, Molly! What the hell are you doing here?" he asked in disbelief.

"You told me to come here at four o'clock."

"Just like the devil," he said to himself, referring to the Spencer Tracey and Frank Sinatra movie about the volcanic eruption. "Get in here, the pair of ye!"

When the two adventurers had entered the house and Waxy managed to close the door shut, he went to another room and returned with the doll.

Molly didn't hear a thing after that because she was enthralled with her dream come true and could not believe she had a Barbie at last. Her trance was broken by Tadgh who was nudging her.

"He wants his money, Molly."

Molly placed the scrunched-up money into Waxy's hand.

"Pleasure doing business with you, miss. You're a determined little lady coming out on a day like this. Do your grandparents know you two are here?"

Neither of them said anything. They just looked at one another. That was enough to indicate to Waxy to withdraw himself from this situation as soon as possible.

"Right, I see. Well, you better be getting back home as soon as you can because if Debbie doesn't get you, Pa Leonard will. Now go!"

Molly had thought of everything. She had tied a belt around the waist of her coat so she could push Barbie inside against her chest and she would stay safe and snug there. Tadgh had gone to get the bike but abandoned the idea and left it there. Their rapid rollercoaster ride to Waxy's was out of the question for their return trip home.

Immediately their bodies were strained horizontally as they battled to walk against the wind. Tadgh had to help Mollie. He was sorry now he told her to leave her crutch behind.

Waxy watched them struggle from his front window for a moment then let go of the curtain, just like his conscience.

On their way back towards the town, Tadgh signalled to Molly to take a shortcut across the fields. Their attempts to keep any kind of pace were becoming more and more difficult, especially for Molly. The wind was becoming stronger, nearly making it impossible for their small figures to hold firm. Mollie grabbed the branch of a tree to rest for a minute. Tadgh continued on but felt a few drops of rain falling from the dark sky which he sensed was going to turn into something very heavy. He waved back at Molly, who was some blurry distance behind him, and pointed to a shed ahead of them.

Once they managed to get inside the door-less building they picked a corner each, to sit and restore their flagging energy.

Meanwhile Pa Leonard was awoken from his slumber by the noise of a gate banging outside. Elsie was already awake and had gone to the kitchen to make a pot of tea.

"Thank God for the gas cooker. I'll be very surprised if we don't have a power cut but at least we can keep the cups of tea coming," she said with a smile.

"Where are the kids?" asked Pa.

"They must be in their room. They're so quiet. I think they're afraid of the storm. I'll get them to come here to the kitchen."

A moment later she returned.

"Pa, I can't find them."

"What? Sure they must be somewhere, check the rooms."

"I've checked. They're not here!"

"Maybe they went outside to see the wind. Look, I'll have to tie that banging gate so I'll have a look around and check the sheds."

Elsie was waiting at the back door when Pa came back inside, shoving the door shut hard against the wind as he did.

"Jesus, It's brutal out there. I don't see them. Where the hell have they gone to?"

"The Lord saves us! I'm getting worried now. You know Molly was acting a bit strange today, like she was up to something. Why was she so anxious to go to Quirke's shop with you earlier?"

"I don't know. She didn't even come in with me."

"What did she do so?"

"Well, when I came out I saw her over at Waxy Carolan's stall in the market."

"Oh, that flipping Barbie doll! That's what this is all about," Elsie said angrily.

She filled in Pa on the basis of her suspicions and they both agreed the children must have gone up to Waxy Carolan's house. They felt they had no choice but to go after them. However, they then decided that Elsie would stay in the house in case they came back and Pa would head out. They both looked out the window and Pa sensed a wave of trepidation in his stomach, considering how bad the weather had become.

Elsie could feel this too and now started to worry about Pa. "Ask Sammy to go with you – it's too dangerous to go to Waxy's on your own."

Sammy's obliging good nature meant that Pa did not have to ask him twice. Sammy was fond of the two kids and always spent a bit of time with them when they came to stay with their grandparents, which usually meant their poor mother was in hospital again. He could not believe they had gone out into the storm and wasted no time jumping on the tractor with Pa. The heavy vehicle provided them with a safe passage to Waxy's house, crunching over the increasing debris that blew into their path.

Waxy, unsurprisingly, was not very forthcoming with his information. He just about confirmed that they had called earlier to his house and Molly had collected her doll. He said they left again right away and he presumed they had gone straight home.

"Wouldn't you think you would have driven them home in your van, you bollix?" said Sammy angrily. "How did you think two small kids like that were going to walk home in this wind?"

Waxy just shrugged his shoulders. "If ye were that concerned about them, ye shouldn't have let them out in the first place. So don't be mouthing off to me now you can't find them."

Pa walked away with a worsening sick feeling in his stomach. He knew what Waxy said was true.

They drove back into town, all the time looking around to see if they could see the children anywhere.

Sammy tried to convince Pa to go to the gardaí and raise the alarm. "Look, Pa, ordinarily we would find them and they probably would have turned up for their tea anyway, but you and I are no match for a hurricane, to be out in this on our own." Sammy was mindful that Pa was an elderly man and he was concerned for his safety as well as that of the children, not to mind his own.

Pa read his mind and conceded. He would go to the gardaí.

Pa explained everything to Sergeant Lamb who in return said very little other than "Right, I see."

Lamb and Tully were frustrated that their satisfactory evening of "sitting it out" was not going to happen. In fact, the complete opposite was now foisted upon them. This was the call-out they were dreading.

According to normal protocol, Lamb would have to initiate a search party comprising of more gardaí, other emergency services personnel and a number of volunteer civilians. But these were not normal circumstances and he already knew the odds were stacked against them.

A phone call to the Garda Station in Castlebar confirmed what he was afraid of.

"I'm sorry, Pa," he said. "I am unable to organise reinforcements at the moment due to the severity of the storm. It's a health and safety issue for all. My request has temporarily been denied."

"No! We can't leave two kids out there! They might get killed!" Pa protested.

"I know, Pa, I know. The best I can do is try and see if a few locals will help us. But you must understand I am not going to put them under pressure to do so."

Sergeant Lamb and Tully made several phone calls around the parish. Unsurprisingly, they got a poor response. While most were on board, they were not willing to go out until after the storm.

However, Nate and Babs Wheatley arrived at the station straight away, followed by Dennis Slattery, Cassie Quirke and off-duty Garda Martin.

Sergeant Lamb briefed his gallant volunteers about the last known location of the children being Waxy Carolan's house and how they could only presume they would have set out for home after that.

They made the easiest decision first. Tully was to drive Cassie Quirke up to Elsie Leonard's house to see if the children had returned and also so Elsie wouldn't be on her own if they hadn't. Babs was nominated to literally hold the fort at the station. Sergeant Lamb instructed her that, if any other emergency should arise in their absence, she was to explain that they would deal with it as soon as possible and she was to ring the station in Castlebar for further assistance. He then went rooting through a box and retrieved two walkie-talkies.

Tully returned and sadly revealed to all that the children had not come back but Elsie was very grateful to Cassie for staying with her.

Sergeant Lamb split the volunteers into two groups, to lessen the risk of losing and having to look for someone else.

They decided to cover two opposite directions in the vicinity of Waxy's house via the town.

"Be careful," said Babs, as the search teams left the station.

But it became clear within minutes of their exposure to the storm that this mission would be in vain. They stayed close within their groups and held on to one another, as individually they could hardly stand upright such was the ferocity of the wind which had got progressively worse. It was impossible to concentrate on anything but their physical stance, never mind to be looking around them. The wind was also so loud they could barely hear what they were saying to one another which made shouting out the children's names futile and they in turn hearing them impossible.

After ten minutes Tully's walkie-talkie started bleeping and flashing. He stood behind a wall for shelter and could barely hear Sergeant Lamb's instructions of *"Abort! Abort! Tully, get your group back to the station immediately! It's too dangerous to be outdoors!"*

The others were already there before them.

They heard Dennis Slattery saying, "Whatever about Bootleg Barbie, there is nothing bootleg about Debbie – she's the real deal."

Sergeant Lamb approached Pa. "I'm sorry, Pa. I cannot risk your life and the lives of these volunteers in this hurricane, it's just too dangerous."

Pa was visibly distraught but understood the situation.

"I promise you, the minute the storm dies down a bit we will be back out there and we'll be able to deploy more searchers," Lamb said. "We'll have them found in no time, but all we can do now is sit it out. They're smart kids, Pa. I bet you they've found somewhere safe to stay and will pop out themselves as soon as they can."

Dennis, who was feeling guilty that his remark about Bootleg Barbie might have been slightly insensitive, invited all the volunteers to come back to the pub where there was more room and comfortable seating. They all appreciated the offer as nobody wanted to head home in the storm, but they also had a sense of duty to stand by Pa, being the good neighbour he always was to them, so he wouldn't have to suffer this turmoil on his own.

Meanwhile Tadgh and Molly were still in the shed. They weren't talking to one another because Molly knew that Tadgh was angry with her for bringing him out and Tadgh felt like he had nothing to say because he knew it wasn't really her fault.

Molly sat on the wet floor with her head buried in her arms which were resting on her knees. The shed was cold and damp. Its vacant entrance and broken window meant the agitated wind swirled and screamed vigorously around them. The roof was leaking and, at the lower end of it, at the gable, it was lifting every time a gust attacked it.

This did not go unnoticed by Tadgh who also had been observing the showers of rain. And he noticed that when the thick rain appeared it seemed to chastise the wind momentarily. Tadgh saw this as their chance to make a break for it.

"Molly, when the wind goes down again with the next shower of rain we need to make a run for it."

"No, I don't want to go out," she replied without looking at him. She was scared.

"Molly, it's not safe to stay in here. I think the roof is going to blow off. Can you not see it lifting and hear that beam creaking?"

"But where can we go? We're too far from home." She looked up at him.

"I know. We're near town so we'll try and make it to there. Come on! It's starting to rain."

Molly did not think about it because, if she did, she would have lost her nerve. She followed Tadgh out the door after checking that Barbie was still secure.

It was near impossible for them to walk in the wind and hold firm, especially for little Mollie. She struggled to follow Tadgh up through the field, holding on to the back of his jacket. He was right – she could see the back of the town close by so she tried to persevere as best she could, using her arm to shield her eyes from all the flying debris.

When the rain ended, the wind whipped up again with a vengeance. They had to stop behind a stone wall and grab on to it to keep their balance.

"*Molly! We'll head for the round tower first!*" Tadgh shouted to her, pointing towards the historic landmark close to the town square. He knew she would need another rest before they decided what to do next.

Tadgh made it to the door of the tower with great relief.

"*Molly!*" he called out. "*Give me a hand to open this door – it's stuck!*" He grimaced as he tried to prise it open. "*Molly!*"

He looked around to see where she was. He could not see her.

"*Molly!*" He scanned the field in front of him and turned from side to side and all around. He couldn't understand it. She'd been right behind him. It was like she'd vanished into thin air. He got really worried and started running back.

Then, suddenly he realised what must have happened and his heart started to pound. The well! He could just about see the circumference of it level with the surface. It was just like a hole in the ground, unguarded, no boundary or wall to indicate and warn of its location. This was why it was of the upmost importance to the locals to keep it covered – because it was such a hazard. But on this occasion Tadgh could see the forgotten covering, just a sheet of galvanised iron held down by block of cement by the side of the well, not on the top of it.

He ran to the well and peered into it. She was lying awkwardly half-in half-out of the water at the bottom, her head on the bottom stone step.

"Molly! Molly!"

She didn't respond. Blood was trickling down her face from her head. Her eyes were closed. *Was she dead?*

He looked away, put his hands to his head and started rubbing it hard. What was he to do? Would he go for help or try to pull her out? He couldn't leave her like that – he would have to try and pull her out on his own.

Carefully he stepped down two protruding stone steps positioned diagonally on the inside of well. The bottom step where Molly's head lay had blood on it.

Stepping into the water, which was about two feet deep, and hunching over her, he called her name again. *"Molly? Can you hear me?"* She was unresponsive. He grabbed her by the shoulders and turned her around. She was lifeless and therefore heavier than he thought she would be. The right side of her face was covered in blood. He put his arms under hers and pulled her up with all the strength he had, staggering back onto the first step. With his arms still round her, he sat there holding her on his lap until he caught his breath and more momentum. With a second heave he managed to prop both of them on the next step.

The last bit was the most difficult. He stretched up and, using his left elbow for leverage against the rim of the well, he roared out in exasperation and strain as he hauled her out over the top with him. He lay on the ground beside her, exhausted, but it wasn't over yet. He needed to get them both out of danger.

They were very near the round tower. He dragged her by the collar of her coat, stopping every few feet to rest his aching arms, until they reached it. After another infuriating battle, he managed to open the door. With the little strength and might he had left, he pulled her inside and propped her up against the wall.

He could see she was breathing but unconscious and still bleeding.

"Molly, you're going to be OK," he said. "I'm going to get help. I'll be right back."

He didn't know if she could hear him or not. He hurried to the open door but suddenly the wind banged it shut in front of him with such force that it rattled a timber rafter in the roof which came crashing to the ground and lodged itself in the stepwell of the closed door. It just missed Tadgh by inches and frightened the life out of him.

Once his heartbeat calmed down again, he tried to lift the fallen piece of timber to the point where he hurt his back pulling and pushing but it proved too heavy for him and he was unable to budge it. Feeling utterly defeated, he crawled back to Molly and stooped over her. He called her name again but there was still no response.

Tadgh started to cry. He was only ten years of age after all and this was a living nightmare. He knew they were trapped and that no one would be able to go out in this ferocious storm to find them. His little sister was seriously injured, maybe she was dying, and there was nothing he could do or think of to do. He was scared. He looked around him. There was very little in the tower but somebody had dumped an old pair of polyester curtains and a mat there. The curtains smelt of soot but at least they were dry. He removed Molly's sodden coat and boots as carefully as he could and placed unscathed Barbie down beside her. After manoeuvring Molly onto the dry mat, he wrapped one curtain around her and draped the other over himself when he lay down beside her. All he could do was put his arms around her to keep them both warm. Then he, like everyone else, listened to this monster and the terror it was unleashing around them.

Only a short distance away, in Slattery's pub, Pa Leonard and the others waited, desperate to find the children but not knowing how close they were.

Dennis Slattery's family had lit candles around the lounge, not in anticipation of an imminent power-cut but as a vigil of hope to keep the missing children safe. Dennis generously served up tea and sandwiches. Drinks were offered but everyone respected the seriousness of the matter and, because of a potential sudden call of duty, they abstained from indulging.

Babs noticed that Pa didn't touch a thing to eat and pressed more tea and sandwiches on him.

"No, thanks. I couldn't eat a thing."

"I know you're sick worried about them, but Sergeant Lamb was right. They will have found shelter somewhere to stay until this blows over. Or, who knows, maybe they even made it back home by now and you are here worrying over nothing."

Pa did not engage with that wishful thinking even though he knew it was intended kindly.

"Babs," he said quietly and emphatically, "do you know how hard it is to watch your own daughter fighting for her life and it's no one's fault? But now we may lose our grandchildren too and it's all *my* fault."

"Nonsense, Pa. This is not your fault. You have helped rear those kids since they were tots. They are a credit to you and Elsie. The only fault you have is that you nurtured a great sense of bravery and courage in them, so much so that they boldly went out even in a hurricane." She laughed. "Seriously, Pa, it's those virtues that will get them through tonight, you'll see."

Every now and then the lights flickered. Candles and flash-lamps were on standby as well as holy water and endless decades of the rosary. They flickered again and then suddenly the whole town went black like a sinking ocean liner.

As the evening and the night rolled on, so did Debbie. Her evil eye was now looking directly down on the West Coast of Ireland, as she wreaked untold havoc in her path. The rolling radio reports were the only source of information for all who were locked down. Each report was more and more alarming as they informed the frightened listeners of how close the storm was getting and the escalating ferocity of the wind. Many farmers chose to release their animals into the open, fearing that their sub-standard barns and sheds might not be able to withstand the storm. Their suspicions were proved right: everything was on the table for Debbie. She spread herself over the landscape with a savage appetite. While the animals were left to fend for themselves, people took refuge under beds and under tables, small children were put in closets. The noise was as unnerving as the event itself. Some describing the sound like a freight train, others like a relentless howling scream. It was something that most people in this country had never experienced before. Some gusts of wind kept their momentum for up to ten minutes at a time. People were petrified. External doors were flung open like an evil entity was entering their homes. Creaking timber beams chilled the blood of the residents underneath. Parents glanced at one another helplessly but said nothing for fear of further terrifying their children who were already covering their ears with their hands. Some had their eyes closed too – they could not bear to see or hear the danger all around them.

Outside it was a very violent environment. What hadn't been battened down was now circulating in the open. The trees were creaking in pain and being stretched like rubber until they snapped and were tossed around like loaves of bread. Some power lines were ripped clean off their poles and the wires were left spitting electricity like a Circus Master's whip. Light-weight objects were frequent missiles while heavier ones were doing considerable damage when they tangled or crashed into more grounded structures.

Tadgh continued to hold on to Molly as they sat in the pitch dark. The distant street lamps, which up to a point had provided Tadgh with some sort of comfort, were no longer shining in on them. Now he felt in complete isolation. Molly had still not roused from her unconsciousness and in the dark he couldn't make out if the wound on her head had stopped bleeding.

The searchers in Slattery's remained as they were. Some stretched themselves out on the lounge seats and, while they may have closed their eyes to rest, they did not sleep, imagining how this night was going to play out. If they dared think about this hurricane coming to an end, they wondered what would be the state of their homes and that of their loved ones?

The natural alarm clock the next morning ironically was the silence followed by surprising but reassuring choral birdsong. People were afraid to think it was over. It was like they were afraid to wake the beast again so slowly they shoved the chests of drawers away from their doors. Children crawled out of their hiding places and they all nervously looked outside. It was a dream-like experience. The calmness was surreal and the idyllic blue sky was cleansed of any trace of the brutality it had endured.

Everyone's property was affected. The aftermath of the storm was hard to take in. Roofs were ripped off in part or in full. Smashed slates lay strewn on the ground and crackled underfoot. Walls were blown down, fences vanished altogether, while smaller objects littered everywhere like a tide that had gone out, retching its contents behind it.

The town required a major clean-up. Stop signs were blown down. Rubbish bins had tipped over and rolled away, spilling all their contents which had been sucked up into the vortex of the hurricane and dropped elsewhere. Domestic appliances, like a banjaxed washing machine and an old steel sink, had made their way into the town square. A water pipe had burst and was flowing without confinement. More dangerous were the exposed power lines and telephone lines that had snapped, leaving the town and its hinterland isolated and without any means of technical communication.

It was heart-breaking to see most of stalwart mature trees that had graced the town throughout the years now slaughtered to the ground with their roots prised from the anchoring earth. In the countryside many minor roads had been completely blocked off due to fallen trees. Any crops that had not been harvested by now were flattened to the ground, ruined, without any part to salvage.

On the coast, boats and trawlers were whipped from their moorings and extensive damage done at the marinas where boats had crashed into one another, causing some of them to sink altogether. Beach huts and mobile homes were wrecked and broken into pieces, strewn on the shorelines.

The radio reports during the day announced endless accounts of nationwide damage and tragically a death count began and increased with fifteen people sadly losing their lives.

When the storm abated satisfactorily, Pa Leonard and his volunteers got to their feet. Sammy went off and got Sergeant Lamb and Tully and they all gathered together in the square. None of them were paying any heed to the blue skies or the birds – their focus was back on finding the missing children. They stood at an edge of the square that was not covered in as much debris and discussed what the best course of action would be and the possibility of drafting in some more searchers.

Their voices were enough to rouse Tadgh who was in an exhausted slumber, still huddled beside Molly. He listened carefully and was so relieved when he heard her breathing.

He listened intently again and this time he was sure he could hear voices too. It was Grandad! He got up and ran to door. He picked up a fallen plank of wood and started bashing the door as hard as he could.

"*Help!*" he yelled. "*We're in here! Help!*"

It was Nate who heard the shouting first.

"*Shh*, lads, what's that noise?"

"*Help! Help! We're in here!*" cried the muffled voice they could suddenly hear.

"*It's Tadgh!*" said Pa, surging through the others. "Where is it coming from?"

"Sounds like it's coming from the tower," said Nate.

They all ran to the door.

"*Tadgh, is that you?*" called Pa.

"Yes, Grandad."

"Is Molly with you?"

"Yeah, but she's hurt."

"That's OK, lad. Can you open the door?"

"No, it's blocked with a rafter that fell down."

"OK, stand well back, Tadgh, and we'll open it."

Nate and Sammy looked at one another and on Sammy's nod they jointly shouldered the door. On the third attempt they opened it enough to let Tadgh out.

Tadgh ran straight into the waiting arms of Pa.

"I can't wake Molly up!"

Sammy went in, lifted Molly up and carefully carried her out.

"She fell into the well and she hit her head," said Tadgh.

The blood had dried on her face and head but it did not disguise the open wound that had split her eyebrow open. Her eye had swollen repulsively to the point where it had closed.

Pa spoke to her and she responded with a moan.

"She's coming around but she's in a bad way," said Sammy.

"We can't call an ambulance," said Tully. "The phone lines are down. We'll drive her to the hospital in the Garda car."

"What if there are fallen trees on the road?" asked Dennis.

"Don't worry – hell or high water, we'll get her there," Sergeant Lamb assured him. "Babs, you might sit with Pa in the backseat of the car and comfort her on the way. Tully, make sure the rope is in the boot in case we need to pull anything out of our way on the road."

Tully went and brought the car. They wrapped a Foxford blanket softly around Molly and placed her in the car.

By now other people had ventured out of their houses and started to walk around the town like zombies, seeing the apocalypse for the first time. However, their curiosity was sharpened when they noticed the gathering of gardaí and others around the tower. Fearing a personal tragedy, they quickened their pace and headed towards them.

One of these onlookers was Waxy Carolan.

As the group conversed among each other the Garda car drove away to the hospital in Castlebar. People could not believe it. They were shocked to hear that two young children were out in the middle of the hurricane on their own and they felt so sorry for Molly on hearing that she had fallen down the well and been seriously injured. Their own sleepless night and structural damages did not seem so significant anymore and they considered themselves lucky by comparison.

Eventually, after the presumed sequence of events had been discussed, the crucial question arose. Who didn't cover the well after using it last?

The chat murmured out to a flat silence.

"Waxy, you were the last one here to leave the square yesterday. I saw Mutey motion to you to cover the well. Did you cover it?" asked Sammy, straight in there.

"*Um*, God, I can't remember – was I the last one?"

"*You fucking idiot!*" shouted Sammy, lunging at him, catching the collar of his jacket and pinning him against the wall. "That little girl could have been killed! You should see the state of her eye, she'll probably lose it!"

"It was an accident! I forgot. I was in such a rush to get out of the storm like everyone else."

Sammy tightened his grip and banged him against the wall a second time. Nobody tried to stop him. "Accidents don't happen, they're caused. Is it not enough that little girl's mother is dying, she herself had polio and now her poor face could be disfigured too as a consequence of you not giving a toss about anyone other than yourself?" Sammy slammed Waxy against the wall again, his head hitting it hard. Then he spoke quietly to Waxy. "I'm sick of your wheeling and dealing and the rest of the dirty tricks you're turning. Well, your card is up this time. I'm not turning a blind eye to your blackguarding anymore. So you'd better watch your back, Waxy, because I know exactly what knives to throw at it." With a final heave he threw Waxy into a heap of strewn rubbish on the ground. "That's where you belong – in the dregs, you dirty runt! Nate, can you run me up to Elsie Leonard's so I can tell her what's happened? C'mon, Tadgh, time to get you home."

Sammy never took his eyes off Waxy until he turned to walk away.

The next day Sammy, Nate and Babs went to visit Molly in the hospital. The phone lines were still down so there was no way of communicating to see how she was. When they arrived at the appointed visiting hour, the Leonards were already there. They were all in a jovial mood, brought on by the relief that Molly was making a good recovery. She was sitting up in the bed playing with Barbie who had survived the whole ordeal unscathed.

The visitors noticed the bandage across her right eye but didn't comment. While Babs chatted with her about her new doll, Pa leaned over to Sammy and quietly revealed that the doctors didn't know yet if she was going to lose her eye or not.

"It could be worse," was all Sammy could offer. He didn't know if it could or not, considering all the burdens this child had endured so far in her short life. Had she not suffered enough?

Tadgh appeared happy in himself. He was reading a comic and swinging his legs from the edge of the empty neighbouring bed he was sitting on.

"A reward?" Nate asked, nodding at the direction of the comic.

"You couldn't be mad at them," said Elsie. "They're only kids. We did tell them off and warned them never to leave the house like that again without telling someone but, look, their common sense will come with time and only then will they look back at the dangerous thing they did during one of the worse storms ever. They're lucky to be alive. We haven't told their mother yet and we probably wouldn't tell her at all only for Molly's eye – there's no hiding that."

Sammy spoke to Molly for a while and admired her lovely new doll.

"You should have called her Windy," he teased. "And will Barbie not get lonely on her own when you go back to school?"

Molly shrugged and smiled shyly at Sammy.

"I think she'll miss you a lot," Sammy continued. "But I have an idea." With that he handed her an oblong-shaped parcel.

Babs helped her tear open the wrapping paper.

"*Oooh*, who's this?" asked Babs.

"*It's Ken!*" Molly squealed in delight. "*Barbie's boyfriend!*"

"Well, as long as Ken keeps Debbie out of the picture I'm sure they will live happily ever after," said Sammy, laughing.

CHAPTER 5

A Royal Appointment

December 1961

"No, I don't think it was Waxy. Nate and Sammy had a stirring of bad blood between them if you ask me."

"It was brewing for a while," said another patron in Slattery's pub. "Sammy was rubbing Nate up the wrong way, especially after that fiasco that happened last June. You know they had words about that?"

"*Ooh*, was there a bust-up?" asked another.

"You could say it was a *royal* bust-up alright."

When the public announcement hit the airwaves on Radio 1 that Princess Grace of Monaco was coming to Ireland to visit the birthplace of her grandfather, Jack Kelly, at Drimurla, Newport, County Mayo, German native Frieda Huber was more excited than anyone else. Grace Kelly was her idol and neither hell nor high water was going to stop her from meeting the Princess, seeing that this was the nearest she was ever going to get to her.

"In fairness to Mrs. Huber," said Cassie Quirke who was sitting on a low stool across from the bar, "she did an awful lot of fundraising to raise money for one of the charities that was close to the Princess's heart, the one that she was a president of, too – the Red Cross. You see, the 'Save the German Children Society', which Frieda was passionately committed to, received a lot of money during and after the war from the Red Cross. Coincidently, Frieda does translation work for the German Embassy so she persuaded the embassy to let her translate a letter of gratitude from them into English and set about raising some money for the Red Cross, to present to the Princess in person. It was her way of giving something back and, boy, did Frieda know how to liberate the moths from the purses and wallets of the locals here! My God, she organised twenty-five card drives, pub quizzes, cake sales, door-to-door collections, raffles, church collections outside Mass. She really got the momentum going. Even Mutey, God bless him, gave her the takings of his fruit-and-veg stall one weekend. The only thing holding her back was physically getting to Drimurla in Newport. She didn't know where that was, so I think that's when she asked Sammy."

June 1961

One day Sammy was delivering post to Frieda's house. He had a very important registered letter for her from the German Embassy.

She was overjoyed when he handed it to her. She hugged him in excitement. "Oh my God, I can't believe it's here!" she exclaimed.

"Is it a ticket to the Connaught Final?" joked Sammy.

"What? No, it's my golden ticket to see a princess! It is official permission from my embassy to translate a letter of gratitude from them into English, to give personally to Princess Grace when she comes to Ireland. Sammy, you are going to have to help me. How on earth am I going to get to

Drumoland in Newport the day she is going there? I don't have a car –
I can't drive."

"Drimurla, you mean, Frieda – but I never even heard of the place before
this Princess Grace visit."

"I know, but you know people and you know people who do drive."

"I bet Nate would know," suggested Sammy.

"Yes, please! Do ask him!" she said excitedly.

"What's in it for me?" asked Sammy, teasing.

"What do you mean, what's in it for you? You Irish are so funny," she
said, flirting.

"Maybe I could get a golden ticket too?"

"Are you serious?"

"If I figure out a way to get you there, you have to take me to meet the
Princess too," suggested a cheeky Sammy.

"OK, fine." With that, she planted a kiss on his cheek and closed the
door.

Sammy smiled from ear to ear. He was surprised by this amorous
expression of gratitude. In the past he had viewed Mrs. Huber as he viewed
the Princess herself, beautiful but unattainable. But, maybe if he played his
cards right he might have as much chance as the next fellow, or more.

This encouraged him to talk to Nate Wheatley about where exactly this
place was, which he presumed Nate would know, and, secondly, convince
him to drive them there.

"The 15th of June – what day of the week is that on?" responded Nate,
moderately interested.

"It's a Thursday."

"Ah, Sammy, what about my rounds? My customers will be waiting on
me. Frieda Huber doesn't buy anything from me."

"Ah, feck it, Nate, you're not a heart surgeon. They'll survive for a few hours. You have plenty of time to give them advance notice. We'll be home early and you can do your rounds when you come back."

"Are you taking a half day, Sammy?"

"No, I have a few days' annual leave to take so I'll be grand."

"That's the Civil Service for you. Different ball game when you're working for yourself, Sammy."

"Get over yourself. Look, I know this sounds a bit superficial and flimsy to you but in three weeks' time this is all people will be talking about. Forget about President Kennedy. Princess Grace is the new show in town and when are the likes of us ever going to get the opportunity to meet royalty like this again? You're the one who'd be treated like a king afterwards because everyone would be dying to talk to you to know what the visit was like."

Sammy knew Nate's soft spot – his weakness was the fear of missing out on anything. And the power trip of the popularity earned would do wonders for his ego. Sammy was right – it became too much for Nate to ignore so he agreed he would drive Mrs. Huber, Sammy and himself to Newport.

"Great! We'll head west on the evening before, make a night of it. It will be a bit of craic if nothing else," said Sammy, walking away rubbing his hands in glee.

"On the Wednesday? No way, Sammy . . . *Sammy!*" shouted Nate after him, but he let him go. While one part of him thought this would be a sissy palava, the other part of him was rather excited about it.

Sammy only had his hand on the rickety, red, wooden gate leading up to Frieda's house when she dashed out to meet him. She was delighted when she heard he had procured transport for them but he told her that Nate wanted to go down the night before because he wanted to get a good secure parking spot for the truck. Frieda didn't care or give a second thought to Nate and his parking issues but readily agreed.

"So we're all set then?" asked Sammy.

"Nearly. I just need to get something personal and local for the Princess."

"A picture frame with me in it?"

"*Ha, ha!* You are funny, Sammy. No, I need something Irish, something unique – but not you!"

Sammy grinned, flattered. "What were you thinking of?"

"A book. I know she loves art and literature. In fact, I believe she already has a collection of Irish literature so I would love to give her something like a copy of *Ulysses*."

"Why? Do they not have proper doorstops in the royal palace in Monaco?"

His humour was not appreciated this time by Frieda, who ignored him.

"But, of course, she would already have that book and indeed all the books written by the great Irish writers," she said.

"What about *An Irish Childhood*? Do you remember a few years ago – the schoolmaster – well, I know he was well retired by then – but he wrote that book and launched it in Slattery's."

"*Mmm*, not really ... have you read it?"

"Yes, it's a nostalgic narration of a typical childhood experienced by the middle and lower-class children growing up here in Ireland over the last century."

"Is it any good?"

"All a bit too familiar for me but, the more I think about it, it would be ideal for her. It would give her an insight into the kind of lifestyle her own grandfather endured growing up in challenging times typical to the West of Ireland, compared to the comfortable upbringing she was fortunate to have growing up in America."

"You are a genius. Where can I buy this book? It would be perfect."

"I'll ask the schoolmaster when I'm on my rounds tomorrow. He could sign a copy for her, making it even more personal for Her Royal Highness."

"Sammy, this is wonderful! How can I ever repay you?"

"A cup of tea wouldn't go astray."

"I'm more of a coffee drinker but come on in anyway."

When the big day arrived, Nate drove to Frieda's house first. He was saved a trip to Sammy's because he was already at Frieda's.

"*Guten Tag*, Mr. Wheatley."

"Ah, hello there!" replied Nate, not having a clue what Frieda had just said to him.

"I am so grateful to you for doing this. It's like a dream come true for me, I'm such a fan of Grace Kelly."

"That's alright, Mrs. Huber. It's years since I've been to that part of the country and it's a lovely spot."

"Please call me Frieda."

"OK, as long as you call me Nate."

"Hey, what about me?" joked Sammy.

"I'm capable of calling you a lot of things but let lazy not be one of them. Now shut up and pass me one of those bags and we'll get going," responded Nate. "*Whoa*, what the hell have you in this one, Frieda – the Book of Kells?"

"No, that's not Frieda's, it's mine and while you're at it ..." Sammy paused, leant over the wall and straightened back up holding a fishing rod.

"Are you having a laugh?"

"No, just a good time, my friend."

"God, you don't get out much, do you?" mocked Nate.

"Hello, Pot, my name is Kettle, I don't think we've met," retorted Sammy.

"Just get in the truck, smart arse!"

The three of them sat snugly in the front of the truck and set off. Frieda carefully put the copy of *An Irish Childhood* she was giving to Princess Grace on the dashboard.

Nate was quiet. His miniature statue of a dancing Honolulu girl in a straw skirt bobbed on the dashboard.

"What's rattled your cage this morning, Nate?" asked Sammy. "You're in a fouler."

Nate didn't reply, he just focused on his driving.

"Trouble in paradise?"

"Don't mention the war – actually you can, I'd prefer to talk about the war. Oh Jesus, Frieda, I'm sorry!"

"It's OK, Nate," said Frieda. "I'm used to it. But is everything alright?"

"Yeah, it's just the missus doing my head in – she wanted to come on the trip too."

"Ah, poor Babs, you should have brought her," said Sammy.

"I can't. I can only fit three people here in the front."

"Surely one of us could have sat in the back, no?" asked Frieda.

Nate laughed. "No, Frieda, it's not safe. You could get a missile flying at you in any direction –the stuff topples off the shelves sometimes – and it's dark and there is no fixed seating."

"You could have worn a helmet," suggested Sammy, making them all laugh. "Look, tell Babs when you get home that you had a rubbish time. That the digs were awful, you hardly had anything to eat, it rained and you didn't get near the royal couple. Never again!"

"I'd say the priest does overtime when you go to him for confession?" mocked Nate.

"Even the priest says one Our Father and three Hail Marys after he sees me."

Nate wanted to change the subject so decided to brush up on his knowledge of Princess Grace through the encyclopaedia better known as Frieda on her chosen subject.

"It was her grandfather, John Kelly, who emigrated to America and set up a Construction Company. His son, this was Grace's father, who was also known as John, further developed the company very successfully and they became a very wealthy family with a comfortable lifestyle living in Philadelphia. However, her mother was called Margaret and Margaret's parents were German immigrants so we have as much claim on Grace's ancestry as you have. Grace was born in 1929 and became determined to be a serious actress. She starred in some great films that you know, like *High Noon, Mogambo, High Society* and *The Swan*. She won an Oscar for her performance in *The County Girl* but, despite that, she is probably best known for her collaborations with the famous film director of suspense, Alfred Hitchcock. You know he made *Dial M for Murder, Rear Window* and *To Catch a Thief* with her, of course?"

"God, you're right – I didn't think she was in all of them," said Nate.

"Yes, and all by the time she was 26 years of age! I know it's extraordinary. She retired then because she had literally met her Prince – Prince Rainier of Monaco. She was happy to leave it all behind her. There was a hush-hush underbelly in Hollywood that was not very desirable. She became disillusioned with the domineering control the movie companies had over her career. Like other actresses they controlled the amount of money she earned, the way she looked and even her weight. They decided what movies she could and could not make, despite her proving time and time again how talented she was. But, you know, she stood up to those chauvinistic pigs at a time when women's voices were silenced, especially in that precarious industry she was working in, and fought for what she deserved, and I think that is what I like the most about her. She was a modern woman, ahead of her time."

Nate and Sammy couldn't disagree with that. In fact, they were so impressed by Grace Kelly's profile they were looking forward even more to meeting her now.

"So what palatial palace have you booked us into for the night, Frieda?" asked Sammy.

"I know a lady from the school staff in Ballantur and she has relations in Newport. Apparently it's a small town with very little accommodation on offer so one of her relatives has offered to put us up. It's not an official boarding house or anything so she is only going to charge us a modest fee. Is that OK?"

"Fair play to you, Frieda. On top of all the fundraising you did, you managed to arrange this for us too," said Sammy, plamasing her.

"You know what they say: if you want to get something done, ask someone who is busy," replied Frieda.

"So don't ever ask Sammy to do anything for you!" said Nate with a laugh.

"I asked you, though, Nate, didn't I?" said Sammy.

"Guys, you both have been so helpful but there is one last thing I'm worried about. I don't know if I should keep the fundraising donation on me. Do you think it is safe to leave it in this house we are going to, especially if we decide to go out somewhere tonight?"

"*Mmmm*, not sure," replied Nate slowly. "It might be safer in the truck. Why don't you hide it in your book and we'll put it in a box and leave it here, locked in safely."

"Sounds like a plan," said Frieda. "Now, are we nearly there yet? We must be near Dimola now?"

"Drimurla," the two men corrected her.

"It's near the Leg of Mutton Lake," Nate pointed out.

"Why is it called that?" asked Sammy.

"Well, gee, Sammy, I guess it's in the shape of one."

"Mutton – it comes from French *mouton*, you know, meaning sheep," said Frieda.

"But, Frieda, do you know the expression we have here – 'Mutton dressed as lamb'? It's like when older women try to dress and look younger than they actually are."

"Like a lot of women around our way," chuckled Nate, winking at Sammy.

"*Excuse me?*" Frieda protested.

"Don't mind him, Frieda – he doesn't mean you, obviously – you're more like a spring lamb," said Sammy, trying to stop the matter escalating.

"Well, you know what I find here?" said Frieda, more than ready to fight back. "It's the women who go to great lengths to preserve themselves and look presentable, yet men of a similar age who clearly have let themselves go think they have a God-given right to capture a younger woman. *Ha!* It makes me laugh – they are so delusional."

Neither Nate nor Sammy said another word. It could have been Princess Grace herself who was sitting between them, making them feel so chastised.

After an awkward silence, Frieda took the book she was presenting to Grace Kelly from the dashboard and decided to read a few extracts out to them. This led to various discussions but Nate and Sammy both came to the same conclusion, which was that things hadn't changed much between the times described and their own childhoods. While both agreed that thankfully jobs and trades were more plentiful, they equally lamented that children were still leaving school early. Many of those were wholly or partially illiterate and that poor education only qualified them for the inevitable prospect of emigration.

Separately, on a humorous recollection of growing up, Sammy laughed about their entertainment and the popularity of telling ghost stories around the fireplace. These tales frightened the bejesus out of the young and not so young, especially when it was related to areas known to them that were meant to be haunted. People would go the long way around to avoid passing these condemned places at night. He was very amused when he pointed out how, once electrification came to Ireland and an increased number of motor cars on the roads, the ghosts disappeared. He was of the opinion that it was not only the spirits who didn't like the electricity. Apparently the housewives were complaining about it because it showed up every bit of dirt and smoke in the house.

Nate and Sammy continued to reminisce about walking to school in their bare feet during the summer months. Neither of them thought it was a hardship – they agreed it felt more like a liberation and celebration of the holidays ahead. However, one topic they did not agree on was the bog harvest versus the hay harvest. Sammy remembered fondly the smell of the freshly cut meadows, turning the grass over to dry it out then putting it into laps and finally, as it dried further, building it into cocks of hay. It was thirsty work and frequently a communal effort, so rewards of cold bottles of beer or tea were passed around as well as ham sandwiches and biscuits which were brought to the fields by the women if they weren't already working in them. If windy weather was forecast, a rope was thrown over each cock of hay and weighted either side by a stone to keep their efforts intact.

Refreshments were delivered to the boglands too, explained Nate, but not on a regular basis like the hayfields, as the boglands could be situated several miles away from where people lived.

Sammy expressed his disdain for the blisters, wet feet, backbreaking hard laborious work between laying the turf, turning it, footing it, bigger footings as it seasoned and then loading it into bags, creels and trailers before the long hungry walk home.

"But the only ones who enjoyed the benefit of the hay were the animals," Nate pointed out. "At least with the turf you were damn glad to be looking into the fire on those cold wintery nights, satisfied that the hard work had paid off."

As they continued to exchange their views, all of which Frieda found very interesting, time flew and before they knew it they were approaching Newport. The old meandering soulful river on their left looked like it had been doing the same thing since the beginning of time. Up ahead was the impressive but not intrusive seven-arch viaduct dividing the town in two. The place was a hive of activity. Obviously a lot more outsiders like themselves had descended on it to be part of this historic visit.

Nate continued to slowly drive up the road and turned left over the bridge. There was a carnival atmosphere everywhere. A funfair had been set up in a nearby field. They could already see the children flying high in the air in their swingboats and hear their squeals of delight as they swung higher and higher. A beautifully coloured carousel mesmerised more people watching it spinning around than those on it. The chair o'planes were popular too as they swooped up and down, thrilling those who were in them. You could barely hear the twinkly music that was unique to funfairs sounding out from the loud speakers. There was a queue to the 'Hook a Duck'. Surely it couldn't be that hard, thought the revellers who then buckled under the pressure themselves.

Food and drink stalls were trading strongly too. Candyfloss in particular was a huge hit because most people had never seen it before. They were unsure if it was even edible, looking at its fluffy form in an array of pastel colours.

To make the occasion more relevant, a stall was set up selling small Irish flags and the red-and-white Monegasque flags. They also sold plastic tiaras so the little girls could to be princesses for a day too.

"Nate, you missed a great opportunity today. You should have staked a stall here. You would have made a small fortune," said Sammy.

"Don't I know it!" agreed Nate regretfully – but he soon got over his loss when he spotted the perfect parking spot at the end of the street just as someone else was pulling out.

"What will we do now?" asked Frieda as she hopped out of the truck, helped by Sammy.

"I'm hungry," said Nate. "Where on earth would you get something to eat around here? It's so busy."

"Are you serious?" laughed Sammy in disbelief. "You have a mobile supermarket with you."

"I know, but I have nothing fresh like milk or bread for us."

"Well, if it's freshness you want, pass me out that fishing rod," ordered Sammy.

"That's a great idea. Let's have a picnic by the riverside," suggested Frieda. "It's sunny and getting really warm – it would be lovely to sit outdoors."

"Oh my God, if we're waiting for Sammy to put something on the table, Sputnik will have landed in space first!" said Nate.

"Come on, live a little, it will be fun," teased Frieda. "I will go and buy some fresh bread somewhere. You must have something to eat in that big pantry of yours, Nate."

Nate, outnumbered by the spontaneous enthusiasm, shrugged his shoulders and decided to go with it. He grabbed a small cardboard box and started to fill it with strawberry jam, Bourbon biscuits, tinned spam, apples, Colleen sweets and three bottles of red lemonade among other things.

"Do you have a frying pan?" asked Sammy.

"Why? Do you want to buy one?"

"No, stupid, what are we going to fry the fish in? And bring of a box of matches and a knife with you too," ordered Sammy, walking off.

Soon Nate was sitting on the bank of the river, watching Sammy attach some flies to the hook of his fishing rod. "It's getting hot alright. God, I'd kill for a pint," he said.

"So would I, but we'd better eat first. There will be plenty of time for a pint later. Besides, we can't leave Frieda on her own."

"Or maybe *you* don't want to leave her on her own?"

Sammy just smiled back at Nate.

By the time Frieda returned, Sammy had the trousers rolled up and was knee-deep in the middle of the river casting off. Nate was stretched out enjoying the sun and having a drink. He had got into the spirit by returning to the truck for the blanket he used to cover his legs while driving in cold weather. He had also retrieved a secret stash of bottles of beer. He shoved them down into the water at the edge of the river to keep them cool.

"Boys!" Frieda said, rejoicing. "Look, I got fresh bread rolls, scones and butter. Have you caught anything yet?"

"No, Jesus the fisherman is having trouble with the bait!" Nate laughed out loud.

"Hey, where did you get those?" asked Frieda, pointing to the bottles of beer.

"I had some in the truck."

"Are you allowed to sell alcohol?"

"Who are you? The Gestapo?"

Sammy nearly choked his cast off and lost his footing when he heard that historic allegation.

"*How dare you!*" responded Frieda.

"I'm sorry, I was only joking," mumbled Nate who realised he had been far too impertinent.

"*How dare you!*" repeated Frieda, except this time she was louder and more indignant. "I can't believe you have not offered me one!" She laughed and with relief the other two joined in.

Nate was surprised that Frieda was a bit of craic, but was glad that she was. He watched her when she went into the water to dip her feet. She was a liberated strong-willed woman whose fortitude was grown out of a need to survive the hardships of war first-hand and the losses it laid upon her. While she was maturing in years, she was still a good-looking woman. Tall, slim and elegant with auburn wavy hair, there was nothing mutton about her, he thought to himself. Then he turned his attention to Sammy who was wading deeper into the water.

"You have matchsticks for legs, Sammy. God, you're so skinny, do you even get wet in a shower of rain?" he said, slagging him.

"Well, I prefer my matchsticks to your redwoods."

Frieda observed her male companions. She could get lost in Sammy's penetrating blue eyes framed by his wispy black hair. She preferred his trim physique to Nate's cumbersome larger frame. Sammy cycled miles every day on his rounds and, while Nate was equally on the go, the driving meant he did all his mileage sitting down. Nate was lying on his side now and when she looked at his outline she had to bite her lip – it reminded her of the Seven Hills of Rome.

"Frieda! Get out of the water, you'll frighten the fish!" said Sammy. "Oh, hang on ... *I think I've caught something!*"

"The Sea of Galilee has produced something to go with the loaves at last," mocked Nate.

"Never mind the Sea of Galilee, the Brown Oak River has delivered a sizable brown trout – look at that!" said Sammy proudly.

A tasty feast of fried fish, fresh bread and treats was enjoyed and washed down with some more cool beers. All three satisfactorily relaxed in the sun afterwards.

Sammy was delighted with his catch as much as Frieda was impressed. It was easy to tell that fishing was one of his passions. He was so content he got up and broke into song, although the few beers might have contributed to his bravado.

Nate was still longing for a real pint so they decided to go and check into their accommodation before heading down the street to a pub.

Their unofficial guesthouse was cosy and had a warmth to it matched by the cordial welcome they received from the woman who lived there.

Frieda told her companions she would find them later after she changed her clothes.

"Changing her clothes for a while of the night?" said Nate as they left. "Did you bring a change of clothes, Sammy?"

"Yes, I brought a clean shirt for tomorrow. Why? Did you not bring anything at all?"

Nate's silence said enough.

"And I wonder how you are the married one!"

The pub they went to was hopping. You wouldn't twist a sweet in your mouth in it. A traditional céilí band was playing frantically like a well-oiled piston. Its infectious beat caused the happy customers to be induced into toe-tapping or thigh-slapping.

Nate laced straight into the creamy pints of Guinness while Sammy went on the pints of Smithwicks. Frieda, who was conscious of her duties in the morning, had a few glasses of beer shandy.

It was a hot night. Many of the revellers were drinking out on the street as it was more tolerable than the packed sweaty pub. Nate, who was feeling a bit of out of place between Frieda and Sammy, went outside too. It wasn't long before he met someone he knew, and then another, and another. Sometime later Sammy joined him and explained that Frieda had retired for the night.

"Right so," said Nate. "Let the real drinking begin."

Several pints later, the two amigos took their leave and went back to their B&B. They were sharing a room. Nate conked out immediately but Sammy was too hot. He got up and opened the window. After a few minutes he realised that was not going to work because the noise from the street was too loud. The banter, laughing and shouting did not appear to be abating at all despite closing time being called some time ago. He got up and closed the window again. He would have to suffer the heat but at least throwing off the bedclothes brought some sort of ease. This was shortlived, however, when Nate started snoring. Sammy covered his head with his pillow but then he couldn't breathe and it didn't do much to diminish the train in the room anyway.

He got up again and went over and shook Nate. It was futile. If the Russian Army marched through the room right now Nate wouldn't hear them. Feeling completely frustrated, Sammy grabbed Nate's keys and headed for the truck, taking a blanket from the bed with him.

Sitting into the passenger seat, he shuffled left and right trying to manoeuvre a level of comfort. No joy – a few minutes later he was shifting again. He sat up, altogether fraught that the sleep had left him. He reached through the hatch to the back of the truck. On the shelf to hand he could feel the box that had Frieda's book in it. He pulled the book out, disregarding the fact that the money was still lodged in the middle of it, and attempted to read it under the dim light coming from the street lamp shining through the windscreen. It did the trick. Within a few minutes his eyelids were sinking and he loosely let the book fall back through the hatch before he fell fast asleep.

The next morning Frieda and Nate were already seated at the breakfast table when Sammy arrived into the kitchen.

"Where the hell did you go last night?" asked Nate.

"I was afraid of the structural damage to the room we were in due to the vibrations of your snoring. I had to sleep in your truck. Jesus. Nate, how does Babs put up with you?"

"She doesn't complain, unlike you. Here, pour us out a cup of tea while you're on your feet," said Nate, motioning to the pot brewing on the gas cooker.

"It's coffee," said Frieda.

Sammy was helping himself to it – slowly as punishment to Nate.

"Oh, for God's sake!" said Nate, abruptly getting out of his chair and colliding with Sammy. "*Ow! Jesus Christ, Sammy! I'm scalded.*"

"It's not my fault. You went straight into me."

Frieda grabbed a wet cloth from the sink and started rubbing Nate's shirt.

"Get away from me, both of you!" roared Nate. "Look at the state of me! What am I going to do now?"

"It's OK, Nate, you have plenty of time to change before we to meet the Royals," said Frieda.

Nate's eyes met Sammy in a state of panic.

"Here, we'll change first and then come back down for the breakfast," suggested Sammy, winking at Nate.

Once they charged into the bedroom Nate sat on the bed in a state of despair.

"OK, you can have my spare shirt," said Sammy. "I have a tie with me so I'll put that on to look a bit different."

"Your shirt won't fit me. You're like a lath."

Needs must. Nate put on the shirt and stood in front of the mirror. The buttons were under fierce pressure and strained gaps exposed his rolls of skin. He frowned at his reflection and thought of what Frieda had said yesterday. He had let himself go and he conceded that he looked like mutton dressed as lamb now.

The silence from Sammy spoke volumes.

"I'll tell you what, put on your jacket and button it up, and you'll be grand," said Sammy.

The silence from Frieda also spoke volumes.

After an awkward and unnecessarily rushed breakfast they set out for the truck.

"Here, give me the keys, Sammy," said Nate.

After Sammy did the patting-down-dance on himself, he revealed he did not appear to have the keys.

"Where are they?" asked Nate, seriously.

"*Um,* maybe I left them in the truck."

Nate pounded down the street ahead of them.

"*I can see them from here, they're stuck in the back door!*" he shouted back.

"I didn't put them in the back door, I slept in the front ..." Sammy trailed off.

Nate opened the back door and sure enough his fear had been realised. He had been robbed.

"*No, no, no!*" he cried as he hopped inside.

After some shuffling around he returned.

"Nate, my book, the donation, are they there?" asked Frieda with great concern.

Nate held the book up but there was no money.

"*Mist! Willst du michveräppeln?*" shouted Frieda, reverting to her native tongue to express her anger.

"I'm sorry, Frieda, there's no sign of it."

"Did they take anything else?" asked Sammy.

"No."

"Are you sure?"

"Yes! There isn't much demand for tinned soup on a black market here in Newport, Sammy. A few bags of sweets and cards of chocolate are missing so it must have been kids but the little dickheads were mature enough to take the money."

Frieda jumped into the back of the truck to search again.

When she was out of earshot Nate laid into Sammy.

"For fuck sake, Sammy! How stupid are you? And you're the one in charge of important letters and cheques every day. How could you be so careless? What is the poor woman going to do now?"

"I'm awful sorry. We'll figure it out."

A very big crowd had gathered in Drimurla in anticipation of Princess Grace and Prince Rainier's arrival. An entourage of black shiny cars swerved in as per schedule. The bodyguards got out first then numerous gasps could be heard from the crowds as they watched Princess Grace descend from her vehicle. She was striking, tall and elegant, just like she stepped out of one of her Hollywood movies. Her blonde hair was neatly swept up. She wore minimal make-up but a little eye shadow accentuated her blue eyes. Her two-piece pale jacket and skirt were as dazzling as the newly whitewashed thatched cottage she had come all this way to see.

She was joined by Prince Rainier and they chatted at length with its current owner and accepted some tea while they also talked with some of the locals about the time her grandfather and his family grew up there and what it would have been like for them.

All the time the royal couple were under the watchful eye of the clicking photographers and other media outlets. The pace of the spectacle surely would not give Princess Grace a restful opportunity to absorb the history but one would hope on reflection she would consider her family's humble beginnings – their lifestyle and culture, the hardships they endured but, most of all, the fact that like all Mayo people they had a stoic sense of resilience and a belief they would succeed. And, as every man's home is his castle, she might hope that despite all the odds against them they were happy while they were living in it. This was where it all began on her father's side and it was a tribute to her ancestors that she had returned to say "It's OK, we made it". It may not necessarily have given her a sense of belonging as it was a world so far removed from her own but, nevertheless, it was an undeniable part of her identity and one that she could be proud of.

She continued to pleasantly talk with the people who had gathered there and who approached her one by one.

When it was Frieda's turn, Sammy stood beside her while Nate took refuge behind both of them.

"*Gutan Tag*, Your Royal Highness, it is an honour to meet you," said Frieda. "I have been an admirer of you both professionally and personally for years. My name is Frieda. I am from Germany but I came to Ireland with the 'Save the German Children' international campaign and never left. So I have as much claim on your ancestry as the Irish do."

"Indeed you do!" said the Princess.

"May I present you with this book? I know you have experience in being *The County Girl* but this book gives an account of a traditional rural childhood in Ireland and we thought it might provide you with an informative and charming insight into the life your grandfather may have experienced growing up here. Also, we were hoping to present you with a donation to the Red Cross as a thank-you to the Red Cross organisation for its aid during the hardest times of the war in Germany and beyond but ... *em* ... well ... I'm sorry ... we don't have it." Frieda ended abruptly.

"We drank it all last night," Sammy whipped in.

Much widened eyes and blinking ensued from everyone with the shock of this impertinent revelation, until Prince Rainier burst out laughing.

"Well, there is a first time for everything, *monsieur*," said the Prince.

Frieda slapped Sammy's arm playfully, to show that he was only joking. "Oh no, that's not true, Your Highness. We're ashamed, but the truth of it is that we simply forgot to bring it. We were so excited and we all thought that one of the others had it until we got here. I can see it. It's still in an envelope standing up carefully on the mantelpiece of the fireplace in my sitting room. I am so embarrassed and I do apologise and I assure you I will forward it on to your organisation as soon as I get home."

"I understand, these official visits are still even daunting for me," replied the Princess, diplomatically putting Frieda's mortification at ease. "*Danke. Auf Wiedersehen, Frieda.*"

The mood lightened within the company of the three on their journey home. They had shared a lovely day yesterday, an enjoyable night and got to meet the Prince and Princess of Monaco all within twenty-four hours. The calamity of losing the money had taken a humorous turn and they began to laugh about it. They were on a high and agreed to meet in Slattery's that evening to tell their friends about how it went.

The royal visit had been reported all day on the radio and the locals were dying to hear all about it.

The three amigos regaled the whole story to them when they met up, not leaving anything out.

Their friends laughed out loud when they heard that Sammy had told the Princess that they had drunk away the money that had been raised for the charity.

"Fair play to you, Sammy, no better man!" someone said.

"God, you were skating on thin ice there with that one," said Waxy Carolan.

"Yeah, but at least I broke it and got them to see the funny side of it! It was Nate who needed calming down the most. I thought he was going to kill me after he discovered the truck was broken into. Don't worry, Nate, I'll compensate you for anything that is gone or broken."

"You're damn right you will," replied Nate with a smirk.

"I felt so bad lying to her," said Frieda in earnest. "I told them I could see the money still sitting on the mantelpiece in my sitting room. I was so ashamed."

When all the details had been accounted for and the hair of the dog was straightened, Frieda was the first to take leave from the pub. Nate and Sammy stayed on for another one and continued chatting.

Within half an hour Frieda returned to the pub, flustered and out of breath.

"Are you alright, Frieda?" asked Dennis, the landlord.

"No, my house has been broken into and everything is smashed all over the place!"

"Come on, we'll get the gardaí," said Sammy, taking Frieda by the arm and leading her outside. Nate followed.

Sammy told Frieda to go straight into the Garda Station and tell them what happened and he would wait outside for her. He lit a cigarette.

In her absence Nate turned on Sammy aggressively with his finger pointing in his face.

"This is all your fault, Sammy. You know what has happened here?"

"What are you on about?"

"Someone in there, in the pub, got the wrong end of the stick and heard Frieda saying that there was money in her house on the mantelpiece and decided to steal it while she was down here in the pub. If you hadn't lost the money last night in the first place this would not have happened. God, can you do anything right, Sammy?"

Sammy snapped. He shoved Nate's finger out of his face.

"You listen here to me, Sonny Boy. I don't know what makes you think you can be so righteous because I do know what happened to you in England and I know why you legged it to America. I have never told a soul around here about that so I suggest you get off your high horse or I won't be long pulling the saddle out from under you and your self-acclaimed four-star status in this town won't be worth a penny!"

He stopped when he heard Frieda and the gardaí coming out of the station.

"I'll come with you, Frieda," said Sammy. "You can go home, Nate. I'm sure Babs is dying to hear about the great time you had in Newport without her."

So while the locals in Slattery's had witnessed a cordial relationship between Nate and Sammy inside, it's what a few of them happened to witness outside that set their tongues wagging.

This threat of exposure from Sammy rattled Nate. He had fought internally with his conscience over what happened in London for years. It was still unresolved so he couldn't move on. He hadn't made peace with it and didn't want anyone to know because this was a story about him and he was far from the hero.

CHAPTER 6

London 1949

Nate was born into a family as the youngest of three boys. They grew up in a content household of modest means with a small farm. Without finishing secondary school, his two brothers went to England looking for work as did so many of their generation. There was a noticeable gap in age between Nate and his two siblings so it was Nate who stayed behind and looked after their parents. His father died of old age and his mother suffered a stroke. She lived out her final years in the County Home as her needs were beyond Nate's capabilities. His brothers settled into their new way of life in England, each marrying an English girl and having a family.

Nate inherited the home house and land. He knew full-time farming at the time was a miserable way to make a measly living and part-time wasn't worth the effort at all so he sold the smallholding of land to a local dairy farmer. His brothers in England were furious when they heard of his intention to do this and exaggerated the point that they might want to return home at some point and live there. Nate offered to sell them two sites. They never mentioned it again. Funny how every dream has a price.

Nate worked full-time in Brennan's Yard in Castlebar. It was a Cash and Carry for traders, grocers mostly, and Nate got to know the market inside out. He knew of mobile grocery business owners and was well impressed by how much they bought which indicated how much they sold. They always seemed to be in a good mood too so Nate reckoned they must be satisfactorily reaping their rewards. It was the one business he felt that his own area lacked and he thought a good provisional service like that would do very well. However, he never once saw himself being the entrepreneur of such a venture. He was becoming restless and began to think he was missing out on a greater success to be had elsewhere, such as England. He knew so many people, including Sammy Joyce, who were emigrating because of the lack of job opportunities in Ireland. By all accounts his friends were getting on well and the work was plentiful. He had met Babs at this stage and, while he liked her, his affection was not enough to hold him back. Besides it was becoming a rite of passage to experience and partake in this national exodus. So he decided to go.

His brother had secured a position for him in the building trade even before he had gone over. Nate settled into his job quickly and with ease. His labour was manual work, digging out crushed rock with a shovel in a quarry. After the first few days he was already looking around him and beginning to ask: is this it?

One afternoon the foreman approached Nate and his fellow co-workers and enquired if any of them were able to drive. Nate made it known straight away he was capable so the company set about procuring a driving licence for him to drive a truck. This idea pleased Nate because he felt he was already exacerbated enough with the trials and tribulations of digging stones so to get on the road driving a truck sounded great, considering he was not long in the job, or indeed the U.K.

Unfortunately his jovial outlook was short-lived. On getting the licence and presentation of the truck, Nate was advised that the only place he would be driving was within the confines of the quarry. As it went, the crushing machine broke the rock into smaller pieces. The Hymac loaded the stones into the trailer of Nate's truck and he transported them out to the road for further distribution by someone else. He unloaded there and went back for another load. Over and back, over and back. A day felt like a year. He felt like a hamster on four wheels and knew he could not do this long-term or literally he would go crazy. He didn't mean to be ungrateful, especially when his employer had arranged the driving licence in the first place and he reminded himself that he was at least under cover out of the bad weather. He genuinely felt sorry for the other men who spent all day in cold, wet, harsh conditions, up to their knees in mud, wearing cold wellington boots and oil skins for protection. But that empathy eventually ran out too and Nate felt he had no option but to stick his neck out and see how reasonable the foreman might be if he asked him to assign him to something else. What that was, he had no idea.

After three failed attempts out of fear, Nate put his request forward. It didn't go down well at all. The foreman asked Nate if he was joking. He reminded Nate of the trouble they went to in the first place getting a licence for him and how they had hoped he would be driving for the company for the foreseeable future. Then he told him in no uncertain terms that if he didn't like it he should fuck right off.

It was a split-second reaction when Nate responded by saying that he would "fuck right off then". It took Nate as much by surprise as the foreman and Nate immediately left the quarry with that dreaded 'Oh no, what have I just done?' feeling, but later that evening he felt fine about it. He hadn't known that he had it in him. He was satisfied that he realised the job was not for him and, while it was an unfortunate outcome, it had to be done all the same. He did feel bad about letting his brother down, though, for it was he who got him the job and now he had no job at all. Nate suspected he was going to get to know himself for the first time in his life and, having been pushed out of his comfort zone with the potential to bring some upheaval upon him, that was something he felt he was ready to take on.

After a few conversations at a Job Centre in London, Nate was advised to figure out what kind of a job he did want. He never had that choice before. At home you just took what you could get without even thinking about it. He knew he liked helping people but did not want to get his hands too dirty. He wasn't fond of getting cold or wet either. He was a "people person", the lady at the desk told him when he told her he liked meeting and talking to people. He liked that term, "a people person", but his enthusiasm waned in confusion when the lady advised him of a position as a delivery driver for a shop.

"But that is exactly the job I left behind me in Ireland! Why would I want to do this over here? That's a step sideways not forward, ma'am."

"How many people worked in your former place of employment in Ireland, Mr. Wheatley?"

"Five or six."

"And how many other branches did it have nationwide?"

"None," said Nate flatly, not understanding her questioning.

"Mr. Wheatley, the employer for this vacancy is Colbert's. It is one of the biggest grocery stores in London. It employs up to two hundred people and the Colbert family owns eight of these stores across the country. What I am trying to tell you is that a position with this progressive company could reward you with several promotions through the ranks during your career."

"Career? Is that not the same as a job?"

"A job is for people who want to move sideways, a career is for people who want to go forward, do you understand?"

Nate had seen the light.

"Mr. Wheatley, you are in a very good position to apply for this. You already have very valuable experience working in a similar environment and you may even have an advantage over the other candidates because you have a qualified driving licence for a truck. You've told me that you like meeting and greeting people so make sure you mention that at the interview. If successful, Mr. Wheatley, and you prove your worth in the short-term, you would be entitled to apply for other promotions as they arise all the way up to top management. I believe they are very good employers."

Nate thanked the lady for all her help and bounced out of the Job Centre with a can-do attitude.

Nate stared at the envelope for a good while before he opened it. He knew it was from Colbert's – they had their stamp on the back of it. He had done the interview the week before and told them everything the lady in Job Centre told him to, and more. He didn't know how it went. He had never done an interview like that before. He nearly had a heart attack when he had to sit at a table with two people sitting on the opposite side. It was so formal and terrifying. If he had known that in advance he probably wouldn't have gone.

Ripping open the envelope, he scanned the contents of the letter as quickly as he could until his eyes settled on what he wanted to read.

"We are pleased to advise that your interview has been successful and we are looking forward to you joining our dedicated team here at Colbert's."

Nate punched the air and let out a *"Yahoo!"* He felt ten feet taller. At last he thought, he was about to start living.

Nate took a disciplined approach to his work. He was all "Yes, sir, no, sir, three bags full, sir". He was a bit apprehensive about being himself yet. He observed that there appeared to be a lot of pomp and ceremony to the business, more than was necessary in his opinion, but his attitude changed when he realised that Colbert's were going the extra mile for their customers because their customers were going the extra shilling for their groceries. Colbert's was sourcing and producing top-quality fruit, vegetables and fresh meat and their delicatessens were fit for the Queen. They carried an extensive range of fine wines, liquors and tobacco too. Nate noticed it was the staff of the great households of London that did the shopping there, mostly on behalf of their wealthy owners whom Nate expected the Colberts must be on a par with, such was the reputation of their thriving business. Mr. Colbert himself used to walk around the store and yard frequently and, to be fair to him, he knew every member of his staff by name.

"Oh yes, Nate – one of our best drivers by all accounts, making all those deliveries in jig time, I hear. Well, come on, old boy, *chop, chop*, don't spare the horses, as they say!"

Nate smiled and nodded in return then jumped back into his truck, nearly afraid to make eye contact with Mr. Colbert, never mind talk to him.

"He's alright, you know, the old man," encouraged George, Nate's accompanying delivery man.

George had taken Nate under his wing because he could tell he was a fish out of water in this pool of classes just like he was himself when he joined Colbert's. He told Nate what was what, who was nice and who was not. After work, he explained that some of the women they met were all lipstick, powder and paint, but the quieter more dignified girls were the real ladies. In fact, it was George who introduced Nate to one of those ladies – Lorna.

Lorna, without clinical diagnosis, could be described harmlessly as having a split personality. One version of her knew exactly how use her demeanour to manipulate men and get what she wanted and Nate was no exception. He fell hook, line and sinker for her. She was very pretty with long, curly, fair hair and blue eyes, she had an enviable figure and turned herself out well, considering she didn't earn very much. Lorna was a singer by profession and was known as 'Valentine'. This was her stage name when she sang in the Belvedere Club. Her performances were theatrical and powerful enough to emasculate the gaze of her manly audiences. She believed her talent deserved to be heard in more salubrious venues by more uptown clientele, rather than the back-end soggy-carpet venue she was currently working at. Secretly, she dreamed of being famous and revered by men who would wine and dine her in beautiful locations and lavish her with frivolous gifts.

But then there was the other Lorna. The one that came from a working-class family in Yorkshire and this was the Lorna that liked Nate. Because of their similar backgrounds, she didn't have to pretend to be anything with him, although she did start wondering if he wanted to shoot for the stars as high as she did and, as of late, she began testing him.

After a lovely sunny Sunday afternoon wondering around Hyde Park, Nate and Lorna sat on a wooden bench, eating tubs of strawberry ice cream.

"This is the life, isn't it, Lorna? It's the simple things in life that count."

"Yes, I've had a lovely time."

"I can't even bear to start thinking about Monday morning already. Why does the weekend go so fast and the rest of the week can't even get out of first gear?"

"Pity about you! I work at the weekend, remember? Singing my little heart out. I can't wait for Monday to come because it's my day off."

"Thanks a lot, you definitely know how to make people feel better. While you are turning over in your scratcher in the morning, I'll probably have four or five runs done around the city."

"Ah, poor baby!" teased Lorna in a child's voice. "I know, why don't you ring in sick and spend the day with me?"

"I can't do that, sure there's nothing wrong with me."

"Nate Wheatley, you are as honest as the day is long. Just pretend, tell them it's something dodgy you ate and you're vomiting."

"Charming."

"Seriously, Nate, they'll know then you'll be back in again the next day so they won't dock your wages."

"How do you know?"

"Nate, please ... please, pretty, pretty please! Just one day to spend together ..." she tailed off in a baby voice again, trailing her fingers across his round face.

"Ah, I don't know. You'd have no luck for that kind of thing."

"Well, you'll have no girlfriend either," she responded, getting angry.

"Don't be like that."

"If you cared about me you would do it," she added, turning the screw on him.

"I do care! Oh for God's sake, right I'll do it, but only because the weather is nice."

"You're the best, Nate!" She smiled, throwing her arms around his neck and kissing him all over his face.

They met up again the next day at lunchtime. It was hotter than they expected. Both of them had taken their jackets and Lorna had an umbrella. She was grateful for it now because she could use it to provide shade for her fair skin. They were drawn to the water so they headed down by the River Thames.

Nate had felt awful guilty ringing in sick earlier that morning. Gail in the office who answered the phone seemed duly concerned and wished Nate a speedy recovery before telling him to drink plenty of liquids. But after a while of fun and frolicking by the water's edge with the apple of his eye, he soon forgot about work altogether. They took a boat out on the river and Nate practised the new skill of rowing which left him exhausted. His arms were killing him and he had worked up an appetite.

"Oh Nate, that was brilliant!" said an exuberant Lorna, oblivious to his aching limbs. "What will we do now? How about a horse and carriage ride in the park?"

"I'm starving – let's get something to eat and then we'll see."

"I know the perfect place, it's called The Vale," said Lorna whose eyes were all aglaze at the thought of it.

"Never heard of it."

"What? Honestly, Nate, I sometimes think you walk around with a box of over your head. The Vale is one of best new restaurants in London. The decor is meant to be as tantalising as the food. Sounds amazing."

"Sounds expensive."

"Please, Nate, how often do we get to treat ourselves?"

"I don't know. Where is it?"

"Lyme Street."

"*Lyme Street? Are you mad?*"

"Why, what's wrong with that?"

"It's the street where I work, at Colbert's," replied Nate, annoyed at the lack of interest and awareness Lorna had clearly shown about his job despite all that he had told her about it.

"Well, I didn't know where Colbert's was, did I?"

"No, but you knew where Lyme Street is and this fancy restaurant."

"I'm sorry, Nate, but some of the other girls at the club have been taken there and I feel so left out when they talk about it," she said, pouting.

Nate looked at Lorna, flabbergasted that she could not join the geographical dots together.

"*Lorna,* I work on that street. I rang in sick this morning, remember? Do you want me to get caught?"

"No, of course not. You won't get caught because we'll go in the side door from Mill Street," she replied, still determined to go.

"It's too risky. Surely to God there are plenty of other restaurants in the whole of London where we can go for something to eat?"

"Yeah, but there are none like The Vale," she said, turning on the waterworks. "And it's my birthday next week, so this could be my present and if we go before five o'clock it's cheaper than later on in the evening. We can sneak in from Mill Street and no one will see you, I swear."

Nate didn't know whether to believe her or not about her birthday. He didn't know exactly what age she was other than she was younger and prettier than he was.

"But what if someone from work is in there?"

"They won't be because they'll all be at work, silly!" Lorna grabbed him by the arm and started dragging him along.

He was beginning to lose his appetite.

The pair cautiously walked up Mill Street. Lorna used her umbrella to shield Nate's head.

The restaurant was located on the first floor. Inside, Lorna followed the waiter while Nate handed the umbrella and jackets to the maître d'. Again, Lorna vexed him when he saw that she had chosen to sit by the window opposite Colbert's.

"Ah Jesus, Lorna, we can't sit here! Do you want them to see me?"

"Relax, no one is going to see you up here from down below and, look, the sun is so strong they have pulled down the blinds in the upstairs offices. If anyone comes in we'll just say you are over the worst of your illness and you've heard they serve good chicken soup in here."

Nate looked around the fancy eatery and could tell this was not the type of place that served chicken soup. He stared at Lorna, thinking show business was definitely her calling.

They ordered some food and Lorna ordered some wine. Nate eventually began to relax and enjoy the view out of the window. He literally had never seen his workplace from this vantage point before. He looked at the colourful window displays which were very eye-catching. He watched the people fleeting into the shop, all of them carrying a parcel or box on their exit. He also observed the yard to the left-hand side of the adjoining store where he himself worked mostly. It was busy as usual, with a flurry of trucks leaving with deliveries and others arriving with stock to drop off. He was impressed by the turnover and the diligent work ethic of the staff and felt good about being part of that. The business had a good name and a successful attitude.

Suddenly, this rosy outlook was smashed when Nate saw a bit more than he was expecting. He blinked twice and then squinted to focus and leaned closer to the window.

"*Lorna, Lorna,*" he whispered, "*I think Colbert's is being robbed! Look!*"

They peered across to the yard and sure enough three opportunistic robbers, obviously choosing a rare quiet but prime and selected moment, climbed into the back of a truck and carried out between them a crate of tobacco and a crate of French red wine. They had almost got away with it when they were sprung by an employee who yelled at them. One of them made a run for it. The second one tripped and fell, forcing the third one to drag the two crates on his own out the gate and around the pillar where the first guy was now waiting to help him. The fallen robber bounced back up on his feet despite been caught by the scruff of neck by an employee. He twisted and turned in the tussle and punched the worker straight in the stomach, winding him so he fell to the ground. Then he kicked him hard in the side and ran out of the yard.

Nate and Lorna watched them make an advantageous getaway down the street without threat. A policeman's whistle could be heard. A fat policeman almost ran to the scene and when he did he went straight to the aid of the injured man.

"Oh my God, Lorna," said Nate, rising to his feet.

"*Sit down, Nate.*"

"I can't sit here and do nothing. I think that's Eddie who's down, the poor bugger. And I think I know who did it."

"*Sit down, Nate, you're making a scene,*" Lorna hissed.

"Are you serious? Did you not see what just happened? I'd better go over there."

"Are *you* serious? You go over there now and you will lose your job. Listen to me!' She tugged him towards her to focus him. "If they see that you're alright and there's nothing wrong with you, they will sack you!"

Nate slowly sat back down. He could see his colleague Eddie getting back up on shaky feet.

"It's a lousy robbery," she said. "All they got was two boxes of stuff, big deal – and look, your friend is fine. This is not worth losing your job over, a job you like. This was not your fault."

This was the Lorna that Nate liked, the sensible one. It still turned out to be a costly evening though. Now, with several staff and police swarming the street and yard, it meant that Nate and Lorna could not leave the restaurant for ages so they had to order dessert, coffee, and more wine.

Nate went to work the next morning, feeling awfully guilty about what had happened the day before. He pulled himself together as he entered the yard and decided to play it cool.

A warm welcome awaited him from George when he entered the canteen.

"Ah, Nate, my old friend. How you feeling, *eh*?"

"I'm fine, George – just something dodgy I ate, I think, knocked me for six, could hardly get out of the bed yesterday morning."

"Must have been something foul alright, mate – you've the stomach of a goat."

"That's for sure, I've seen what you have put in it," said another staff member called Simon Thomas.

"Anyway, enough of that – you'll never guess what happened yesterday," continued George.

"What?"

"We were robbed."

"*What?*"

"Yeah, *daylight* robbery. In the yard. The Napoleon Company had just arrived with their delivery of booze and tobacco when these two goons ran into the yard and jacked two boxes right out of the truck while the driver had gone into the office with the delivery docket."

"I don't believe you!"

"Eddie grabbed one of them but he turned on him and he copped a right waltzing, the poor old beggar, but he's OK, thank God."

"So did they get away?"

"Yeah, with the two crates."

"Did ye call the police?"

"There was a bobby up the street who heard the commotion but they were well gone by the time he arrived."

"*Wow, wow, wow!*" said Nate, trying to sound amazed. "I'd say it was them Blake brothers that did it."

"Why them?"

"Well, they're always skulking around here, aren't they? And it's not the first time they've struck the yard."

"Honestly, how they managed to get two heavy crates out so quickly, I'll never know," said George.

"There were three of them," said Nate, stunning himself.

"Three? What makes you say that?"

"I mean, there must have been more than two – another one of them somewhere hiding around the yard," Nate said feebly, trying to dilute his theory.

"But how did they know to target that truck?" asked George.

"They probably tracked the Napoleon truck across the city, knowing well it carries the red wine and tobacco," said Nate.

"Hang on a minute," said Simon, halting the conversation. "For someone who wasn't even here, you sure seem to know a lot about the robbery."

Nate could feel the sweat pouring through him and his face turning red. "Well, I mean, I'm guessing it's the Blakes, who had help, that's all," he said, trying to sound matter of fact.

"Oh right ... but how did you know it was red wine they took?"

"*Em*, well, with Napoleon's being a French wine merchant I just presume that's what they went for, or was it the shite – I meant the white?" he added humorously, trying to diffuse the tension that had suddenly arisen.

Simon in one swift move jumped off the box he was sitting on and stood a little too close in front of Nate.

"Bit of a coincidence that you were 'sick' yesterday, mate, on the day we got robbed and yet you seem to know more about it than anyone."

"You're barking up the wrong tree, Simon. I swear I don't know what I'm talking about. I'm just saying."

"I'm watching you," threatened Simon, releasing his stare and walking away.

"Ah, you've done it now, Nate," George said. "You'll feel a hole in your back from that fellow's eyes boring into it. Once he takes a set on someone, it sticks. Never mind – that's why no one likes him anyway. Take no heed, lad. Now, come on and give me a hand. Your holiday is over. As a matter of fact, I'm going to take it easy today seeing as I had to do everything on my own yesterday."

CHAPTER 7

Flotilla on the Thames

After a few days no one was talking about the robbery anymore but George was right about Simon who had persevered in observing Nate with a suspicious eye. Truthfully, he had every right to, considering that Nate could identify the thieves, knew that there were three of them in total, saw exactly what they took and most importantly witnessed one of them assaulting Eddie. The latter was the worst part that gave rise to the turmoil in Nate's conscience and he knew that the perpetrator should be arrested and charged for that alone. But he said nothing and cowardly accepted it was too late, because if he did come forward now all of the staff would lose respect for him.

But the guilt wouldn't leave Nate so he tried to find another compromise and endeavoured to take Eddie under his wing. Eddie had arrived from Montego Bay in Jamaica a few weeks earlier. In Nate's opinion he was given the crap jobs within the store and the yard to do. When Nate could, he would offer him a hand. He found out that 'Eddie' wasn't even his real name, it was Akoni Dacosta and they only called him Eddie at work because they felt like it.

However, in spite of Eddie's challenges at work, he did not warm to Nate's feathers and turned down his assistance on numerous occasions. He thanked Nate but, with an inward determination, he was going to make his own way in life and just wanted to keep his head down, his mouth shut and get on with the job.

ele

Lorna, on the other hand, was the one person Nate was turning the cold shoulder to. He would never say it to her but he felt the burden he was carrying was her fault for persuading him to take the day off work dishonestly, seeing the whole robbery and not getting justice for Eddie who endured the physical brunt of it.

Things were stilted when Nate and Lorna met up again. She could sense his reluctance to engage with her so she tackled him head on about it.

"I don't blame you, Lorna, but I think there is still something we can do. I should go to the police and identify the robbers."

"We have been over and over this, Nate. If you go to the police and tell them everything then your career is over and you're the one who keeps going on about the great prospects Colbert's have for their employees."

"Well, then *you* should go the police and tell them you saw everything and you know you the robbers are."

"Me? No way! I'm not going to wing this on my own. Why should I? Eddie is your friend, not mine."

"Because we need to do the right thing," pleaded Nate.

After a few silent moments in mutual thought, Lorna changed her mind.

"You know, maybe you're right. I mean, this would definitely make the newspapers and along with publishing my name they would say what my occupation was, as an upcoming talented singer. Like they say, there is no such thing as bad publicity."

"Are you serious? Is that all you can think about – yourself?"

"Excuse me! So it's all right for you to protect your prospects but I can't protect mine? I know well you blame me for all of this, starting with the restaurant. I just wanted to take you somewhere nice, to have a taste of the good life for a change."

"Well, Lorna, maybe you and me have very different appetites for what we want. You seem to have a very high-flying taste for things compared to me."

"You can say that again. I'm actually getting a bit sick of your limited ambitions," finished Lorna, storming off.

Nate didn't go after her. In fact, they never saw each other again.

After a few weeks Nate's conscience has settled considerably. He was thinking how well he was getting on at work and was becoming quite popular. He was even cheeky enough now to hold a conversation with Mr. Colbert and always tried to inject a bit of humour into their chats, for likability.

His efforts began to pay off because one afternoon Mr. Colbert walked into the yard, calling the staff to gather round. He informed them that the annual flotilla on the River Thames was going ahead on Sunday and like every year his store would be represented by having food stalls on the banks. His clerk would take the names of anyone who wanted to participate and organise the tempting food and beverages they would sell. They had done this for the last seven years and it had proved to be very lucrative for the business, not to mention great publicity.

However, it was not the only source of advertising they used. Mr. Colbert was a keen sailor and he owned a handsome sailing boat. On an occasion such as this he had banners printed for the sides that ran the length of boat deck: *Colbert's Food, Wine & Tobacco Merchants*. They were tied to his boat which was named *The Regent*.

After his initial talk to the staff, he singled out Simon Thomas.

"Mr. Thomas, I hope I can rely on you to be the skipper again this year?"

"Aye, aye, Captain Colbert – it is a pleasure to sail on the *Regent*."

Then Mr. Colbert turned to Nate. "Nate, would you fancy doing a bit of driving on water for a change?"

"I don't know anything about boats, sir, but I'll give it go." The satisfaction he felt knowing that this would vex Simon was bringing the devilment out in Nate.

"Oh dear, if that is the case you might be better as a deckhand. I am inviting a few friends on board for the race and we will be having some refreshments so perhaps you could assist with organising that. Bring someone with you to help with setting up tables, food and drinks, that sort of thing."

George stepped forward, grinning from ear to ear, but was ignored.

"Eddie, yes, Eddie, bring Eddie with you," finished Mr. Colbert. "Won't be all work, I promise – then you can enjoy yourselves, gentlemen, like everyone else."

Eddie knew he wasn't like everyone else and this was a poor attempt to make up for the assault on him during the robbery, so it didn't impress him in the slightest.

On the day of the race the sky was grey and cloudy, a scene very familiar to Londoners, everyone praying that the rain would hold off.

Nate and Eddie arrived early and set up the catering. Then they assisted the ladies in all their finery up the platform and onto the boat.

Mr. Colbert was dressed like an old sea captain, albeit a wealthy one – all he was missing was a pipe. Simon was hovering on the top deck at the boat's wheel. He was dressed all in white, canvas shoes too, hair slicked back. Nate thought he looked like an idiot. Then, looking around him he noticed how all the patrons were dressed in as much nautical costume as one could imagine.

The boats were decorated with bunting flags from bow to bridge and beyond. Scarves, ties and flower wreaths adorned many of them too. The whole river looked like a floating flower bed at the height of summer, exploding in colour. There was an obvious air of anticipation and giddiness. The horns of the boats rang out randomly as the impatience grew. The majority of the boats were not there for first prize but merely to be shown off by their wealthy owners who celebrated the day in style.

Nate admittedly did not know a lot about boats but was very taken with the *Regent*. She was built out of a dark wood with gold fixtures and fittings all so shiny, so clean. She was sturdy and calm, making Nate forget all about the dread sea legs he thought he might unfortunately encounter during the course of the afternoon. Eat your heart out, Lorna, he thought, smiling to himself. How much the Prima Donna would have loved all this palava!

A foghorn rang out and the crowd roared from both land and water. The race had begun.

Even though when looking forward it all appeared to be going in slow motion, yet when one looked more close to hand these boats were trashing their way through the water with a robust speed. A wave of patience eventually descended on the more leisure-minded sailors like those of the *Regent* who let the real competitors take off, so Nate and Eddie went about serving crustless sandwiches and sparkling champagne to Mr. Colbert and his guests.

Nate then retreated to let them feast in peace but decided to have a snoop around the boat. He was reluctant to go upstairs to where Simon was steering but he knew the view from there would be worth the usual wrath he received from him, so he paid no heed and up he went.

"Ah, just in time, Paddy! Get over 'ere, will ya?"

"What's up, Simon, are you alright?"

"I'm bloody starving and in need of a drink. Here, take the reins, she's all yours."

"What? No way. I don't know how to steer a boat!"

"It's not hard – even you can do it. There's nothing to do really right now, just keep her straight," said Simon flippantly as he bolted down the stairs.

"*Where are you going?*" cried Nate after him as he grabbed the wheel.

"*To join my own class!*" Simon shouted back up.

What a jackass, thought Nate, furious – but not for long. He couldn't believe the panoramic view he saw before him. It was amazing, stunning, biblical. Hundreds of boats hurtling forward with pride and panache. Nate felt privileged to be part of it and knew this spectacle would be something he would never forget. He continued to enjoy this vista for some time until a smaller boat ahead began to bother him. She was veering into the *Regent*'s path and Nate was not sure where the brakes were, so to speak.

"You alright there, sailor?"

Nate turned around and for the first time in his life he was actually glad to see Simon.

"Great timing! Come here quick – we getting too near this boat ahead!"

"Oh, get out of the way, Paddy, and go back to your four wheels!" said Simon who stormed up and took the wheel, leaving quite a whiff of liquor lingering in the air behind him.

Nate was relieved and, speaking of relief, he was bursting for the toilet. He made his way downstairs to the bottom deck as quick as he could, despite the small steps being an encumbrance to his big feet.

On his return back up the stairs he dared to wonder if it would be appropriate to join the guests. How about if he casually sauntered near the sandwiches and perchance they might invite him to join them and a wonderful evening would ensue?

He was just back up on deck when suddenly there was an almighty jolt, so powerful it threw him over the edge sideways. Hitting his head on the gilt-edged railing, he fell into the cold water.

Nate opened his eyes. All he could see was white everywhere. Had he died? He focused his gaze. He was looking at a ceiling, then a wall, then other beds and stripy pyjamas. He realised he was in a hospital.

"Nate, Nate, you're awake!" a voice whispered.

He turned his banging head slowly and saw George sitting by the side of his bed.

"Am I alive?"

"Yes, my old mate, thank God. How are you feeling?"

"Like I got hit by a train."

"Actually, it was a boat, kind of. Can you remember?"

"Why are you whispering, George?"

"Trust me, keep your voice down. This is serious, Nate. What do you remember about the crash?"

Nate slowly pulled himself up in the bed.

"I ... I ... oh yeah, the boat race. I was on the boat, there was a bang and I fell over."

"Were you steering the boat, Nate?"

"Yeah, I was, George. You should've seen me," said Nate with a smile of nostalgia on his face.

"Oh, I see," responded George, looking disheartened.

"But I wasn't driving when the bang happened, Simon was."

"I knew it! That conniving pig! Nate, Simon said you were steering and caused the crash."

"What? No, it's the opposite. I was the one who warned him of the danger ahead and that we were going to crash into the boat ahead of us."

"What happened then?"

"I left him to it. Sure, I don't know how to steer a boat. I went to the jacks. What's wrong? Aren't I alright? Did the boat get damaged? Oh God, I'm getting fired, aren't I?"

"It's a bit more serious than that. A woman drowned, Nate. She was one of Mr. Colbert's guests. And young, only twenty-four years of age, poor thing. She fell overboard too when the boats collided. Some people jumped in to save her as she couldn't swim, but they didn't get to her in time. She drowned. It was all over the papers and the news. Mr. Colbert even closed the shop as a mark of respect yesterday. There's a black ribbon and note on the front door."

"What day is it?"

"It's Tuesday. You've been unconscious for the last two days. You hit your head on something, they think, when you were falling over. Luckily, the water police on standby hauled you out."

Nate was rendered speechless, trying to take in the shocking news of all this tragedy at once. After a moment he spoke again.

"So you're saying that Simon is blaming me for this?"

"Yes, that's why I'm here trying to warn you. There has been a criminal investigation launched by the police and, the minute they know you are awake, they'll be in here like the Hound of the Baskervilles to question you."

"But I'll just tell them what happened."

"Where was Simon when you were steering?"

"Downstairs, trying to be something he's not with the guests."

"So plenty of witnesses then. Where were you when Simon was steering, at the time of the crash?"

"Coming out of the jacks."

"Did anyone see you?"

"No."

"So no witnesses then."

"Is that bad?" asked Nate, already knowing the answer.

"Simon obviously heard and saw you using the toilet and knew that no one else did so it's his word against yours that you were steering the boat because no one can prove otherwise."

"But the police – Mr. Colbert – they'll have to believe me."

"You have nothing to convince them. We all heard you telling Mr. Colbert that day that you know nothing about boats and yet here you were steering, allegedly, when the boat crashed into another boat. Nate, mate, I don't think you have a leg to stand on. You could get into serious trouble for this."

"But I didn't do anything wrong!" said Nate, frustrated.

"I believe you, but you could be charged with manslaughter for this and go to prison for a very long time."

"It's not going to come to that. Why are we still whispering anyway?"

"No, it's not going to come to that and we are whispering because I don't want the nurses to know that you are awake yet."

"But surely that's a good thing?"

"No, Nate," said George who was the one getting frustrated now. "I told you – the minute they know you have come around, the police will be in here on top of you and they will probably arrest you."

"So what am I supposed to do?"

"Play dead."

"What?"

"Go back to sleep as you were. I'm going to go home and get you clothes and shoes. Your keys are in the cabinet beside you. I'll be back again later for the evening visit and I'll help you escape."

Nate started laughing at the silliness of it all.

"Escape? And where exactly am I supposed to go?"

"America."

"Have you lost your fecking mind? That's nuts. I am not going to America. I could go to Scotland or Wales."

"No, Nate, you can't – they'll be looking for you all over the U.K."

"Well, I'll just go home then."

"You can't go there either. They have your home address on your work record, remember?"

"But America, it's so far away. That's a bit extreme, George."

"I know, but I have thought about it and they speak English there and you could get a job easily. It doesn't have to be forever and it may be safer to travel back from there to Ireland when the heat is off you. You can set sail tonight. I'm assuming you have some money saved up? If not, I can help you."

"Thank you, George. You're a great friend. But I'm OK I have some money put aside."

"Good."

"But how am I supposed to get to the ship, when the heat is on?"

"When I come back this evening we'll pull the curtain around the bed and I'll help you sneak out. Remember you said to me once 'May you be in heaven half an hour before the devil knows you're dead'? That's how we're going turn the heat off."

At half past six sharp George was back at Nate's bed. Nate had lain like a stone at the bottom of the river since he had left earlier. George pulled the curtain around the bed which was not at all unusual during visiting hours.

Nate changed into the clothes George had brought him, then he grabbed his keys as George gave him directions to the exterior door up the corridor on the right.

Nate did not waste any time except to shake the hand of George firmly.

"Thank you, George. You're not only a good friend to me now but you have been kind to me since I arrived and I won't forget it."

"There isn't a bad bone in your body, Nate, and you don't deserve what's coming to you, so God speed, my old friend, and I wish you the best of luck."

Nate absconded out of the hospital, leaving the closed curtain behind him. Visiting lasted for two hours and the staff would assume George was still there and would alert them if he recovered consciousness, so this provided him with a lengthy window of opportunity to leave.

He went straight back to his digs and pulled out his battered brown suitcase. He hadn't thought he would see it again so soon. Frantically he threw what minimal clothes he had into it. Then he got the tobacco tin which he had hidden in the lining of suitcase and began to count the notes in the roll of money he had stored in it. Sitting on the bed, he wondered if he even had enough earned to sail to America. He broke out of his tortured mind for a moment and asked himself what was he doing? How had this happened? This was so unfair, madness. But then the sense of dread returned. He could imagine Seedy Simon accusing him of the tragedy and Nate knew he had no one on his side of the story. He could not go to jail for something he didn't do.

Unheard by Nate, his flatmate had walked into the house and stood leaning on the jamb of Nate's open door.

"Nate, are you coming or going there?" he asked, looking at Nate in his disarray of packing. "Where have you been? I know you were going to that boat race and I heard about the accident. Did you see it? Who was the girl that drowned – did you see her? Was the boat damaged? What about the other boat?"

Nate thought his head was going to explode with all these questions torturing him. He couldn't stand it. He got up, suitcase in hand and hurried out the door saying nothing to no one.

George had come through for him again – his information was spot on. A ship was bound for New York that night. Nate got his ticket and boarded in a trance. He pulled the collar of his coat up around his face and watched his back. No one appeared to be paying him any undue attention. Everyone was preoccupied with their own individual momentous occasion which they were experiencing right now. They were relishing excitement and healthy apprehension in equal measure on the eve of their long journey into the unknown.

For Nate it was a very sombre and numbing experience. He hadn't even dwelled on the fact that this was the first time he was back on a boat after the crash. He stood at the rails on deck for a long time and watched as the bright lights of London got smaller and smaller. He lamented the good life he had just started there and mourned the life of the young woman that had tragically ended.

CHAPTER 8

Island-hopping

If Nate thought London was big, then his mind was blown away all altogether when he reached New York. It was huge. Street after street, row after row. How far would you have to go to see a green field, he wondered. He hadn't yet discovered Central Park.

He lived in Brooklyn on a street called Bay Ridge Parkway. A home from home, there were so many Irish people. But at work there were so many different nationalities from around the world it made Nate realise the Irish were not the only ones escaping their burdens. After a while everyone became oblivious to each other's backgrounds and just got on with the job.

His initial work contact proved to be spot on. He was asked very little about himself other than "How soon can you start?", and that was such a relief to him, exactly what he was hoping for. He got a job on the last stage of construction of the Brooklyn Battery Tunnel. This was a solution to allow thousands of vehicles to drive under the city, such was the expanse of the metropolis congestion that was devouring itself. Nate came to this party late – it was due for opening in May and now there was a real push on to get it finished in time.

He was assigned to the smelly and dirty tarring machine. He didn't have clean fingernails in ages and he swore the stuff was seeping into his skin. Like London, the money was good, but hard-earned.

One slobbery wet Monday afternoon Nate was waiting for the tar to heat up before spreading it on the road. He heard a click. He was standing at the mouth of the tunnel in a trance, absorbing the news that his employment would be terminated at the end of the week because now it was the turn of the electricians to come in and light up the tunnel. He heard another click. He took his shovel to test the consistency of tar and started to mix it.

Click, click!

What the hell is that? he thought.

He looked up and around and squinted at a man who was down on one knee with a camera in front of his face.

Nate stood up straight and held the shovel at his side like a Samurai solider.

Click, click, click, click!

"Can I help you there, mister?" asked an annoyed Nate.

"No, please carry on, man, don't mean to disturb you."

Nate, not sure what to do, went back to his task in hand, wondering should he let this guy take his picture. What did he want them for? Should he tell his foreman? Maybe he was up to no good.

Click, click, click!

Nate turned around and the photographer was right beside him.

"Ah here, what's this about? What are you taking pictures of me for?"

"No, seriously, man, this is great, and you're Irish! Don't let me interrupt you."

"I'm not lifting another finger, *man*, until you tell me why you are so trigger-happy with your picture-box there."

"OK, calm down there, John Wayne. My name is Max – Max Grundig." He extended a hand to shake with Nate. "I work with *Globe International Magazine* and we're doing a story on the snowballing construction that is going on in New York right now and the people behind it who are turning this city into one of the most innovative places in the world. I mean, you guys don't even realise what a contribution you are making to the skyline of this great city. It's historic."

Nate started at him blankly. He had never thought of it like that, he was just doing his job. He thought of Max, his dog at home who shared his name with this intruder.

"Sorry, look, I didn't mean to sneak up on ya. I want to do some interviews too with all the great nationalities that have come together here on this construction. Are you a talker?"

Nate smiled. That was one international skill he had no difficulty with and was flattered that someone from *Globe International* might want to talk to him.

"What do you want to know? I mean, I'm not going to get into any kind of trouble talking to you, am I?"

"God no, I have full permission from your project managers who are delighted to have us on board. I mean, this is a great story for us and great publicity for them. It's a win-win."

"Right, but where's the win-win for me?"

"*Ha, ha*, there's no flies on you."

"If they are, they're paying rent."

Max laughed out loud. "What time do you clock off?"

"Five o'clock."

"How about I buy you a beer and we can have a chat? Where's handy around here and I'll wait for you there."

"Havana Bar, right around the corner."

"Great, see you there."

Nate punched out at five o'clock on the dot and ran to the galvanised temporary washroom. He took off his dirty overalls and washed his hands and face with the carbolic soap. He pulled on his jacket and left.

Havana Bar was a far cry from the idyllic landscape of its namesake homeland. It was rough. The type of place where even the women spat. It reflected its clientele – hardworking and hard-drinking.

"Thanks for meeting me," said Max. "I'm so sorry, I didn't even ask you your name."

"It's Nate. Well, Ignatius – Wheatley."

Max took out his notebook and wrote it down.

Maggie, the barmaid, dropped a bottle of beer and a meat roll on the table for Max.

"You hungry?" Max asked.

Nate nodded.

"Can we have another, sweetheart?"

"Sure you can," replied Maggie, flashing Max a cheeky grin.

Nate hadn't realised she had bad teeth. He had never seen her smile due to the sullen reception she gave to most people. She was a real New Yorker. Straight-talking and tough, which she had to be to discipline these often drunk and lecherous customers. But Nate realised that she could see that Max was a handsome man with an air of adventure about him. He could tell Max could sweet-talk any sour mouth.

A pair of aviator sunglasses sitting on his head chastised his windswept blond hair. He wore a white shirt in dire need of ironing but, matched with his cargo pants, he looked like he was always on the pulse of where the action was.

A bottle of beer appeared on the table for Nate. What he wouldn't give for a pint of cold porter but bottles were all the go here so he had to make peace with that.

Max went on for an age, telling Nate about the story he was writing. 'The Hands that Built America' he was calling it. He explained the irony of how all other nationalities were coming here from their home countries, ravaged by poverty and destitution to make another country the best in the world. He spoke with passion about all the new builds in New York, their innovated avant-garde (whatever that was, thought Nate) and futuristic designs. How these architects were pioneering all this new technology, the likes the world had never seen before, and his magazine was eager to document this extraordinary revolution. He had interviewed several more people who were contributing to this metamorphic rise, from the like-minded architects to the people on the ground who were all encapsulated in this very special period of time.

Nate was succumbing to Max's charms as much as Maggie was. He was so interesting and knowledgeable, but not in a condescending kind of way. He possessed a warm generosity of sharing what he knew and Nate felt at ease with him. His adventures were a hard act to follow and Nate struggled to reiterate his own life story to him (leaving out the bad bit about London, of course). He couldn't sell himself like Max could. He didn't share that self-confidence that only Americans can exude so shamelessly. He told Max he grew up in a small town called Ballantur in the West of Ireland. How he had lived there all his life until he went to London and then America to relieve himself of the minimal existence he was experiencing at home because there was no work, and how he was forced to seek a better life elsewhere like everyone else, and like everyone else what he wouldn't give to return home in the morning, despite his country's failings. He lamented and spoke of the shame he felt when he sold his parents' lands and left Ireland, considering how long it took to free Ireland from British occupation. He was in America to earn good money and make a life for himself. Honestly, he didn't care about, or think about industrial revolutions, gigantic leaps forward to the building of a new city and being a part of that, until now. Maybe in years to come he would look back or drive by all these magnificent man-made advances and say, yeah, I was part of that.

They continued to talk about this new age for a while and then Nate suggested a proper drink for the road before they went their separate ways.

They went and sat at the bar.

"Maggie, two whiskeys, please. So where is home for you, Max?"

"Hawaii."

"Honestly?"

"Yeah, well, I am originally from San Francisco but now I live in Oahu."

"Oahu? I thought you lived in Hawaii?"

"There is more to Hawaii than just Hawaii, Nate. Hawaii is made up of eight islands, Hawaii, Oahu, Maui, Kaho'olawe, Moloka'i, Lani, Kauai and Niihau."

"Well, I never knew that."

"Have you heard of Honolulu? It's the capital and it is on the island of Oahu. Ever heard of Mauna Loa?"

"Who's she?"

"Not who, Nate, *what*. It's a volcanic mountain. It has terrorised the people of Hawaii for centuries – ask my wife – she's from there.'"

"You're married?"

"Yep, to a woman called Ilima, named after the flower of Oahu, and we have two kids. Haven't seen them in ages – in fact, I'm heading home tomorrow. So I know what you mean, Nate, when you speak of homesickness and missing family. In fact, Oahu and Bale-lane-toor, right?"

"No, it's Ballantur."

"Yeah, that's what I said."

"Yeah, but its pronounced BAL. Oh, never mind." Nate went on to describe Ireland in general.

"God, you cannot pronounce my places and I can't pronounce yours," said Max, laughing. "We have much more in common that you think. Our islands sound so similar. Small local communities that care about each other. People who have great affection and connection to the land and sea. A strong sense of honour and tradition among families. But, seriously, Nate, you should see Hawaii, it really is heaven on earth. We have long-range mountains and in our cooler seasons the tops can be covered in snow, so white it nearly matches the white sands of our never-ending beaches. I live in Pearl Bay, called after the beautiful warm sand that is massaged by the lapping tropical sea water. We eat coconut, pineapple, banana, papaya, starfish, *mmm mmm!* Oh, and the women are so tasty too. Beautiful, long brown hair, straw skirts swaying in the music, wearing wreaths of orchids around their necks."

"Sounds just like Ireland," chuckled Nate, "minus the tropical bit, the exotic bit and the women wearing straw skirts – but it is green!"

"And when you go back to the Emerald Isle you can do it with pride," said Max, taking the reel of film he had used earlier out of his shirt pocket. "This story is every Irishman's story of how they got up from the gutter to the gods and you, Ignatius Wheatley, are the reflection of that and I am going to make sure you are the representative of that journey.'

"*Here, here!*" toasted Nate. "Maggie, same again!"

The two men continued to talk a lot and drink a lot in equal measure and on the spur of their departure Maggie presented the bill.

"*Oh shoot!*" said Max, whose hands were dancing around his pockets. "I thought I had more money on me." He stood up and staggered.

"Don't worry, Max – *hic!* – sure it's the least I can do – *hic!* – for you and your magazine," hiccupped Nate, unfolding his dollar bills to cover the lengthy tab of food and drinks. His inebriated coordination made him drop the money and slowly he swayed over it on the ground before picking it up.

Max gazed at the money in Nate's hand.

"Actually, Nate, I feel terrible asking you this, but the thing is I work freelance so they don't pay until you print. You couldn't sub me a few bucks, could you? I just want to take something home to the kids."

Nate was taken aback at this but how could he say no? Max didn't leave him with much choice.

"Here, Max, safe journey."

"Thank you, man, I won't forget you."

"Well, be off with you! What're you waitin' for?"

"I'm just waiting for the door to come around again."

Nate woke up on the sick bed of Cúchulainn the next morning. Even his hangover was hung over. Oh never again, he scolded himself. He pulled himself up in the bed and let the flashbacks of the night before start flicking through his mind. Max, Havana Bar, *Globe International!* The latter was good pain relief and he was very excited about it. He heaved himself out of the bed and went to work.

Friday evening came quicker than he liked. His contract was finished today and while he was sure he would pick up another job he hated the insecurity of not having something else already confirmed. He decided to head to Havana Bar and get chatting to some of the lads there to see if he could get a few leads.

"A beer please, Maggie."

Maggie plunged a cold beer on the counter.

"Is your friend joining you this evening? You were getting on like a house on fire here on Monday night."

"No, he's gone home – to Hawaii."

"Oh right, so neither of you two goons realise that he left this after him then?"

Maggie turned around to the back counter and took down a small canister from the top shelf.

"That's Max's reel of film," said Nate anxiously.

"I thought I saw you guys messing with it alright. Found it on the floor when I was sweeping up the next morning."

"Oh no, Maggie! What am I going to do?"

"Why? What's wrong? You look like you've just seen a ghost."

"Max is a photographer for *Globe International*. He took photos of me working on the tunnel and he was going to use them and write about the likes of myself working there."

"*Wow*, that's something!"

"He can't do the story if he has no photographs," said Nate

Maggie felt sorry for Nate and could see he was shattered so she poured him a whiskey.

"Here, you look like you need it. OK, calm down, let's think for a second."

"Can't I send them to *Globe International* with his name and a note?"

"You want to put something that precious in the U.S. mail?" asked Maggie. "Especially when he isn't even there."

"No, I'll take it myself to the *Globe International.* Do you know where it is?"

"It's all the way over and above in Washington D.C. Honey, you'd be quicker going to Hawaii."

"Maggie, I don't even know where Hawaii is," said a discouraged Nate.

Maggie turned around again to the back counter and moments later pulled out an old stained beer-sponsored map of the United States of America.

"There's Washington . . . and there is the Hawaii Islands," she said, trailing her fingers across the distance.

"Jesus, they're both on the other side of the world! How would I make it there on my own?"

"Nate, look at me. You made all the way over the Atlantic Ocean, didn't you? On your own. You can do this too. You just got to ask yourself if it's worth it. This is supposed to be the land of opportunities, remember? It's no good to no one if you don't take the opportunities it presents you with."

"How would I go about getting there?"

"By train, dummy!" Maggie pointed to the map. "New York, Philadelphia, Columbus, Indianapolis, Denver, Las Vegas, Los Angeles. Then from Los Angeles you can get a boat to Hawaii."

"I'd be going all the way across America," Nate said in awe. "How long would it take?"

"A few days train-hopping for sure and then it takes a couple of days to get there by boat, I think."

"What! That long?"

"No disrespect, Nate, but I don't think you can afford to fly or if you could you wouldn't be working in the tunnel, honey."

"You can say that again. I don't even think I can afford to go by land and sea."

"Well, like I said, Nate, only you can decide how important this is to you."

Nate sat and he thought and he thought. He had no work on the cards so there was nothing committing him to stay here. It would be a great opportunity to see this huge country, the plains of Denver to the deserts of Las Vegas, just like the cowboys in the movies. And now he could be the star of his own story. He didn't mix with a very learned or articulate collective of people at home but everyone had heard of *Globe International* and to see one of their own in such a prestigious publication would make him a local legend forever. So he had to decide if he could justify his self-indulgence or if he was sacrificing his dignity on a journey that could turn out to be very expensive and futile.

"Well, have you decided, Nate?" asked Maggie, collecting her empties.

"I have. I'm going to go."

"That's what I was hoping you'd say! Send me a postcard."

Nate had plenty of time to think while on his arduous rail journey. He stayed over a night or two in some cities because his bones could not tolerate the constant discomfort of the rattling tracks – *clickety-clack, clickety-clack*. Most days were made bearable by the pleasant company of the other commuters. He even got offers of work which was such a great comfort to him as he was conscious of his fragile budget. At least he could work his way back to New York if he had to. His main worry right now, though, was locating Max. Deep is the hole of doubt. All he knew was that he lived on the Oahu Island somewhere around a Pearl Bay. He feared he might be too late and his mammoth effort useless. If Max had flown home he would have had nearly two weeks on him at this stage and even without the photographs surely the resourceful Max would write his story about somebody else

Nate reached the island of Oahu by cargo ship. He bartered passage for working on deck for the six days it took to get there. He was green by the time he disembarked and cursed the big comfortable cruise ship he saw moored at the harbour, laden with wealthy American tourists.

He took a bus to the city centre.

Honolulu, he repeated to himself. He rubbed his hands in giddy glee. If his friends could see him now! Of course he had heard of Honolulu but truthfully he'd had no idea where it was and now here he was! He sat and looked across a city square. It was bustling. Far more hectic than the impression Max had given him. There again it was the capital so that had to be expected. There were people everywhere. So many tourists and so many American sailors in their crisp white naval suits which had not gone unnoticed by the local girls. The city women wore long dresses and white gloves. Nate wondered and hoped when he got to the more rural locations he would see the girls in the straw skirts.

But for now it was late afternoon and he was tired. His appetite had returned with vigour so he decided to take refuge in Honolulu and commence his mission with more energy in the morning.

The staff in his guesthouse could not have been more helpful to him when he was checking out. Thank God they spoke English, he thought. He had heard some of the native tongue and was at a complete loss. He made brief

enquiries about Pearl Bay and got instructions on what bus to catch to get there. He felt positive about the next leg of his trip.

Half a day later he arrived at Pearl Bay. It looked to be smaller than he imagined. He saw an open-air café. He sat on a wicker barstool and ordered a beer there before he nervously asked the barman about a Max Grundig. The barman was not so sure and suggested asking the fishermen down at the pier who were visible from where he was sitting.

Nate knocked back his drink for a bit of courage and approached the gathering of people. After he engaged in pleasantries, one of men liaised with him in broken English.

"Max Grundig? I'm looking for him. Do you know where he lives?"

The local turned to his comrades and a flat conversation in their own language ensued. When nothing was forthcoming, he had another go.

"Max Grundig, he's married to Ilima, they have two children?"

Again a round of discussion took place.

"Wait here," said the man and he walked away up into the vegetative hinterland.

Ten minutes later he returned with a woman walking behind him.

Nate's heart started beating faster. The man ushered the woman in front of Nate.

"Ilima?" Nate asked.

The woman looked at Nate and said nothing.

"Max Grundnig?" Nate added.

The woman took one step back from Nate, drew her right fist closed and punched him hard on the face.

He was stunned. He'd had a few scrapes at school in his time but this left him ringing.

"What the fuck?"

"You are a friend of Max?" Ilima enquired.

"Yeah," said Nate, cradling his jaw back into position.

"Then you are no friend of mine."

"Clearly, but do you know where I can find him?"

"You joke? I haven't seen that useless animal for two years."

The locals spoke among themselves while at the same time trying to pacify an emotional Ilima and then led her back up the beach.

Nate was left reeling by the water. He squatted down on his hunkers to steady himself.

Unbeknownst to Nate, an elderly American couple who were walking on the beach had witnessed the altercation and stopped to see if he was alright.

"You OK there, son? That's quite a rattle you got."

"Jesus, I just wanted to ask her something. I only arrived here today. I don't know her from Adam!" Nate churned this out as quickly as he could to demonstrate his harmlessness.

"But I heard you asking about Max, right?" asked the woman.

"Yeah, I'm only looking for him to give him something – what the hell is wrong with her?"

"It's a touchy subject. Here, you'd better come up to the house with us, your nose is bleeding," said the man.

Despite the awkwardness of the situation the couple introduced themselves as Hank and Betty. They were two retirees from Connecticut who had relocated to Hawaii more than ten years before. They had socialised in the past with Max on account of their mutual link to mainland USA.

Nate related his story to them over an iced tea, sitting on their sea-view front porch.

Hank and Betty told Nate that Ilima was not joking when she said she had not seen Max in two years.

"Max came here to do a story and fell in love with Oahu and Ilima," said Hank. "She went against her family's wishes by marrying him. The couple were happy at first but Max was always coming and going, working for the magazine, a real fly-by-the-seat-of-his-pants kind of a guy. It was tough for him because, with him being freelance and the high standard of its publication, they didn't always print his stories. I guess he had to follow the action and he started coming back less and less. Oh, I don't know, Nate, I'm only guessing. I don't what happened to him. But I am sorry, son. Sounds like you were taken for a ride."

Nate thanked the couple for their help and left the reel of film with them.

Never mind the rattle to his face, he felt that he had been sucker-punched to the stomach too, not to mention the sadness in his heart that made him feel nothing more than a fool. He was angry with himself for believing such rubbish in the first place. Why on earth would a magazine like that or indeed any paper, even a local one, want to know about a village idiot like himself?

He followed the directions Hank and Betty had given him to a guesthouse on the island. Crestfallen, he went straight to bed even though it was still bright outside.

There is something about the dawning of a new day that brings an ongoing freshness to our daily monotony. Nate still felt raw and wondered what his mother would say – "May all the bad luck of the year go with it," or "Offer it up". Nate didn't have much faith lately, considering all that had happened to him.

He sat outside the bar he had first come to yesterday and ordered breakfast from the same waiter. Eating outside, he thought, smiling to himself. What would his mother think of that? Vulgar, most likely. He took out his train timetables and set about studying them to travel back to New York.

The waiter placed his food on the wicker table. "You leaving so soon? You only arrived here yesterday. You white men, always rushing! Why? You always in a race to be the first ones to die," he said laughingly.

Nate was amused and influenced. Maybe the waiter was right. He reflected on the rapid endurance race he had taken to get here and it was all for nothing. He looked up and down the beach. There was definitely a slower pace of life here. And he was tired. Maybe he could spend a few days here for a holiday? When he thought about it further he realised he had never been on a holiday in his life and, seeing that he had come so far to such an iconic destination, it would be a sin not to explore it. So that is what he decided to do.

A few days tuned into a week and a week turned into another and then another. Nate was really enjoying himself. He was eating manna from Heaven and felt like he had entered through the gates of Paradise. He was spending very little money because there was nothing to spend it on. He did buy a small Honolulu doll that was a symbol of the dancing girls in the straw skirts that Nate was so shy of in real life. He also bought and wore a floral-pattern shirt that made him fit in rather than stand out.

Finally, he bought a postcard for Maggie.

Dear Maggie,

Well, I made it. Hola from Oahu. Max turned out to be the greatest conman and took me for a fool. However, I have spent the last while licking my wounds by eating, drinking, swimming and nothing else. It's lovely here. Far cry from the Havana!

Take care, Maggie

From Nate

XX

Yes, eating all the delicious fruit and vegetables and drinking rainbow-coloured cocktails were enough for Nate not to miss the Guinness and sullen dinners. He didn't miss the hard work either and dared to start thinking of living on the Hawaii Islands. The wages here were dismal but so was the cost of living so that balanced out and he believed he could get a job transporting all the rich American tourists around– they would love him. But firstly he would continue sightseeing the various islands before committing to a sight he would like to see on a more permanent basis.

He embraced the national cultural practices such as wearing no shoes in the house. Raw fish was nearly always the dish of the day, which did take some getting used to. He observed the traditional physical greeting of a kiss on the cheek even on the first meeting, regardless of gender, or touching foreheads or noses together. He laughed to himself when he thought what his own locals would have made of this at home. The raw fish would have raised enough eyebrows but the touching of noses was completely something else.

He did some island-hopping. He intended to stay for a while on Hawaii Island, the biggest of them all, because there was so much to explore. He travelled to the south of island and laid his suitcase there.

One balmy evening, on the 1st of June, he went to a bar for some food and cocktails. It was a typical open-air restaurant and very popular with the tourists. They had the female dancers in their traditional dress, swaying to the *hula kahiko*. Nate was mesmerised.

In the interval these beautiful girls collected glasses from the tables in the hope of earning a few tips. Nate obliged and, while he was convinced all the cocktails were very tame, he had a bit more bravado than usual.

"You're a great dancer."

"Thank you, kind sir."

"What's your name?"

"It's Nana."

"Oh very nice, *hic!* I'm Nate."

"Nana and Nate, it has a nice ring to it," she answered cheekily. "Where are you from, white man with the golden hair?"

"Ireland, I'm Irish. It's a lot like here, you know, very green." He didn't even hear what was spurting out of his mouth because he was too busy leering at her long brown wavy hair which matched her dark smooth olive skin and brown eyes. Her straw skirt swept the ankles of her bare feet while the fragrant flower wreath she was wearing brought his attention back up to the brassiere she was wearing, which appeared to be made out of coconut shells.

"Sounds beautiful," she said.

"*Ahem!*" Nate cleared his throat, not knowing what to say next.

He was getting hot under the collar but he was not the only one.

Suddenly, in the distance, a fissure appeared in Mauna Loa. She was getting ready to blow. This hadn't gone unnoticed by the locals who were very in tune with their landscape, especially as this was not first time this mountain had erupted. A siren rang out and the band ceased playing immediately. Patrons were advised to remain calm, return to their homes and quickly pack some essential items in the event that an evacuation was necessary.

Nate did as he was told. He went and picked up his bag before returning to the centre of the village where everyone else was gathering. All eyes were on Mauna Loa who appeared to be getting more agitated. Down at the seashore boats were being prepared.

Nate could see the neon-orange lava starting to spit out and seep down the side of the mountain. Smoke and ash was now blowing down to the village and he could sense an uneasiness within the crowd. He was terrified. The bubbling streams of lava began to widen and move with speed. Another siren rang out and this time the officials began to direct people to the boats and ordered an immediate evacuation.

Nate did not need telling twice – he jumped into one of the first boats to be pushed out to sea. All the people could do then from afar was watch Mauna Loa scar their beautiful island. The smoke and ash began to get so thick that it got to a stage where they sadly could no longer even see Hawaii or indeed any of the islands.

They appeared to be lost at sea but, after a long time bobbing on the endless dark ocean, eventually they could see lights coming towards them.

"*Rescue boats!*" Nate heard someone cry out.

They were like suspended lights in a darkened room. When these boats got near enough people hopped across to each one assigned to a specific island. Most of the residents had family on the other islands so they would go and stay with them. A young American couple told the handler of Nate's boat that they were due to leave Honolulu tomorrow and sail back to the mainland of the United States. The handler pointed to a ship beyond them and told them it was bound for San Diego and he would try and get them on that so they would not have to go back via Honolulu at all. Nate overheard this and had a bite at his conscience. This might literally be his ticket out of here, but he didn't have a ticket. Watching the ferocious Mauna Loa had put the fear of God in him and all the beauty in the world could not romance him to stay here any longer. He bit the bullet and told the handler he was due to leave for the mainland too and he did not care by what means. After a lot of negotiation, Nate and the couple were rowed over to the big ship. The honest-to-God couple had their travel tickets in hand. Nate pretended to search his bags for his ticket and rolled his eyes to heaven while trying to look like he couldn't find it. The sailor said nothing and just beckoned him onto the ship. Several hours and a few more displaced passengers later, the ship set sail for San Diego.

When Nate arrived on dry land he thanked the Lord. Then he boarded a train, then another and then another and kept going until he reached New York. There was no desire to rest his rattling bones from the shaky carriages on the way back. He was just grateful to have escaped the poisoned island with his life.

In the weeks that followed Nate tried to come to terms with the ordeal. He was staying at a former work colleague's boarding house in New York and could not stop reading the newspapers every day about the crisis and damage Mauna Loa had caused. The pouring lava had scorched the telegraph poles and wires, severing all communication to and from the island and it was several days later that the true extent of the destruction it had caused was feeding through to the media. The rivers of fire had destroyed villages and displaced all the residents. It burned its fertile forests, lands and wildlife. People's livelihoods were lost and all their belongings gone forever. Sometimes it's not the thing itself that matters but everything else. Most families were lucky to escape and, just like their ancestors before them, they would rebuild and rebound. As soon as they could, they started to return to Hawaii, pulled back by nothing more than resolve and resilience. 'Malama'Aina' they called it. It meant taking care of the land. They were going to heal and soothe the wounds of their island. They were going to live among the loss and start restoring their lives.

This inspired Nate. He decided he had enough adventure in his life already, considering what had happened to him in London, New York and Hawaii.

To hell with it all, he thought. I'm going home to take care of myself.

CHAPTER 9

To Whom It May Concern

December 1961

Foggy, frosty, damp and freezing, well, no change there then, thought Caitlín as she walked away from her cottage. She was glad she had slept as well as she did because yesterday was so intense she needed it. She cautiously hoped today would be better but knew the reality of it – it wouldn't be.

Ordinarily the station was like an icebox but it was tropical compared to outside and she was glad to be in out of cold once she arrived. As she was settling down at her desk, she spotted Babs Wheatley sitting in the hall.

Tully was already at his desk.

"Morning, Seán."

"Morning, Caitlín. Ready for another crazy day? Lamb is already here and so is Detective Cullen. They've brought Mrs. Wheatley in for questioning so no doubt they will be giving you a shout in a few minutes to join them."

Caitlín looked over at Mrs. Wheatley. She definitely hadn't had a good night's sleep – she looked terrible. She was miles away, lost in thought.

As far away as Italy, in fact, as she pondered what her life would have been like if she married Rosario Fratelli instead of Nate and moved there.

When Babs was younger and living in Westport she was very taken by a young man called Rosario. He and his family had moved from Naples – via Navan, then on to Westport – and opened up a chip shop. Their cousins in England had opened up two in the North of England and they were doing a bomb selling this new convenient, fast and tasty food that the locals couldn't get enough of.

Westport was proving a great success for this Fratelli family too, although Rosario might have a lot to do with that, as all the local girls fancied the pantaloni off him. He was of medium height which was unremarkable but it was the dark skin, dark eyes and longer hair that made him so different to the natives. He knew how to speak to the girls too. He always made them feel special and beautiful, especially Babs whom he appeared to have more affection for than the others. Twenty-year-old Babs had a healthy figure but it was her long, blonde, wavy hair that made her so exotic to her Mediterranean pursuer.

"You go in!" said Madge.

"No, you go in!" said Babs.

Even though both of them were dying to go in.

"I love the way he undresses you with his eyes," said Madge, swooning.

"Oh Jesus, you go first so," urged Babs.

"Why?"

"Because you're probably wearing better underwear than I am!" said Babs, giggling.

"Yeah, but it's not my knickers he wants to see, is it, Babs?"

Babs smacked Madge hard to alleviate her own embarrassment.

Over the next few weeks Babs got over her flutters and flusters to the point where she and Rosario started going out together. Babs used to be in awe listening to him telling her all about his childhood growing up in Naples. They had orange trees, lemon trees and olive groves that literally grew in their back garden. The sun shone from April to October as they splashed their days away on the beaches of the Mediterranean Sea among the thousands of tourists that swam with them and waited in the long queues for the gelato. So exotic and wonderful, thought Babs, who couldn't understand why anyone would want to leave all of that magic and come to a dowdy and damp Ireland. He missed his beloved soccer team, Napoli. He couldn't get his head around the Gaelic games. Between the picking the ball up, pucking it, punching it and frequently punching each other, he couldn't see any rules at all.

All Babs had ever known about Naples was that the Mafia lived there and they were bad people because she had heard that in the news and read it in the paper. According to Rosario, his extended family were victims of their brutality. They advised them to pay "protection money" when in fact the only people they were being protected from was the Mafia itself who found various demeaning ways to thwart them from continuing on an ordinary course of business or profession. While Babs' family had a favourable inclination towards Rosario, with him been a Catholic displaying a good set of traditional family values, at the same time they would have preferred to see Babs settle with a nice local lad. But Babs knew herself that there was nothing nice about a lot of them.

One Friday evening Babs was to meet Rosario at the clock in the square as they so often did. He didn't turn up. She walked as slowly as she could pass the chip shop more than once but could not see him there either. She decided that he must be sick.

After a few worrying days she got the courage to go into the chip shop and ask Mrs. Fratelli where her son was. She was told that he had been sent back to Italy to help his uncle run his olive farm. She was so blunt about it that Babs didn't know whether she should believe her or not, especially when Mrs. Fratelli would not give her a forwarding address to write to him. She dismissed Babs hastily and Babs began to think maybe it was because Mrs. Fratelli's heart was broken as much as her own was smashing into pieces. It took Babs a long time to get over her Rosario.

The following year Babs started working in a café in Castlebar. Every Friday Nate Wheatley and his work mates from Brennan's yard came in for their lunch as a treat to themselves and every Friday Nate ordered the exact same thing; a mixed grill. Babs used to have it written down in her notebook even before he finished asking for it. She noticed there was always a bit of nudge, nudge, wink, wink, from the giddy boys while they were there. She reckoned one of them fancied her but couldn't be sure which one. In any event she did not encourage it.

A couple of months later Babs handed in her notice. She couldn't tolerate her ignorant bosses anymore. When she saw an advert on the window of another café up the Main Street looking for a waitress, she applied immediately and got the job.

And there, on the first Friday of her new post, who walked in only Nate Wheatley on his own and sat down at a table.

"Are they no longer doing the mixed grill down the street?" enquired Babs.

"Oh they are, but I hear the staff are a lot nicer in here."

Nate and Babs smiled at each other knowingly.

But, sadly, for a second time Babs was let down when Nate decided that he wanted to emigrate to England. Of course he had asked her to go with him but her mother was not well and she didn't want to leave her and, truthfully, she felt she did not possess the same sense of adventure as Nate did at that point in time.

After that Babs decided she was never going to wear her heart on her sleeve again and resigned herself to a lifetime of singledom.

But fate had other ideas, it seemed, when two years later Babs was reluctantly attending a social dance in Castlebar with her sister and she bumped into Nate. He was back from his travels for good. She didn't know whether to kiss him or kill him. But the talk came easy and before she knew it she had agreed to meet him again ... and again.

They subsequently married and life with Nate was stable but predictable. As long as she was living and breathing, he didn't seem to notice much else. He worked hard, long hours, but the fruits of his labour were of no advantage to Babs.

She got lonely. Sammy Joyce used to talk to her every day in a way that reminded her of how Rosario used to make her feel – excited and appreciated. He asked her about her, not small talk about the weather, or politics, or any other mundane topics. No wonder she felt drawn to him. But nothing ever happened and when she heard he was fooling around with Mrs. Huber too, well, she felt mortifyingly foolish. The remorse and guilt for her actions and what they manifested into, with her husband now behind bars, was unbearable. She wondered if he would ever forgive her.

"Mrs. Wheatley, please follow us," said Sergeant Lamb, showing her into an empty office.

When all the screechy chairs had been pulled up to the table, Detective Cullen introduced himself, Sergeant Lamb and Garda Kennedy.

"Mrs. Wheatley, I know this is difficult for you but you must understand that we need to ask you some questions. Where were you between 7 o'clock and 9 o'clock yesterday morning?"

"I was at home."

"Can anyone verify that?"

"No, I was still in bed."

"Did you see Nate yesterday morning at the times I have just indicated to you?"

"No."

"When did you last see him?"

"It was the night before. We had a row when we came home from the pub, he left the house in a rage and was gone to work when I got up."

"Did he return to the house before he left on his route?"

"Yes, yes, he did."

"How do you know?"

"I could see he had breakfast."

"What did he eat?"

"*Em* ... he made tea and ate some brown bread and cold chicken."

"Do you know where he went to when he left the house after your row?"

"No, I don't."

"You said he left the house in a rage?"

"He was angry with me but he didn't go off and kill Sammy Joyce if that is what you are implying? He's not a murderer."

"I'm not implying that at all, Mrs. Wheatley," replied a calm Detective Cullen. "Now, perhaps you could describe your relationship with Sammy Joyce."

"There was no relationship with Sammy Joyce," replied Babs in earnest.

"But you were caught in a compromising position with Mr. Joyce in Slattery's which was witnessed by my colleague sitting here beside me."

Mrs. Wheatley blushed and began to cry. "It was only a kiss, nothing else ever happened between us! I swear that is the truth."

"Can I put it to you that you must have established some form of a relationship with him to lead up to the tryst you shared with him in the pub?"

"He called with the post every day and we chatted. He always made time for me, he was kind and nice. I acted on impulse. I don't know what came over me. I didn't even know he was seeing Mrs. Huber so I don't know why he would be bothering with me, a married woman. He made a fool out of me."

"So you hated him after hearing he was in another relationship?"

"No, no, the poor man is dead, he didn't deserve that."

"You mentioned a Mrs. Hubur – what can you tell us about Sammy's relationship with her?"

"Nothing! I didn't even know he *was* seeing her until Nate told me last night. I don't know who else knew."

"Finally, do you drive, Mrs. Wheatley?"

"No, I never learned. I wish I had."

"Thank you, Mrs. Wheatley. We will be in contact with you again if we have any further questions. We must insist that you remain within the locality for the time being."

"But what about Nate? Can I see him? When is he coming home?"

"All in good time, Mrs. Wheatley, rest assured he is being taken care of."

After Mrs. Wheatley had left the station, the team concluded that she had not much to offer as a witness, never mind a suspect.

Their deflated mood was suddenly turned upside-down when a member of the search team rang into the station.

"*I found the bag, the postman's bag!*" he declared, badly out of breath. "There was still some letters in it and a few more scattered around it at the brink of the river!"

"*Kennedy! Have you that incident room set up yet?*" bellowed Sergeant Lamb.

"I didn't get a chance yet, sir," replied Caitlín.

"Well, get on it – we have vital evidence here to examine."

Caitlín had limited props but she and Tully pulled two tables together and covered them with sheets. On the mounted blackboard Caitlín drew the timeline of events, details of the victim, details of the suspects to date that included Nate Wheatley, Babs Wheatley and Waxy Carolan. Photographs were still being developed and forensic tests outstanding.

Sergeant Lamb and Detective Cullen joined them.

"Where was the bag discovered?" asked Detective Cullen.

"At the bridge, a mile outside the town," Tully informed them. "The suspect driving the truck must have flung it out the window. He obviously meant to throw it into the river but miscalculated his aim and the weight of it. It was lying right at the brink. It was open with a few letters inside and others scattered around it. The search team reckon the rest of the post probably blew into the river and any of those letters are well disintegrated by now. They followed the river for several miles on but found nothing further."

"The addressees will have to be notified that these letters and their contents have become evidence as part of a murder investigation and the letters will be released to them in due course," said Sergeant Lamb. "However, I suspect with us being in the run-up to Christmas there might be money in some of them that people may be depending on. We can consider that on an individual basis and perhaps make an allowance to release it on compassionate grounds if necessary, so make note of the people we need to let know. Right, let's have a look then."

After pulling on some white gloves, very very slowly and carefully Caitlín and Tully laid out the damp letters and one package. They had still been intact in their envelopes. They opened the package first. Inside was a plastic sealed collection of toys called 'Stick 'Em Up' containing a sheriff's badge, a plastic gun and holster with a roll of snap rounds with a note to wish *Little Jack, my favourite cowboy, a very happy Christmas from Auntie Josephine in County Westmeath*.

"Well, Auntie Josephine was one step ahead of us," said Detective Cullen. "She knows it is the lawless Wild Wild West here alright."

Tully then unfolded the first of the letters and he and Caitlín proceeded to read and dissect them in turn.

Bank of Ireland
Main Street
Castlebar
County Mayo

9ᵗʰ December 1961

Mr. Seán O'Brien Snr.
Castle Road
Ballantur
County Mayo

Re: Loan approval

Dear Mr. O'Brien,

We are writing to inform you that regretfully your loan application has been rejected on this occasion. As a valued customer, please do not hesitate to contact us in the future if we can offer you any further assistance.

Yours sincerely,

Andrew Hickey

Andrew Hickey
Branch Manager

27 Claridge House
Brook Street
London W2K 4HR

1st December 1961

Dear Mother,

I hope this letter finds you and everyone at home well. We won't feel the time pass until the Christmas now. You should see the shops here in London. They are all lit up with decorations, it looks like a completely different place altogether. I was wondering if Dad and the Committee had put the crib up in the square yet but then again I think they leave it nearer to Christmas week. People at home seem to have the good sense not to fall for all the craziness like they do here. You'd swear the money is burning a hole in their pockets, they can't spend it fast enough. It's a shopping frenzy. I have been tempted myself but I know you would put money to better use rather than me sending presents over. Sure I don't know what to buy the young ones anyway. I am enclosing £100. I have worked hard all year at the hotel and we are getting a Christmas bonus so I am blessed to share my good fortune with you. Like I thought, I am working over the Christmas. People here come to the hotel for their Christmas dinner, can you believe it? All dressed up to the nines, knocking the brandy and champagne back to beat the band. I wouldn't fancy it myself, to be honest. I'm already missing you and Dad fighting over whether to have a goose or a turkey, the smell of your boiled fruit cake and the lovely red candle you put in the window. I am going to go out now and buy a candle to light for my window so every time I look at it I'll know our 2 candles will be burning together. May its light shine upon us for the New Year.

So happy Christmas to ye all. I'll be home in January so you'll have to make another cake especially for me!

God bless, Mam

Caroline XXXXXX

8th December 1961

Dear little brother Paul,

I hope you are well. I'm home now about 2 weeks and will never forget the boat crossing coming home as long as I live. The sea was so rough it was splashing over the sides. Everyone was sick with nowhere proper to get sick, if you know what I mean. I will never leave this country again unless I can afford to fly in an aeroplane.

Dad will collect you at the bus station in Castlebar at half six. You can congratulate Irene on her engagement! It was so funny, Paul! Didn't Seán Clarke come down to the house last Friday night and propose to her! She burst out crying and I burst out laughing. Dad was very diplomatic, thanked Seán for his kind intention and how of course Irene would give it due consideration. I think Dad was more inclined than Irene, saying she could do a lot worse and how he had a good farm of land. Mam told her not to mind him, those days were over and she could marry whoever she wanted. Poor thing was in shock for a few days but is beginning to see the funny side of it now too.

That's all for now. If you come back with a posh accent we won't be long knocking it out of you because we don't want you having notions about yourself, now that you're a Civil Servant. There is nothing civil about you. Hà, ha, only joking.

Martin

—ell—

Silesians Fathers
Bow Street
Youghal
County Cork

7th December 1961

Mrs. Bridget Lenihan
The Fairgreen
Ballantur
County Mayo

<u>**Mission for Black Babies in Africa**</u>

Dear Mrs. Lenihan,

A sincere thank you for your generous donation. May God bless you during the Christmas period and the New Year ahead.
We enclose our annual calendar which we hope will be of some use to you.

Thank you.
Yours sincerely,

Fr. Maurice Franklin

Irish Sweepstakes
R.D.S
Ballsbridge
Dublin 4

6th December 1961

Mr. John Cawley

Kiltimagh Road
Ballantur
County Mayo

<u>Irish Sweepstake Registration No. 240221</u>

Dear Mr. Cawley,

We are pleased to inform you that you have won £50.00 in our monthly Sweepstake draw. Please see cheque enclosed made payable to your good self.

May we take this opportunity to wish you a very happy Christmas and continued good luck throughout the New Year.

Mise le meas,

Diarmuid Darcy

Diarmuid Darcy
Financial Controller

2nd December 1961
7 Signet Walk
Queen's Road
Manchester
M8 1UF

Well hello, Nora!

How are you? Are you settling into the hat factory? You must have a bit of craic from there by now.

Nora, the fashion over here is amazing. I love going into town watching the local girls to see what they are wearing. They're all into miniskirts and high-knee boots, hairbands and so on. You can get tights in every colour of the rainbow. It's so easy to spend all your wages on clothes, there are so many shops. I've bought loads already, Mam will kill me. I will bring home a few bits to you during the summer. So don't get fat! I'm still working in the hospital. The money is grand but you work hard for it. We have good craic. There are some good-looking fellas working here too. Some of them are very posh. One of them, a doctor, never leaves me alone. He was on about the Christmas party we will be going to and he told me he would like to kiss me under the mistletoe. Jesus, Nora, you should see the state of him. I wouldn't kiss him under a general anaesthetic! He must be 40 if he's a day. He's so thin, one eye would do him!

Anyway, I won't be home for Christmas. I have to work it this year. It's grand anyway, there will be loads of parties to go to. Beats Slattery's any day. Sorry, I don't mean to keep rubbing it in but why don't you move over here too? We would have so much fun. Go on, throw your hat in!

Write back to me immediately.

Deirdre

7ᵗʰ December 1961

Dear Winnie,

I am writing this letter slow because I know that you cannot read fast. Can you believe it's this time of year again already? Go mbeirimidbeo go léir ar an am seo arís!

Hasn't the weather turned awful cold and no sign of it improving? I knew it was going to be bad, the bushes were too plentiful of haw berries, nature's way of providing food for the birds. At least it will kill the germs. Don't they say a green Christmas brings a fat graveyard?

We'll be down to you for the New Year. Joe has a side of bacon for ye. He was at Mrs. Whelan's funeral yesterday. She was sick for a long time. The poor woman was hanging on like a loose button there at the end. There was a great turn-out, must have been a couple of hundred mourners but despite this of course Joe and Willie pointed out who wasn't at it, and how they should have been at it!

Looking forward to seeing you all soon. Have a very happy Christmas. I was going to put £10 in with the letter but I had already sealed the envelope.

Your loving sister,

Mary XXX

C/O Tom Collins
Vernon Boulevard
Jackson Avenue
Long Island
New York 11103
USA

25th November 1961

Dear Father,

I am very disappointed that you have not answered my last letter. I wouldn't ask if I was not awful stuck. I still have not found any work since the last place went wallop. The guy I owe the $500 to found out where I live and if I don't pay up he says he will break my two legs.

I don't know what people were on about, it is not easy to get work over here. There is every cut of a fella looking for it, brown, black, white and yellow. At least I speak English and can write but I don't know how some of the other poor buggers get on at all. There are not many other people living around here anymore. All the other Irish seem to have got on and moved out. There is a lot of sickness in the flats and no one seems to be working. Some folk live in such squalor it would make you wonder how bad things were in the country they came from to tolerate what they are putting up with now, but I guess they thought they were coming to the land of opportunity too.

I go to the pub every night to see if I know anyone from home to ask them about work but nothing has turned up so far.

Happy Christmas to ye and I hope to hear from ye soon
Chris

———

London Metropolitan Police
Scotland Yard
London
SW12 2JK

1st December 1961

STRICTLY CONFIDENTIAL

Mr. Ignatius Wheatley
Spring Road
Ballantur
County Mayo
Éire

URGENT
Re: Miss Hillary Rogers, deceased.
Case No. 1238HR

Dear Mr. Wheatley,
We refer to the ongoing investigation in the above mentioned case.
It is imperative that you contact us immediately to discuss this matter further.
We look forward to hearing from you.
Yours sincerely,

Sup. Daniel Ramsey

Superintendent Daniel Ramsey
H.RM. London Metropolitan Police

ele

"Well, most of that was a load of nonsense," concluded Sergeant Lamb.

"No, Frank, we have a second reference to an alleged incident involving Nate in England," said Detective Cullen.

"Tully, get on to the Metropolitan Police in London straight away and find out what the hell this is all about," ordered Sergeant Lamb. "The rest of the correspondence doesn't reveal anything suspicious with regards to the suspects or any other potential suspects."

"But it does throw up a big question," said Caitlín. "I mean, it looks like maybe the killer was looking for something particular and knew it was going to be delivered by Sammy Joyce. It was something that they were prepared to kill for ... so maybe Sammy was not the motive, maybe the letter he was delivering was instead and that is why they stole the bag."

Detective Cullen raised an eyebrow at Sergeant Lamb.

"Then, as I said before," Caitlín continued, "the other side of the dice is maybe they did want to kill Sammy and only stole the bag and tossed it away so we would think it was a letter they were after and not Sammy."

They all left the incident room silently.

Caitlín slunk back to her desk and sighed.

"You alright there, Caitlín?" asked Tully.

"I don't know. I don't know if we are near the shore or all lost at sea."

Chapter 10

All at Sea

Tully's phone call to the Metropolitan Police proved futile. The officer who was overseeing this case was not on duty. Nobody else appeared familiar with it as it was a historic archived file and he was advised to ring back.

Nate was brought in for questioning.

Caitlín was called in with her notebook as usual.

"When can I get out of here?" Nate asked straight away.

"Unfortunately, Nate, we have to detain you for further questioning," said Detective Cullen. "We need to ask about the period of time you lived in England and in particular an alleged incident that happened there." He knew he was winging it a bit – he had not much to go on at the moment other than Pa Leonard referring to it vaguely and an unexplained letter from the Metropolitan Police in London.

However, it was enough to make Nate's heart race and he thought he was going to have a panic attack. After all those years he had tried to put it behind him, dreading the day when it was going to catch up with him and now here it was.

"Nate, we recovered a letter from Sammy Joyce's postal bag," continued Detective Cullen. "It is addressed to yourself from the police in London and it refers to an ongoing investigation into the death of a Miss Hillary Rogers. We have received information that you may have had some difficulties while you lived in the U.K. and we were hoping if you would confirm if the two are connected in any way?"

Nate didn't know what to say. He just stared at them for a moment. He knew he could not avoid the truth coming out now, so he resigned himself to "what will be will be", and recounted the whole story and its unfolding tragedy which led to the death of the young Miss Rogers. He went on to explain how he believed he would have been blamed for it, considering the hostile relationship he had with Simon Thomas whom he worked with at Colbert's Store and this is why he fled the U.K. and went to America.

Nate did not feel any better after releasing that burden after all those years because he thought no one would believe him now any more than they did back then. Now he felt like he was the one who was hit by a truck. All of this was so surreal to him. Two massive accusations in two days. It was overwhelming.

"We're sorry to hear that, Nate, and thank you for telling us. No doubt it was a very difficult time for you," said a compassionate Caitlín. "Is this the first letter from the police in London?"

"No, I've had a few to say they were re-investigating the case and they would be in touch. I haven't got in contact with them yet."

"Have you anything else to tell us? Now is the time, Nate. You're in a lot of trouble," said a stern Sergeant Lamb.

"I think I need a solicitor," replied Nate.

After that bout of questioning, Sergeant Lamb instructed Tully to sit on the Metropolitan Police until someone there spoke to him. He then turned to Detective Cullen and asked him what he thought.

"It's not looking good for Nate though it could be all lies. As well as being possibly charged for one murder, now he could be charged for two.

Either way, Frank, we can't keep him for much longer for this one. We either charge him or let him go."

Caitlín and Tully sat into their car and decided to go into Castlebar for lunch. They felt that they both really needed a break from it all, but there was no getting away from it.

"So what did Nate say?" asked Tully.

"Oh God, he was telling us that when he was in the U.K. a woman drowned on a boat he was steering ... or not steering. Anyway, he said he got blamed for it and legged it to America. I don't know if the case ever closed which is why the police in London are probably writing to him but he could be in very serious trouble. Imagine, you're accused of a murder one day and the next day you're accused of another one. It's unbelievable. He has no real alibi for the murder here and now he may be responsible for the death of someone in England too. I wouldn't like to be in his shoes right now. It's a lot to stomach."

"Well, if I don't get something into my whinging stomach soon, I won't be fit for it either."

"What do you fancy?" Caitlin asked.

"Something substantial. I'd say it'll be another long day."

"You're right, maybe something with eggs – an omelette or a quiche?"

"Quiche? Where do you think you are, ya mad yolk? Did you get it? Yolk?"

"Yeah, you're hilarious, Seán," replied Caitlín. "Did you hear there's a circus coming to town?"

"What? What are you on about?"

"They're looking for a clown – any chance you'd apply for it?"

They both laughed but the joviality was short-lived.

Tully turned up the radio. The One O'Clock News on Radio 1was breaking its lead story.

"A man has died following a hit and run outside the town on Ballantur in County Mayo. He was named locally as forty-five-year-old Samuel Joyce who was a postman for the region. He was fatally hit yesterday morning by a vehicle while on his morning rounds. RTÉ News understands that An Garda Síochána have stepped this up to a murder enquiry and they have arrested a local man who is currently being questioned at Ballantur Garda Station."

Caitlín and Tully were silent. While they were used to hearing tragic news reports like everyone else, when it happened on their own watch it left them with a sick sensation in their stomachs from the exposure and vulnerability of doing a job that was under the scrutiny of everyone right now.

When they got back to the station Detective Cullen had further investigations to be followed.

He directed Caitlín and Tully to return and interview Sammy's relatives, the Coyles. Given that the Coyles had some time to absorb the news, he thought they might be in a better frame of mind to talk about Sammy now before the emotion of his funeral. He and Sergeant Lamb were going to speak to Mrs. Russell, the postmistress. They all agreed to meet at Sammy's house after their respective interviews to conduct a search of it, to see if there were any clues to be found there to assist them.

Caitlín and Tully walked up the gravel path of the front drive of Coyles' house.

"Well, here we are again," said Tully.

"Yeah, and there is that stink again," said Caitlín, then she was distracted by the front door opening without them even knocking on it.

After a cordial welcome from Ralph Coyle, he invited them straight into the kitchen.

Mrs. Coyle or Nancy, as they had come to know her, was still baking for Christmas. She was surrounded by a veritable Christmas bonanza.

Caitlín and Tully's mouths dropped open. Their eyes lingered over the plum puddings, meticulously iced Christmas cakes, mince pies, sherry trifle and chocolate Yule logs. There were also very creative pine-scented centre table-pieces. They were woven with evergreen fir, sprigs of red-berry holly and red ribbon, with a red candle standing in the middle of the decoration.

"*Wow*, that is some production ye got going on here," said Tully in awe.

"Oh, that's all herself, the cooking and the gardening – her forte no matter what time of the year it is," said Ralph proudly.

A bashful Nancy laughed heartily. "It's not all for us. The Committee always get me to do a few Christmas cakes and floral decorations for the 25 and whist card drives. And with Sammy's funeral on Thursday I'd thought I'd bring a few things to Slattery's for the gathering afterwards."

"Have the funeral arrangements been finalised?" asked Caitlín.

"Yes, I was just on the phone with your sergeant there before you arrived," said Nancy. "The post mortem is finished and they are releasing the body. So I rang Slattery's Undertakers in Ballantur and we arranged for the removal from the morgue Wednesday evening followed by the burial Thursday morning after 11 o'clock Mass. We were going to wake him in his house but, bearing in mind our unfamiliarity with Sammy and indeed his community, we didn't think that was appropriate, so he will go straight to the chapel Wednesday evening."

"Would it be alright to ask you a few things about him?" asked Caitlín sympathically.

"Did Sergeant Lamb forget something?" asked Ralph.

"No, it's just easier to chat to you personally about it. We understand it is a sensitive time for you. Could we start by you telling us a bit about him?"

"Well, that's just the thing," said Ralph. "We don't know much about him at all, I'm afraid."

"You were his first cousin, Ralph?" asked Caitlín.

"Yes, his mother and my mother were sisters and they are both dead. They never got on with each other so myself and Sammy's paths never crossed. It's a pity really, because the funny thing is, well, it's not funny at all, but we were both only children, similar in age, so it would have been nice to have known one another."

"But can you confirm you have another aunt in America?"

"You've certainly done your homework, Garda. Yes, we do, or we did. My mother, Sammy's mother and our aunt in the U.S. fell out years ago when they were young women, before myself and Sammy came along, so my family had no connection with the aunt in the States."

"And what about Sammy's mother, did she and your aunt in America communicate?"

"I couldn't tell you. I'm sorry, I'm not much help to you at all. You'll have a cup of tea?"

"No, no, thank you," said Tully. "We need to get back to the station."

"May we ask who is responsible for the funeral fees then, considering the circumstances you have just shared with us?" asked Caitlín.

"Dennis Slattery told Ralph today that Sammy had already provided for his own funeral arrangements," said Nancy.

"Really?" responded Caitlín, surprised.

"Years ago he did it, not lately," said Ralph. "I know, it's a bit morbid to be thinking about something like that, especially when Sammy wasn't even old, but his father died young from a heart attack when Sammy was only a small lad so I would say maybe that was always on his mind."

"But did he not have any relatives on his father's side?" asked Tully.

"He had an uncle, who was a bachelor, never married, had no kids and didn't he suffer the same fate? So clearly there was a history of heart problems in the family," said Ralph.

"Right, right," said Tully. "Were you aware of Sammy being in a relationship with anyone?"

"What? With who?" said Ralph, sounding pleasantly surprised.

"OK, we'll leave it there," said Tully with a laugh. "Right – we'll be in touch, probably after the funeral unless something of significance comes up in the meantime."

"Do you think we could get a suit of clothes from his house?" asked Nancy. "Dennis Slattery is going to lay him out for us."

"The house is being searched this afternoon, so if you give the station a ring in the morning we should be able to organise that for you," said Caitlín.

Meanwhile, Detective Cullen and Sergeant Lamb had called upon Mrs. Russell, the postmistress. Mrs. Russell repeatedly told them how saddened, shocked and incredulous she was about the whole thing.

After some time, Detective Cullen got to ask her about Sammy's recent behaviour and whether or not she had noticed anything different about him.

"*Em* ... not really. I mean, he had been the same Sammy here with me for twenty years. He took over from Finbar Rattigan who should have been put out to grass years earlier. We nearly had to get a ladder to get him up on the bike at the finish, he had got so stiff in the legs."

"Very good, but we just want to know about Sammy," said Sergeant Lamb.

"He took longer than Finbar to do the rounds because he was such a chatterbox, the Lord have mercy on him. He would talk to a stone in the wall. He was a happy-go-lucky kind of a fella."

"Did you see him on the morning before he was knocked down?" Detective Cullen asked.

"No, he was long gone on his round before I opened up the Post Office. It's not for me to speculate, but if I had been humiliated in public in the local pub the night before carrying on with a married woman of loose morals, I certainly would not be too keen to face the neighbours the next day either, if you know what I mean. In any case, he left early."

"So he didn't appear unusually bothered or worried about anything recently?" Cullen asked.

"No, he might have even have a pep in his step if anything, but I think that was down to Mrs. Huber." She smiled at her two interviewers.

"And what about Mrs. Wheatley? Did he ever mention her?" asked Sergeant Lamb.

"*Ooh*, do you think he was having an affair with her and that is why Nate killed him?"

"We don't speculate, Mrs. Russell," said Sergeant Lamb pompously. "We only deal with the facts and if you don't believe you have useful information for us we'll be on our way."

Mrs. Russell blinked at him, taken aback at his rudeness. "I have nothing else to say," she said sharply.

"Right, come on, Detective Cullen."

Lamb and Cullen started to walk back to their car.

"That was a complete waste of time with that eejit," said an annoyed Sergeant Lamb.

"Well, if you had not been so short with her, the cage door might not have come crashing down and she might have shared more information about him."

"What? The likes of that old curtain-twitcher clearly knows sweet feck-all. The woman we really need to question is that Mrs. Huber. Her name keeps coming up."

"Fine, but we're doing a search of Sammy's house now, remember?"

They both slammed their car doors as they sat in. They were getting tired and cranky. Frustrations were beginning to make them crack and they felt more pressure now because the murder was in the media.

Caitlín and Tully were waiting for them at Sammy's house on the outskirts of the town and they all went inside together. The evening had grown dark early so they switched the lights on. It was a typical bachelor's lair, functional with no frills. An old stained oilcloth covered the small table in the living room. A small cup of cocoa half-drunk was left on it. Beside that was a loaf of bread that had gone rock-hard. The fridge was in the living room too with several unidentified items shrivelled up inside. A well-worn fireside chair with the foam oozing out of the arm was on one side of the hearth, while a heavily laden clothes horse stood on the other.

"This won't take long by looks of things, or lack of things," said Detective Cullen. "Tully, go through the dresser there – Kennedy, you go through the back kitchen cabinets and drawers. Myself and Sergeant Lamb will check the other rooms."

Twenty minutes later they reconvened in the living room.

"Nothing of significance on our turn-over," said Sergeant Lamb. "How about you, Kennedy?"

"No, sir, there was nothing of interest in any of the presses."

"Tully?"

"Just the usual – bills, receipts, payslips, coupons and a bundle of old letters between his mother and the aunt in the States. It looks like when Sammy's mother died the aunt continued to write to Sammy instead but other than the weather, local deaths, births, marriages and other similar dribble there seemed to be no red flags in any of them."

"Right, come on, there is nothing here – lock that door after you again, Kennedy," ordered Lamb.

His bad mood was further exacerbated by the lack of any clues. He began to feel anxious because if nothing was washing up now he felt the whole thing might slip away on them.

"Let's call it a day, lads," said Detective Cullen. "Tomorrow evening is the removal and the next day is the burial so out of respect we will have to be very discreet in our enquiries and movements, which I know is frustrating because we are under a lot of pressure with time being of the essence and all of that. But don't worry – something will turn up. The Coroner's report should be back so maybe there will be something in that. See ye tomorrow."

Babs Wheatley sat at her kitchen table and stared at the empty space where Nate used to park his truck. Old Max the dog lay there now, wondering why his master was not coming home. What had she done, she asked herself, with her head in her hands. She had ruined his livelihood, his life and her own. If she thought things were dull and mundane in the past, the future had become unimaginable.

Nate stood on his cell bed and looked out through the caged window. What he wouldn't give for a breath of fresh air, he thought. He had to crane his neck to get a view. He could see his truck still parked in the Garda yard. He remembered the day he bought it.

Once he had decided that he was going to set up a new mobile grocery business after his return from America, he knew he needed a vehicle that would require specific modifications to hold all his saleable products secure while in motion. After enquiries at a few local garages at the time, he was made aware of exactly what he wanted – which was a truck with built-in shelving of various dimensions. Big shelves on the bottom and smaller ones towards the top. Surprisingly, being directed to a circus didn't perturb him. The circus was in Castlebar and one of its staff members had brought this vehicle to a garage in the town for maintenance. However, they were reluctant to spend too much money on it because apparently the act it was associated with was going to be axed and they might no longer have a need for it. The affable circus manager was delighted with Nate's interest and happy to show it to him because it was of an acquired taste. And, sure enough, the minute Nate saw it he balked. He laughed out loud and asked the manager if he was joking, before further asking him if a few clowns were going to jump out of the back of it. It was purple which was fine, but it was the huge painting of a yellow dragon on each side that stumped Nate.

"There's no way I could be seen driving around in the likes of that. Are you mad? Can you imagine what my customers could say? Here comes the Dragon in the Wagon! Or, are you spitting out much fire today or, no wonder you're early, did you fly here?" Nate laughed at the absurdity of it.

"You might be amused, sir, but this is the Year of the Dragon in the Chinese calendar. It only comes around in twelve-year cycles. It will be very lucky for you. Besides, can't you just paint over it?"

Nate didn't care much about oriental prophecy but he knew the manager had a sensible solution by suggesting to redecorate it. He knew having to source another truck and then to go and get someone to do the shelving would cost a fortune. A can of paint was cheap so he agreed the buy the truck and took it away with him. But he never got around to buying the paint. The more he looked at it, the more he liked the dragons and felt that covering them over would be like defacing a symbol of something meaningful. He decided to weather the slagging which ceased over time, well, at least to his face. The locals came to regard the truck and its dragons with affection and couldn't imagine Nate driving anything less ordinary. But the truck was over ten years old now and Nate began to wonder if his luck was running out. His big mobile talisman was losing its spark.

CHAPTER 11

Duty Calls

In Caitlín's and Tully's absence earlier in the day a radio crew had descended on the town of Ballantur. Locals and other members of An Garda Síochána were interviewed and recorded. A report was prepared and aired on the RTÉ Six O'Clock News that evening.

"The man who was killed here in Ballantur, County Mayo, has been named as forty-five-year-old Sammy Joyce. He was the postman for the town and the adjoining townlands. It is understood that he had commenced a round of postal deliveries early Monday morning when he was hit by a vehicle. An Garda Síochána suspect foul play and the investigation has been stepped up to a murder enquiry. A local man has been arrested on suspicion of murder and is currently being questioned at Ballantur Garda Station.

Sergeant Frank Lamb made this appeal earlier today: 'We appeal to all members of the public to come forward if they believe they hold any information regarding the untimely death of Mr. Joyce. While we are detaining an individual presently in connection with the incident, we are still open to all lines of enquiry.'

Locals were shocked on hearing the news: 'Can't believe it, we're all shocked, nothing like that ever happens around here, it's such a quiet and peaceful town.'

The parish priest of the town, Father Morrissey, had this to say about the deceased: 'Sammy was a gentle soul, well known and well liked. We are very saddened by this dark and heartless cloud that had descended upon our tight-knit community at this particular time.'

The funeral of the deceased man will take place on Thursday and instead of looking forward to the Christmas period the residents here are instead mourning the loss of a cherished member of their locality."

Caitlín turned off the radio. She didn't know if she was listening to it as a mourner or a custodian. She sat down at her desk and stared at her cap and reconsidered why she wanted to do this job in the first place.

She had three brothers and no sisters. She was a bit of a tomboy, always keeping up with the boys and never letting them outdo her just because she was a girl. Her days outside of the schoolyard in Ennis were spent jumping into the river during the summer, cycling freewheel down the steep hill at the broken bridge (always forbidden), and playing a bit of hurling when the numbers were scarce. She loved climbing trees and rolling down the gorse hill but didn't like plucking off all the chicken weed she picked up on her clothes on the way.

1959

When the State announced it was allowing women to join An Garda Síochána for the first time, Caitlín got very excited about it. She had endless rows with her mother over her potential career choice. Her mother kept telling her it was no job for a woman and asking did she want people to be laughing at her. She encouraged Caitlín to follow the lead of her brothers and get a good sensible job with the Civil Service, just like their father. Caitlín's mother was a housewife and her father had worked in the Department of Agriculture all his life. But Caitlín knew she was not academic enough and found the thought of constraining herself to a desk all day shuffling forms suffocating. Being "on the beat" appealed to her energetic side. She knew the unpredictability and varying nature of it would always be one step ahead of her curiosity and that's what she wanted to chase.

Her father openly agreed with Caitlín's mother that she should take on a normal and reliable role in life, pointing out it would only be until she got married and had children anyway. But quietly he supported Caitlín because he quite fancied telling friends, neighbours and colleagues that he proudly had a daughter who was going to be one of first banghardas in the country.

"Don't be worrying. She'll probably be chained to a desk anyway – they won't put a woman out on the street," he assured Caitlín's mother when they realised they were not going to change their daughter's mind.

Caitlín's mind had been made up during the innocent days of her childhood many years before. Particularly as a result of her many tree-climbing and cycling escapades that literally set the wheels in motion to determine her future career.

There were five ash trees in the field to the right-hand side of her primary school. Only the brave (and those wearing trousers) would firstly jump over the school wall at break time (without being seen) and then with safe, slow, measured steps and dexterity pull themselves up into the never-ending branches of the high trees which were dappled in the sunlight. In fact, so experienced were these hardened climbers that Caitlín couldn't remember a single occasion where someone fell or hurt themselves.

Once that challenge had been worn out, a new stake was declared by Tommy Tobin. Tommy was in sixth class and he was wild, bad-tempered, bad-mannered and a bully. Nobody liked him but he never went away so at best he had to be ignored and tolerated at the same time. Tommy suggested that they take on a new tree-climbing challenge.

"So you run across the road and climb the trees in Hanrattys' orchard without being caught."

"But, sure, that's no good – those trees are old and tiny," said one of the gang, as all the kids stared at their targets.

"Yeah, but you have to rob five apples while you're at it, don't let the teachers see you and get back here as soon as you can. We'll do a count for everyone so whoever is the fastest wins the game."

"But as well as the teachers spotting us, what about the Hanrattys?" asked Caitlín.

"Those feckers are old, they won't even see you. If they do they're hardly are going to run after you," said Tommy, sniggering.

They all stood silent, contemplating the risk.

While Caitlín wouldn't deny she was tempted by the rush of it all, deep down it did not sit well with her. Despite being only seven years old, she knew it was wrong. She had on numerous occasions, while daydreaming out the window of her classroom, seen the elderly Mr. and Mrs. Hanratty pruning, picking and contemplating their fruit trees. She knew this was stealing so she decided to say no.

"Ah, you're only a girl anyway, what do you know?" said a disgusted Tommy.

"Right so, you go first then," said Caitlín's playmate, Joe, calling Tommy out.

Foolhardy Tommy didn't even think twice and just went for it. The kids starting counting 1... 2 ... 3 ... 4 ... He bolted across the road, cleared the wall, disappeared altogether for a minute but then his blue woollen pullover became visible in one of the trees. He began picking the apples off and shoving them into the upturned end of his jumper. His concentration overrode his awareness because he failed to see Garda McManus walking casually down the road. Both of their minds were elsewhere until suddenly Mrs. Hanratty's dog made a violent raid of barking at Tommy.

Mrs. Hanratty, who was exiting her outhouse, screamed out loud.

"Get away from them apples, you bleeding thief!"

Tommy let go of his jumper and his grasp and jumped down from the tree. With falling apples scattering everywhere he made a run for the wall to escape.

The garda, who was now wholly aware of the commotion, gave chase.

"Hey, get back here now!"

All the kids' voices counting aloud faded away as they watched with open mouths how badly this had gone. Tommy made it back to the exterior wall of the school where all the bikes were parked and he grabbed one. He jumped on and started cycling off as fast as he could, standing upright to get as much power going as he could muster.

Caitlín saw it was her bike he was on.

"Hey, that's my bike!" she yelled after him and gave chase herself, following in line after the garda who was after Tommy and now the other kids in the pack joined in too.

The teachers who were all in the tea room saw the commotion passing by their front window and they ran outside immediately. They were alarmed to see that Tommy was heading straight down the steep hill towards the broken bridge. They feared that he would kill himself at the speed he had built up.

"Tommy, slow down!" yelled one of them.

It was too late. Turning into the bend at the bridge he squeezed on the brakes. The bike skidded severely, crashing into the stone wall. Tommy was flung in the opposite direction and landed heavily on the ground, face down.

"Are you alright?" gasped the out-of-breath garda, kneeling by the injured boy.

Tommy groaned. The garda gently rolled him over.

The teachers, Caitlín and other children now stood around him too.

"Oh my God, is he alive?" asked the schoolmaster.

Tommy groaned again.

"*Tommy, Tommy, can you hear us?*" the schoolmaster asked urgently.

"Yeah."

A sigh of relief was exhaled by all ages but now Caitlín's focus went to her bike. It lay on the ground in a more motionless state than Tommy. She walked over slowly to it as if trying not to wake it up. The chain had come off, the front wheel was buckled with several spokes broken. Oh, how she hated Tommy Tobin!

Tommy was now standing up and began to hobble back up the road towards the school, flanked on both sides by the teachers who were looking more like prison guards walking an inmate back to death row. Tommy was in so much trouble and, boy, did he know it!

Good enough for him, thought Caitlín to herself as she tried to stand up the disfigured bike and wondered how she would fix it and where would she get the money to do it. Would Mam and Dad be angry with her? There was no way she would get another one – this one was a hand-me-down from one of her brothers but she didn't care about that – it was hers now and she loved it. She went to push it but it would not budge because of the buckled wheel. She decided she would have to ask Santa Claus for a new one.

"Is it yours?"

Caitlín turned around and saw the garda standing behind her.

"Don't look so worried, little girl," he said. "You'll be able to put a new chain on it, a new wheel and it'll be good as new. Give it here to me."

He picked it up, put his arm through the frame to rest it on his shoulder and began to walk on.

Wow, he's so strong, thought Caitlín and followed him back up the road.

"What's your name and address? I'll drop it to your house for you later."

She told him her name and, after rhyming off her address, she gave a weak "Thank you", unsure if she should be even looking such an authoritative figure in the eye.

——*ell*——

Later that evening Caitlín was sitting quietly at the kitchen table, doing fractions as part of her homework. Her mother had nodded off on the fireside chair.

Caitlín had told her about the bike after she walked home from school. Her mother wasn't mad – she knew it wasn't Caitlín's fault but the fault of "those bloody Tobins". She had started a rant about them that Caitlín had heard so many times before.

The Tobins actually lived down the street – at the "bad end" according to Caitlín's mother who had often said how they brought the tone of the street down. The house was run-down with many domestic items strewn in the front garden. Luckily, as her mother continued to point out, they themselves lived at the "good end".

"How could it be any other way? Tommy's father, oh yeah, neither use nor ornament that fella is. Every penny he gets he flushes down the jacks in McKiernan's bar because he never leaves it, flipping useless!" she used to say.

Now Caitlín wasn't getting on too well with the common denominator and was delighted to be interrupted by the sound of a car pulling up outside the house. She looked out through their discoloured net curtain.

"*Oh my God!*" she squealed.

Garda McManus from earlier that day was getting out of his Garda car. She saw him walk round to the boot, from where he lifted out her bike.

She ran outside.

"Hello, Caitlín, here is your bike back as good as new. We had a few stolen bikes at the station for ages which had never been claimed so I replaced the chain and the buckled wheel for you."

Caitlín just stared at him in amazement.

"What is that smell … smoke?" he asked, swinging around.

Then, without any warning, an explosion went off at a neighbour's house and the back of it went up in a ferocious fire.

The garda ran towards the house with Caitlín following.

"*Quick!*" he yelled to her. "*Get me a blanket!*"

Caitlín ran as fast as she could back to her house and whipped the blanket from the back of the chair her mother was sleeping on.

"*Wake up, Mammy! Barretts' house is on fire!*"

She ran after the garda.

He grabbed the blanket from her and muttered to himself, "I need to wet this".

"Over there!" said Caitlín, pointing at a barrel under the downpipe at the side of the Barretts' house.

The garda made straight for it.

By now a few neighbours had gathered but watched helplessly as the fire burned out of control.

Then they heard voices from inside the house, screaming *"Help, help!"* The thick smoke inside was probably causing the family to lose their orientation and blinding them as they sought to get out.

The garda tossed his cap behind him and put the wet blanket over his head and shoulders. He kicked the locked front door open and ran in. Immediately five family members fled out into the front garden, falling to their knees on the grass, trying to breathe. All had come out except the garda.

"The fire brigade and doctor are on their way!" someone shouted in the background.

Then suddenly out staggered the garda, carrying an elderly man, the grandfather. He put him down on the grass but the injured man was unconscious and did not respond at all, no matter how many times they called his name or tapped him gently on the cheek. The garda took the man's head in his hands, opened his mouth and blew into it. He did this repeatedly and eventually the grandfather started to sputter and cough.

A sigh of relief was shared by all.

The fire brigade arrived and put out the fire which was reported to have been started accidently by dodgy wiring or something of a similar nature. The ambulance arrived too and all the family members were treated for smoke inhalation, with no long-term harm done. They were all taken to relatives to stay for the night. Everyone on the street continued to stand around until the whole thing wound down.

Eventually the half-soaked garda turned to leave as his fellow colleagues were on the scene now but Caitlín ran after him.

"Your cap," she said, handing it nervously up to him.

"Oh, hang on there a minute," he said, placing it on her head. "I need you to be my clothes hanger." He bent down to tie his wet loose shoelaces.

"You're as handy as a small pocket, do you know that? You'd make a great garda."

Caitlín was beaming from ear to ear and all her neighbours and family smiled too at her cuteness wearing the oversized Garda cap. She couldn't believe how powerful one person could be in one day. This man was a doctor, a fireman *and* a garda. She believed she had seen the Holy Trinity.

CHAPTER 12

December 1961

Sofia at the Window

At the sideline of the football pitch in Ballantur, where the young lads were training, a different train of thought was being exercised by a few locals who again were speculating on Sammy's death and who might have been responsible for it. Yet again, Waxy's name came up and this time the recollection of an art heist in the locality was the basis for analysis.

1957

"It's the type of rain that wets you twice."

"What are you on about, woman?" asked Sammy of his postmistress who was looking out at the weather through the dusty venetian blinds of the front window of the post office.

"It's so heavy when it hits the ground it bounces back up and wets you again."

"*Ha, ha*, it's coming down strong alright. I hope to God I don't have any parcels to deliver today?"

"You have, not one, but two."

"Feck it, it's a scourge trying to keep them dry on a day like today. Can't we leave them until tomorrow?"

"No. We cannot. What kind of a service would that be?" replied the postmistress, vexed at his non-compliant attitude. "Besides, one of them is for the Wentworths and you know Mrs. Wentworth wouldn't be long reporting us for tardiness."

"Who's the other one for?"

"Waxy Carolan."

"Oh, for flip sake! I'm sure it's as urgent as it is moral."

"That's none of our business – we're just doing our job."

Sammy reviled that comment in his head, considering he was the one heading out into the pouring rain, not her.

Mrs. Wentworth was outside the house in her brown waxed caped coat, gathering provisions from the back of her green Landrover, when he arrived.

"Good morning, Mr. Joyce. Gosh, it's raining cats and dogs!"

"You better not stand in a poodle so."

"*Ha, ha!* Sammy, your humour is sunshine! What have you got for me there?"

"A parcel. I tried my best to keep it from getting wet but it's like trying to keep fish dry in a river on a day like today."

"Don't worry, Sammy. I think it's a box of records my granddaughter sent over from London. She's coming over in a few weeks with her friends to stay here. Be a darling and leave them under the lady in the hall for me."

What? Leave them under who? Sammy blushed and forgot to close the flap of the post box on the bike. He scurried up the stone steps and walked through the wisteria-laden front door. He had never been inside the Wentworths' house before, despite all his years delivering post to them. However, the mystery of the lady was solved immediately. There was no mistaking the very large painting of a woman hanging up on the left-hand side in the entrance hall. Sammy left the parcel at the bottom of the frame.

Continuing on with his round, he cycled down the Hazel Road, up by the old Mill, through Cnoc na Gréine and screeched to a slippery halt outside Waxy Carolan's.

"How'ya, Sammy. Come in out of that rain. I wouldn't like to be in your *wet* shoes today. What have you got for me?"

"Here, it's another parcel," said Sammy, handing it over.

The mulched wrapping had receded extensively at all four corners, much to Waxy's annoyance.

"Oh for fuck sake, Sammy, it's soaking!"

"Sorry, Waxy, it's impossible to keep anything dry today. Maybe it's OK on the inside, whatever it is?"

"It's a stack of magazines! And now they're all wet and stuck together! How will I be able to sell them like this? You lot should compensate me for this."

"Come on, Waxy, I have my limitations on a day like today!"

"Well, then, why don't you join the twenty-first century like your colleagues and drive a bloody van? Oh, hang on a minute, it's because you don't know how to drive, you backward bozo!"

The driving issue was a sore point for Sammy. Even the postmistress was able to drive. It touched a nerve and Sammy retaliated by reminding Waxy that he was far from perfect himself. "Well, I know what drives you! I am sick and tired of turning a blind eye to the commodities I deliver to this house."

Waxy didn't reply. He was too engaged in prising apart his glossy magazines.

Meanwhile, Sammy continued to berate him. "I mean, if it's not cheap cigarettes from Spain, it's banned books from England, illegal films from France and God only knows what else. I should be going to the gardaí with them not to –"

Sammy was silenced mid-sentence as Waxy dropped open the centre spread of one of the magazines. *Playboy*. Sammy stared in a stupefied trance at the scantily clad woman blowing a kiss directly to him.

"Looks like cars aren't the only thing you don't have much experience with, judging by that expression," Waxy said with a laugh. "You know these magazines are very hard to come by and very dear to buy but, seeing, as you rightly pointed out, that you carry a very discreet service, how about I gift you one of these very eye-pleasing exclusive publications?"

"Well. I don't know. I mean. It's just that –" Full sentences eluded Sammy.

"I hear you, Sammy boy. Here, take it away with you and we'll say no more about it." Waxy winked as he shoved the rolled-up the magazine into the inside pocket of Sammy's coat.

"Right so," replied Sammy who sheepishly turned quickly and walked out the door. He finished his round early that afternoon.

———ℓℓ———

The following few weeks of Sammy's day-to-day duties proved unremarkable. Not even Waxy was receiving anything of interest. No doubt something else illicit was keeping him busy, thought Sammy.

It was the summer season now and once the postmistress had read the back of the numerous photographic or water-coloured postcards, she passed them over to Sammy. This was normally their ritual first thing in the morning over a cup of tea and a Jersey Cream biscuit.

"'*Having a great time! Wish you were here!*' I don't know why people write that," she said, laughing. "The only reason they're having a great time is because the people they are writing to are not there with them!"

The other standard sentiment referred to the weather. Nine times out of ten the holidaymakers were home before the postcard.

"Well, at least this one was sent in good time," she said before passing the last card over to Sammy. "'*Weather beautiful here in France. We'll be home for Bonfire Night. No need for any fires here, it's roasting!*' Where is the year going?"

"Speaking of which, I'd better get a move on – look at the time it is!" said Sammy, attending to the rest of his post.

Sammy's day of doing his rounds proved to be frustrating. He was delayed on numerous occasions which was no one's fault but his own with all the chatting he did with the neighbours.

Waxy Carolan's front door was wide open so Sammy let himself straight into the kitchen with a letter he had for him.

"Ah, just the man I wanted to see," said Waxy. "I need to ask you a favour. I need you to check a form for me."

"What is it?"

Waxy got distracted as he read the contents of the letter Sammy had just given him.

"Waxy ... Waxy!"

"What? Yeah, sorry."

"Hurry up, will you, I'm already way behind today."

Occasionally, in the past, Waxy had asked Sammy to check correspondence for him. Having left school early, he was not a great reader or writer and, while he was fine with the informal stuff, it was the official terminology he struggled with.

Waxy turned the letter upside-down and left it on the table before he made off to the other room to get the form. The draught created from opening another door blew the letter off the table and onto the floor.

Sammy went to retrieve it. He could see a picture of a painting of a lady attached to it, with a brief message: *"Bonfire night is the time to woo your lady and I will pick her up afterwards."*

"What are you doing?" Waxy charged back into the kitchen and snapped the letter out of Sammy's had.

"Relax, would you? The draught blew it off the table. I was only picking it up for you. Gimme that form."

Waxy handed him a nearly completed application for a passport.

Sammy scanned it. "Yeah, it's fine, Waxy. Just sign it there at the bottom and you can let it off. Are you thinking of going away?"

"I feel a bit of good luck is coming my way, Sam, and when it does I'll be out of here so fast I won't even leave a footprint!"

Bonfire Night always fell on the 23rd of June. It was an old pagan tradition to celebrate the Irish Goddess of Summer, Áine, or in more recent times to celebrate St. John the Baptist. But generally it was a bringing together of communities who gathered at crossroads all over the country where one could sing and dance to the music of a céilí band or sit quietly and be enthralled by the climbing amber flames of the bonfire with the sparks perishing into the night sky. Some energetic participants would attempt to jump through the fire and this bravery was normally earned from drinking and convorting around it.

On the day leading up to this special night Sammy watched the children from each village excitedly gather and occasionally pilfer a yield of supplies to burn. They rolled tyres, carried timber sticks, timber boxes and wheeled old flour bags and rags by the barrowload.

Then suddenly like a bolt from the blue something strange occurred to Sammy. He recalled the message on Waxy's letter referring to Bonfire Night but more significantly he remembered the picture attached to it. Where had he seen it before? He continued on with his rounds and while cycling up the drive to the Wentworths' house it came back to him. The picture attached to the letter was the same as the painting of the lady hanging in the hall of the Wentworths' residence. Maybe it was a famous painting that Sammy wasn't culturally aware of – but he was very culturally aware of Waxy's form and he had a bad feeling about it.

Nobody was at home at the Wentworth house so he dropped their post through the letterbox of the front door and peered inside through the side window of the door. He could see the painting and there was no doubt about it, it was the same image. He was putting two and two together and began to wonder if Waxy had the intention of stealing it on Bonfire Night. But there again maybe Waxy had a romantic arrangement tonight with a lady and someone was genuinely collecting her after their encounter? He didn't know what to think so he told his postmistress about his theory on his return. She too did not give Waxy the benefit of doubt and told Sammy to tell the gardaí about it immediately.

He set off to the Garda Station with some reluctance, fearing the kind of reaction he might get. Would they laugh at him or, even worse, take it seriously to the point of reprimanding Waxy for something or another only for his deduction to be baseless and *he* would be the one to cop the punishment for wasting Garda time? Not to mention what abuse Waxy would set upon him. Nevertheless, he put his concerns across to Sergeant Lamb and left the station feeling rather underwhelmed. Sergeant Lamb and Tully hadn't really reacted at all. They listened to his prediction based on his sighting of the letter, thanked him for his information and time and told him they would look into it.

Once Sammy had left the station, though, the graceful swans started paddling hastily underneath the surface.

"Tully, my young man, get ready for your first stakeout. I am going to ring the station in Castlebar and request back-up. It might not only be Waxy involved in this premeditated burglary and in any case this might be the opportunity to put this scumbag behind bars once and for all. Get together some torches, batteries, ropes, binoculars. Oh, and a flask of tea and a few things to eat."

"Yes, sir, all the essentials."

Tully did as he was told and put all they needed in a box. Sergeant Lamb then told him that two members of the Force were being dispatched from Castlebar to assist with the stakeout and they were on their way. He made the decision not to inform the Wentworths as there was no point worrying them unnecessarily. If this operation did not come to fruition, it would not cause any inconvenience to the family at all and the gardaí could lick their wounds privately.

When the back-up arrived, Sergeant Lamb and Tully could not have been more thwarted. A very mature garda and his dog reported for duty. Sergeant Lamb could not make out which of them was older. Garda

Kilbane looked like he was only fit for the bin while his trusty four-legged friend was not far behind him.

"You're welcome," said Sergeant Lamb, "but I was expecting a team of two-legged assistants."

"I know you probably were but with the night that's in it resources are stretched to the limit," said Garda Kilbane.

"That's an odd-looking colleague you have with you."

"Jasper? Ah yeah, he's a cross between an Alsatian and a collie."

"It's not sheep we're trying to find," said Sergeant Lamb without any hint of humour. "It's a petty criminal who may or may not have more than one accomplice in a suspected art heist of a painting from a house of reputable means, and we have received intelligence that it is going to happen tonight."

"Don't underestimate Jasper. Both bark and bite are menacing and he has a better nose than any bloodhound."

"We'll see. Tully, get to our lookout point now. We will follow you shortly once I further brief our new Canine Unit on the details of our operation."

Tully sat down on the woollen blanket he had taken from the car. The covert location was in a field opposite the Wentworth house and he had picked a spot that was conveniently thick with furze bushes, providing both an excellent view of the front of the house and sufficient cover not to be seen. Using the binoculars he looked across at the house. He could see right into the big sitting room and watched a few young men and women of a similar age to himself enjoying themselves. He wished he was with them. The girls had long hair and sallow skin. He imagined it would smell of orange blossom if he got close to them. Occasionally they sauntered by the window, enjoying coloured cocktails in shallow glasses, just like in the movies, oblivious to Tully's watchful eye.

The window was open so he could faintly hear music playing. He started singing along to song after song: "Will You Still Love Me Tomorrow?" by the Shirelles, "Runaway" by Del Shannon, "Blue Moon" by the Marcels and Elvis Presley's "Surrender".

Dusk had started to fall when Sergeant Lamb and the support joined him at the hideout point.

"Anyone see you coming here, Tully?"

"No. Pa Leonard came into the field to check on his livestock but they were lying down at the bottom of the hill so he didn't come anywhere near me. What about ye?"

"We met a few kids getting ready for the bonfire, that's all. Is there anything happening at the house?"

"Not a sausage. I saw a bunch of young people inside who I presume are members of the family or friends. Are Mr. and Mrs. Wentworth there?"

"No. I made some enquiries after you left. Mrs. Wentworth has gone back to London and apparently it's her granddaughter and her friends who are there at the moment."

"What about Mr. Wentworth?"

"Dead, at least six or seven years ago. Mrs. Wentworth moved a lot of the contents of the house back to England after he died but I suspect there are still a few possessions of value there that somehow have come to the attention of Waxy and the letterwriter, who are going to help themselves to them."

Two hours later darkness had descended but the locations of the nearby crossroads were illuminated by the lively bonfires. Laugher and talk could be heard from the various get-togethers, their voices carried on the wind.

Sergeant Lamb had already managed to munch his way through all of their edible supplies, much to the annoyance of Tully.

The guardians were becoming lethargic and began to inwardly second-guess their mission.

At approximately half past eleven, suddenly something was going on.

"Sergeant Lamb! I think the house is on fire!"

"What? Show me!" He snatched the binoculars from Tully. He too could see a flickering light rising at the back of the house and thick black smoke circulating from it.

"Is it real? Is it a ploy? What should we do?" asked Tully, panicked.

Sergeant Lamb continued to scan the house and watched the young people running from the front room.

Then they heard voices outside shouting, *"Fire! Fire!"*

Without further doubt and putting the safety of their citizens first, the gardaí ran out of the field, across the road and up the drive to the house.

Tully arrived at the house first and raced around to the back.

The young people were outside, carrying a plethora of buckets and basins from the greenhouse and filling them with water at the tap.

"Help us! Quick!" called one of them. *"The sparks are igniting some of the dried-up wisteria plant growing up the walls – the whole house could go up in flames!"*

By now Tully's support had arrived, albeit vastly out of breath, and they all made a collective effort passing buckets of water between them to quench the fire, splashing it against the wisteria to dampen its vines. Their teamwork was gradually successful and the fire was brought under control.

The young people whooped and laughed in relief.

"The house could have burned down for sure, if that took hold, "said Sergeant Lamb.

He walked closer to the origin of the fire which appeared to be an old castaway furze bush that had the remnants of old rags strewn upon it. He pulled one of these off with the aid of a handle of a brush and held it up to his nose.

"*Oh, puh!* That definitely has been soaked in diesel," he said, the pungent smell making him cough.

"Don't look at us, sir!" responded a girl who had said she was Mrs. Wentworth's granddaughter. "I don't know where that bush came from – it wasn't here earlier."

Garda Kilbane turned on his flash-lamp and shone it around. There in the dry sandy earth they could make out a track which clearly showed where the bush had been dragged from a pile of disgarded vegetation at the back of the garden.

"Oh God, why would someone try to deliberately start a fire so close to our house?" asked the scared granddaughter, grabbing the arm of her friend and holding on tightly.

Sergeant Lamb and Tully looked at one another.

"*Run!*" shouted Sergeant Lamb at Tully who took off like another spark.

But it was too late. The front door was now wide open. The intruder had knocked out a small pane of glass to the side of it which enabled him to reach inside and release the lock. A vase of fresh flowers lay smashed on the floor, clearly fallen from the hall table. The water from it traced a path of loss around the mangled empty picture frame which had been abandoned on the floor. The wooden carcass had been stripped of the beautiful portrait of the lady like a piece of meat savagely cut off the bone.

Sergeant Lamb, Garda Kilbane and Jasper appeared at the front door, looked at the scene and absorbed the defeat.

"Come on, lads, he can't have gone far!" Tully rallied them.

"Don't touch anything, we'll be back," ordered Sergeant Lamb to the young people who were now standing in the hall, bewildered at what was happening.

The Four Musketeers ran down the steps but halted immediately.

"Which way would he go?" asked Tully.

"He won't use the roads because they're too busy tonight. He'll take to the fields," said Garda Kilbane who sounded like he knew what he was talking about.

They ran down the track to the stables at the back of the house.

"*Look!*" said Tully, pointing to the bottom of the old rust-ridden gate in front of them.

"It's a man's tweed peaked cap. I'd swear it belongs to Waxy. He must have dropped it."

"Give it here," said Garda Kilbane.

He held it up to Jasper's nose and the dog immediately starting barking and pulling on the lead to go. "Turn off your flash lamps."

"Let's go," said Sergeant Lamb, climbing over the gate first.

Then Tully followed and finally Garda Kilbane who sat on top of the gate for a moment to contemplate how much he was out of the energetic league here. Incidentally so was the gate. It broke out of its deteriorated brackets under the weight of its host and both crashed to the ground.

"Oh Jesus, are you alright?" asked Tully, who had run back when he heard the crash.

"*Ow, ow, my leg, it's my ankle!*"

Sergeant Lamb and Tully pulled him free from his tangled fall.

"Go, go!" he insisted. "Take Jasper with you, he won't let you down. I'll haul myself back to the house when I catch my breath."

With time being of the essence and Garda Kilbane claiming some sort of resilience, Tully grabbed Jasper's leash and took off with Sergeant Lamb behind him. The ground was rough and uneven. The hooves of the ponies that grazed there had punctured the earth, leaving uneven tufts protruding on the surface. It was impossible to run on it without potentially twisting an ankle. With only the light of the moon shining on them, their speed was curtailed. Jasper led them along the low stone wall on the right-hand side of the field, then left by the brink of the river at the end, before turning left again along the stone wall on the other side of the field and out onto the track.

They stopped when they realised they had only achieved a loop despite Jasper's enthusiasm.

"We're back where we started. This can't be right," said a seriously out-of-breath Sergeant Lamb.

"But this is the way Jasper wants to go."

"Oh, for Christ's sake, Tully! You're going on the hunch of a dog that is nearly as decrepit as his handler! Useless, the pair of them! Waxy may have slipped through our fingers at the expense of a mascot. Now start thinking like a trained officer and not a bloody dog! He's not here. He's long gone. We'll go back up to the house and I'll ring it in first thing tomorrow morning."

"Can we not go to Waxy's house and search it?"

"He won't be there, Tully, and besides we need a warrant to do a search and we're hardly going to get one of them authorised at this hour of night, are we?"

After taking statements from the granddaughter and her friends, Sergeant Lamb and Tully assisted Garda Kilbane into the car and brought him to the Accident and Emergency Department at Castlebar General Hospital. The granddaughter had already telephoned Mrs. Wentworth in

London and Sergeant Lamb instructed that he would speak to her as well in the morning to get specific details of the painting that had been stolen.

Tully tossed and turned when he went to bed eventually that night and wondered, if he had used better judgment over the dog, would they have managed to catch their assailant?

Waxy, on the other hand, was sleeping quite soundly. His arms were tightly wrapped around his stolen lady. He turned over on the warm hay high above in the loft of Mrs. Wentworth's stables and dreamt of the night he had just experienced and humorously someone in his dream was singing "Runaway".

Waxy had returned to the scene of the crime. He knew it was the last place the gardaí would have expected him to go and he purposely dropped his cap to seal that opinion. This only made the whole heist all the sweeter. When dawn was breaking he scampered across the fields to his home, hiding his lovely lady in a secret location on his way.

Sergeant Lamb was already in the station when Tully arrived in, looking as rubbish as he felt.

"Had a nice beauty sleep?" asked Sergeant Lamb.

Tully knew how frustrated Sergeant Lamb was and he also knew how much he would take that out on everyone else.

"So while you were turning over for your second round, I have been on the phone to Mrs. Wentworth. She said her deceased husband, Myles, was the art collector and she doesn't know a hell of a lot about the painting other than it is a portrait of a woman in a long dress opening a window in the sunlight. This woman was the actual girlfriend of the artist whom she says was Spanish. His name was Caleb Morales. However, she does believe it is worth a considerable sum of money. I also rang Headquarters in Dublin and spoke with a Detective Brendan Cullen. He is being dispatched here with an Art Expert from the National Art Gallery to inspect the scene. Both he and Mrs. Wentworth are having a phone consultation as we speak to further clarify the identity and value of the painting. In the meantime, you and I are going to Waxy Carolan's house as soon as we process the warrant to search it and we are going to turn that place over until we find it."

One house and three outhouses later revealed nothing at Waxy's premises other than the dignified villain who calmly and coolly told them, as they had expected, that he knew nothing about the robbery. He swore he did not venture anywhere last night and went to bed early.

A debrief ensued in the station after Detective Cullen and his art connoisseur examined the scene of the crime at the Wentworth house.

Detective Cullen led with the particulars of the painting, handing around poor photocopies in black-and-white as he started. "So here are the facts we know so far. A letter enclosing a print of this stolen painting was sent to a petty criminal in this locality with a brief message written on it which roused the suspicions of the local postman who informed this station and led you to believe that it was going to be robbed. A stakeout was rolled out but abandoned when a deliberately set fire broke out at the back of the residence under surveillance. While attending to the aid and safety of the residents at the back of house, it is believed this distraction provided the timeline for the robbery inside the house to occur as all the residents claim they did not start the fire themselves. Thus the suspect made his escape. We are testing for fingerprints so will be able to confirm if this suspect worked alone or if he had help. So what do we know about the painting? I will let my art expert explain what we know and think."

The wizened-looking art expert stood up. His round thin-framed spectacles sat low on his nose. His hair was slicked back so tightly it matched the stretch of the brown pinstripe suit he wore on his lean body.

He began by telling them the name of the painting. "The painting is entitled *Sofia en la Ventana* meaning *Sofia at the Window* – Sofia being the name of the artist's girlfriend, whom he went on to marry. The artist is the famous Spanish painter, Caleb Morales." He then held up a photograph of the painting in colour from a catalogue he had brought with him. "It was one of many portraits he painted of her, but this one was the most striking, painted in 1905. You will notice the rest of the room is dark and the lady in her bare feet has just opened the shuttered window. The dappled morning sunshine is filtered upon her, making her look almost ethereal. She is wearing a long white dress, taken in the waist and she has a red rose pinned in her dark hair. The technique of capturing the sunlight so brilliantly has made this picture particulary revered."

The onlookers were mesmerised into silence.

"However," continued the expert, "I believe the original of this painting is either hanging in an art gallery in the artist's native city of Seville in Spain, or has been bought by the Metropolitan Art Gallery in New York. I will confirm that for you later."

"So you think what Waxy has stolen is a fake?" asked an exasperated Tully.

"Yes – but a very good one. Let me explain. The practice of reproducing paintings by the old masters and other reputable artists goes back for centuries and has been a very lucratative business. Time and time again amateur painters have tried to emulate or surpass the originals. Look, art lovers know they may never be able to afford a famous painting like this and, with so many of these masterpieces considered priceless, having the next best thing hanging in one's home is very desirable. They are willing to pay a lot of money for a good copy. I spoke with Mrs. Wentworth this morning. She recalls her late husband commissioning an artist, she thinks by the surname of Hunter, to paint a replica of *Sofia en la Ventata* about ten years ago. Due to the advances in techinque and the improved quality of oils since the original was painted, she said he was absolutely delighted with it. I am aware of an artist by the name of Douglas Hunter – he's dead now, but he was very good and I believe he created a profitable niche for himself painting copies of the classics. If this painting was done by him and I suspect it was, there would definitely be a market for it. And I wouldn't be a bit surprised if this Waxy fellow's handler doesn't have a buyer lined up for it already. Sadly, though, the painting was savagely cut from the frame, with a knife I suspect, which will affect the current value of it. Cleary it's the work of an amateur not knowing the fragility of what he was handling. There are fragments of the picture still attached to the staples on the back of the frame which enabled us to send some off for forensic testing to confirm the age of the painting."

"*Ha, ha!* So Waxy cut off his nose to spite his face," said a bemused Tully, smacking his hands together.

"It looks that way, but his loss can be very much our gain," said Detective Cullen. "You said you have been after this guy for a while and, even though we know it's a copy, he is still in possession of stolen goods, breaking and entering, larceny etc. If we play our cards right we can come up with a full house."

"What do have in mind, detective?" asked Sergeant Lamb.

"I have my guys in Dublin putting the squeeze on an art smuggler who lives in Rathmines. There have been a few robberies in houses similar to the Wentworths' around the country and we believe he is associated with them. I have a feeling he is behind this one too. How about this? If we pull him out of the equation and convince Waxy that one of us, pretending to be another interested art dealer, is his only chance now to move this picture on, we can catch him red-handed."

"Brilliant. Let's do it," said Sergeant Lamb. "Tully, put the kettle on."

Later that afternoon, the art smuggler in Dublin suspected to be involved with Waxy was arrested by An Garda Síochána and detained for questioning.

Under Detective Cullen's precise instructions a letter was posted from Dublin to Waxy Carolan bearing a clear, concise message: "*Compromised. Phone 01 – 649 3333 to help your lady now.*"

The detective returned to Dublin expecting an edgy phone call from Waxy the next day.

The assigned phone line rang a few times before Detective Cullen lifted the receiver.

"Hello? Peter Walker speaking," he said in a rather posh London accent.

"Hello?" Waxy probed at this unfamiliar voice.

"Hello, yes, who is this?"

"I was given this number and told you might be able to help me."

"Help you with what?"

"Help me with my lady."

"Ah yes, I was expecting a call from you. I presume this is Waxy Carolan I am speaking to? It appears our mutual acquaintance, Hugh, has been detained by the police and is no longer in a position to help you move on your produce. Is it still in your possession?"

"Yeah."

"And how many people would I have to compensate or did you work solo?"

"Just me."

"I see, very good. I am familiar with this lovely lady and have been such an admirer of the original for some time. What kind of money did you have in mind to let her go?"

"I already had arranged three thousand with our acquaintance."

"Good God, old chap! That's a tad tasty, isn't it?"

"A deal is a deal."

"No – that is the former deal you had which is no longer on the table. It's time to renegotiate."

"If you're not interested I will go somewhere else."

"I think we both know you won't. I understand that you are new to this game. You have no contacts so you need me more than I need you."

There was silence on the line.

"Look," said Detective Cullen then, "I'll tell you what we'll do, Mr. Carolan. Let's meet up. I'll have a look at the painting, see what condition it's in and we'll take it from there."

"Where do you want to meet?"

"Ring me back tomorrow at the same time and we'll make arrangements."

"Fine," said Waxy as he hung up the receiver of the pay phone with a bang.

Subsequently, Detective Cullen reviewed the phone call with Sergeant Lamb.

"It got a bit tetchy then. You were lucky you didn't piss him off altogether."

"I had to challenge him a bit, Frank. If I played exactly to his tune he might have got suspicious. So where will we meet him? Do you want us to come to Ballantur?"

"No way. Waxy won't want this going down on his own turf."

"Will we bring him to Dublin then?"

"No, that will only piss him off even more. I doubt he's ever been to Dublin."

"OK – well, then, why don't we meet in the middle? Athlone? I presume he could get a train directly to there?"

"Yeah, yeah, that sounds good. He can get the train from Castlebar."

"Good. Ring me back with the arrival times and I will ring Athlone Garda Station and request a bit of back-up."

Like clockwork Waxy rang "Peter Walker" again the next day. Detective Cullen instructed him to meet him in the public park opposite the train station in Athlone, trying to make it as convenient for him as they could. Waxy appeared to be fine with this location. Detective Cullen further told Waxy he would meet him straight away after he got off the train at half past midday. He went on to tell him that he would be the man in the brown tweed jacket wearing a trilby hat and would be sitting on a bench by the wall.

ele

Other than agreeing, Waxy didn't say much else to Detective Cullen. For once, Waxy felt anxious. He knew he was out of his depth this time and wanted nothing more than to get rid of the damn painting he now was regretting stealing in the first place.

He hadn't slept much the night before and lay awake waiting for dawn to come. At first light he was up and out to retrieve the painting from its hiding place. He scurried across the playground at the local primary school which had been seasonably abandoned due to the summer holidays. Waxy stooped underneath the platform of the slide and gently prised away a flour sack which he had previously attached with thumb-tacks to the timber. He then pinned the flour sack containing the picture to the inside of his long cream mackintosh. He set off for Castlebar railway station immediately before any the locals would see him.

The punctual train screeched to a slow halt in Athlone. A nervous Waxy alighted and got his bearings outside the station. Immediately he noticed the black wrought-iron gate that led into the park and so in he went. His intention was to get the whole thing over and done with as soon as possible, getting his money and getting home. After a lap around the blooming rose garden he spotted his contact – fitting the description he was given, sitting on a wooden bench with his back to a thick laurel hedge. What Waxy did not know of course was that Sergeant Lamb, Tully and two other members of the Force were stooped down waiting behind it.

"Mr Carolan, I expect?"

"Yeah," replied Waxy quietly, looking around him to see if anyone was listening or watching them.

"Relax, man, there's no one here. Hang on, what the blazes is going on? Where is the picture? Why didn't you bring it?"

"I did," said Waxy, undoing the buttons of his coat and revealing what was attached inside.

"*What?* It'll be damaged, man, being carried like that! And I thought it was much larger?"

"Oh, it is – I folded it."

"*What the devil? You can't be serious?* I thought you were a professional? You have never handled art like this before, have you?"

"Yeah, I have," replied Waxy, sounding uncertain.

"Well, Rule Number One, Mr. Carolan, is that you *never, ever* fold an oil painting. It cracks the paint, you idiot! Take it out – let's see how bad it is."

An intimidated Waxy did as he was told and unfolded the picture so Peter Walker could see the full extent of his inexperience.

"Jesus, you are a brute! What did you cut it out of the frame with? A pickaxe? At least an inch will have to be trimmed off the sides to evenly display it again. What did you cut it with?"

"A Stanley knife. Look, I didn't have much time. The family of the owners of the house were there at the time I lifted it."

"*Tut, tut, tut!* And what is all the white stuff on it?"

Waxy hadn't until this point paid any attention to the ancillary debris.

"It's probably just flour from the bag it was in."

"Are you having a laugh? Tell me, Mr. Carolan, were you expecting the new buyer to hang it or bake it?"

"Ah, forget it! If you're not interested I'll get someone else to buy it," said Waxy, folding the painting up again.

"But we both know you won't get someone else, will you? You don't know anyone else in the art underworld apart from Hugh who was picked up a few days ago. Besides, who'll buy it in that condition?"

"You know nothing," said a frustrated Waxy, walking away.

"I know more than you think. Listen to me."

Waxy stopped and walked back.

"You have produced a butchered and flour-covered liability due to your own incompetence. There are more folds in it than a greasy mechanic's road map but you have only brought yourself to a dead end, my friend. I'll give you five hundred for it."

"*Five hundred!* We agreed three thousand!"

"I told you before. You agreed three thousand with your predecessor, not with me. You have presented me with a monster that is now only a shadow of the magnificence it should be. No one is going to offer you any more than that. Can you not see that?"

Waxy knew he was snookered. He conceded to himself that he had made a balls of it and five hundred pounds was still an awful lot of money.

"OK, you can have it."

Detective Cullen took a brown envelope out of his jacket pocket and exchanged it for the painting.

Waxy started to hurry away without another word.

"*Ooooh, Waxy!*" Detective Cullen sang out. "I have a miniature portrait of myself here to show you!"

"Not interested."

"No, seriously, come here – it won't take a second and it might be something you can sell."

A reluctant Waxy walked back to the detective.

"*Ta da!* I would like to present my badge representing my membership of An Garda Síochána where I am one and the same Detective Brendan Cullen. So stick 'em up, mate, you're under arrest!"

Waxy took off running like a hare. Detective Cullen started to pursue, closely followed by the four gardaí from behind the hedge. While in motion Waxy pulled the long encumbering mackintosh off him and left it where it fell. He had shoved the money into his trouser pocket. He ran as fast as he could through some back streets then past the Civic Offices. He glanced back and could not see his hunters so he ran back to the Civic

Offices, thinking that there had to be somewhere to hide inside the big building.

There was no one in the foyer when he went in, only the receptionist at the front desk who looked startled at the dishevelled state of him.

"Can I help you there, sir?"

"Yes, please ... sorry, I'm mad late for a meeting," he replied, considerably out of breath.

"With whom?"

"Ah ... the Planning Department," he said, thinking on his feet.

"Up the stairs and down to the end of the corridor – you'll see a sign ..."

He didn't even let her finish giving her directions for he was up the stairs like a laser. He ran to the end of the corridor where he saw a sign on the door of the Planning Department. Suddenly its door opened and a clerk stopped Waxy in his tracks.

"Flip it, I forgot one of my maps, it's out in the car," said Waxy. "I couldn't go out the back way to the car park, mate? Save me going the long way around?"

"Sure, you can go through the brown door there behind you and that will bring back out outside," said the none-the-wiser clerk.

Unfortunately for Waxy his improvised interaction cost him because down below outside his pursuers saw him engaging with the clerk through the glass windows of the corridor.

"*Quick, up there!*" shouted Tully pointing towards their target above them.

Waxy made a dash for the back exit, ran down the stairs and came outside again. Without knowing where he was going he continued running and turned right up Bridge Street. The River Shannon came into view and he saw it as an opportunity. He could see boats big and small obligingly moored to either of the banks. Waxy's racing mind told him he could try and hide in a boat or between two boats, or under the water if he had to – whatever it took to get away. He ran down the limestone steps two at a time at the side of the four-arch bridge and jumped into the unoccupied boat nearest to him.

"*Stop!*" shouted Sergeant Lamb from the top of the bridge above. "*You're under arrest!*"

The other gardaí were now at the brink of the river.

"*Looks like you have friends in low places here too, Sergeant!*" taunted Waxy as he took a leap of faith and jumped straight into the water. Seconds later he re-emerged and started swimming to the other side.

The gardaí untied a small rowing boat and after jumping in started to row erratically. No Olympic medals to be won there. Their unsynchronised efforts slowed them down pitifully while Waxy impressively swam to the other side before them. Pulling himself out of the water, he stood up and caught his breath. He put his hand in his pocket and could feel the money was still there even though it was soaking wet like the rest of him. He glanced at his pursuers who were nearing the bank so he took off running again. This time he disappeared down an alleyway that led to back of some residential houses. A washing line caught his attention. If he could put some other garment on him to disguise himself it might help. Making a grab for a man's navy jacket, he didn't see the sleeping dog in the back garden and tripped over him. Abruptly roused from his sleep, the big brown mongrel became instantly agitated. The hair on his back became as rigid as the set of teeth that were viciously on show from his snarling mouth. Waxy realised he needed to get out of there and fast. He ran at the block wall and threw himself upon it but not quickly enough. The incensed dog bit into Waxy's left ankle with a vice-like grip.

While Waxy tried his best to kick back and wriggle free, the gardaí arrived on the scene. So too did the bewildered owner who stepped out of his back door and immediately prised the dog away. The gardaí pulled Waxy down off the wall and put a set of handcuffs on him.

Tully smiled and turned to Sergeant Lamb. "Looks like Jasper has friends in low places too." He turned to Waxy. "Waxy Carolan, you are under arrest on charges of larceny, breaking and entering, theft, possession of stolen goods, resisting arrest – shall I go on? You really blew it this time, Waxy. You are not obliged to say anything unless you wish to do so but anything you say may be taken down in writing and may be used in evidence."

Waxy shot him a wild-eyed look of disbelief at everything that had gone wrong on him but said nothing.

"Yeah, you know the real Sofia is happily hanging in the Metropolitan Gallery of New York? But, to be honest, I'd say she'll have aged a bit by the time you get to see her again."

Waxy served three years in jail for his crimes.

Tully was quite content with the A4 photocopy he still retained from Detective Cullen's debrief and hung it on the wall at his desk and occasionally when he looked at it for some reason he started singing "Surrender" to himself.

CHAPTER 13

Doctor Kyros Asclepius

"No way, Waxy didn't kill Sammy over that picture and the jail sentence!" said one of a few customers who were gossiping with Cassie in her shop over a can of bon bons. "You're not thinking outside the box at all. You need to stop looking at the locals. One of our own would never do something like that. I know who did it. It was your man, the odd fellow. Remember that strange doctor from the Mediterranean who came here? He caused all sorts of trouble but nothing that Sammy didn't put a stop to. Remember? It was here in the shop, Cassie, that we first met him."

October 1961

"Dr. *Key-Rose Ass-clip-us*."

"No, it's Doctor *As-Klep-eee-us*."

Cassie Quirke and Babs Wheatley were doing their best to pronounce the name of the doctor printed on the flyers that were left on the counter of Cassie's grocery shop. Out of earshot, the author himself was in the shop too but he was busy talking to another customer.

Babs went on to read the flyer aloud: "*Walk -in clinic for one week only. Astrological Medicine offering alternative treatments for long-suffering aliments such as rheumatoid arthritis, back pain, migraines, skin allergies, insomnia, loss of appetite, heartburn, nasal congestion etc. Open Monday to Friday 10am to 1pm and 2pm to 5pm. Located in Slattery's Guesthouse. All are welcome.'"*

"Ladies, ladies, let me introduce myself personally. I am Doctor Kyros Asclepius. If you, or any of your family and friends have any physical problems they should come and see me at my clinic."

"Hello, I'm Babs, and this is the proprietor of this shop, Cassie. Can I ask you what this Astro-Logical medicine is?"

"Of course, my dear. Its origins go back to ancient Greece where our forefathers believed in the connection between the zodiac signs and the organs in our bodies. Our dates of birth are the basis of our own individual paths throughout our lives. This path is influenced, both good and bad, by the constellation of the Universe so astrological medicine is the most personal, intimate and tailored medicine suited to each individual and what they are suffering from. That is why I highly recommend it, based on such carnal specificity. Now, if you will excuse me I must go and distribute more of my flyers around your beautiful town."

"Fascinating. I'd let him take my heartbeat any day," purred Cassie when he'd gone.

"Yeah, well, I'd get him to test your eyes and ears too. What a load of palava!"

"I'm definitely going to see him."

"I'm not going anywhere near him. Wait – there's nothing wrong with you, Cassie."

"I suffer from tiredness all the time but at the same time can't sleep."

"That's because you are up at the crack of dawn every day and you work hard."

"You should go with your sinuses."

"It's a load of nonsense."

"All the more reason to go. We'll both go. I'll go with my open mind and you go with your reservations and we'll see who fares the best."

The word of this alternative medicine got around and people who were getting no relief from conventional treatments decided to give it a go, resigning themselves to believing they had nothing to lose. Babs convinced Nate to go with his bad back. No amount of stretching, walking or wearing a wired corset as prescribed by his own G.P. was having any effect at all.

Sammy Joyce and Pa Leonard debated about going to see this doctor too when Sammy was delivering the flyers on his round. Pa decided he was definitely going to go.

Sammy thought no more of it than he thought of witchcraft.

"You mean to say that Molly's horoscope healed her after her accident more than the great doctors and staff who nursed her in the hospital twenty-four hours a day?" Sammy saw that Pa was recoiling from this confrontation so he changed the subject. "Molly, come out here – I have a parcel for you!"

Molly hobbled out of the house on her crutch. Her right eye was covered with a patch.

"Somebody is thinking about you, Moll. Look at the big heavy parcel they have sent you," said Sammy, handing it over to her.

Her brother Tadgh helped her rip open the brown wrapping paper.

Astonishment showed on all their faces when they saw a box containing a camera.

"Well, what sick so-and-so would send the poor girl a camera when she has only one eye to use it?" said Pa indignantly.

"*Shhh*," said Elsie Leonard, noting the humiliation on Molly's face. "Don't upset the poor child."

"I think it's a brilliant idea," enthused Sammy. "Who uses their two eyes when they are taking a picture anyway!"

They read the note that came with it. The gift was sent from her aunt in Dublin.

"Vision is not blindsided, Molly. There is nothing to stop you seeing the world like everyone else."

"She's right," continued Sammy. "Don't let your injury hold you back. You show them! You are going to be a great photographer, Molly. No excuses. Get out there and start snapping."

To Babs' lack of surprise Cassie was already sitting in the waiting area of Slattery's Guesthouse in anticipation of seeing Doctor Asclepius who was still engaged with a patient.

"He's *soooo* handsome and oh that accent! I wonder where he's from?" said Cassie to Babs as she sat down beside her.

"Planet Cuckoo Land, if you ask me."

"Babs, if you go in with that cynical attitude you won't come out with any healing."

"You're the one that made me come here, remember? Do you really think the fact that I'm a Gemini is suddenly going to cure something that I've suffered from for years?"

Cassie didn't care about Babs' whinging. She was too busy eyeing up the doctor as he emerged from his consultation room and thinking how dapper he looked wearing an impeccable three-piece suit. It was light grey in colour with a faint pattern of squares throughout. It was accentuated by a crisp white shirt and a red tie. An attire a bit too dandyish for the local menfolk but that is what made him stand out, Cassie thought.

"Look at his hair," she said, nudging Babs. "It's just that little bit longer to show his natural wave. Not like all the fellows around here who get the same universal short back and sides. Trimmed so tight you don't know what kind of hair they have, curly, straight, wavy –"

"Oh, for the love of God, Cassie, will you shut up!"

Thankfully Cassie was the next one to be called in. She felt giddy.

The doctor talked through the double-edged sword of Cassie's complaint which was constant tiredness but still sleeping poorly. He listened patiently to her and empathised that her woes were an unfortunate consequence of her occupation and the long hours she put in. Nevertheless, he assured her he could help her and began by asking what her date of birth was.

"25th August 1903."

"Excellent," said the doctor who began drawing a chart. "So 25 plus 8 plus 1 plus 9 plus 3 equals 46.4 plus 6 is 10. 1 plus 0 equals 1. Your lucky number is 1!"

"Great. What does that mean though?"

"It means if you ever have to pick a number again make sure it's your lucky number 1. Now we need to focus on your natal chart which comes from your date of birth and how the positioning of the planets was then, and now influence your very own state of health."

"Oh, it's fascinating, Doctor," said Cassie, getting excited.

"Your date of birth makes you a Virgo. That means you are in the sixth house of the Zodiac. And this house, which is by the way not a coincidence, controls the nervous system. And it is your nervous system we need to regulate for quality sleep but also to energise you during the day."

"Yes," said Cassie in awe, who felt like she was seeing the light.

Meanwhile the doctor continued to draw a series of lines from dot to dot and squiggles.

"Astrology not only reveals our weaknesses, it also guides us to strengthen them and when the constellation of our stars and planets are in a certain favourable position it makes the cures more potent. And what I mean by that is, certain medicinal herbs and plants are more powerful at one time of the year than another. So, Cassie, I am going to make for you three tailored remedies specifically for your needs, using ingredients that are in your good astrological path right now, to give you optimum relief. Currently, the moon is trining Mars, then Mercury, bringing out the essence of chamomile and lavender. So I am prescribing chamomile tea to drink before you go to bed and I will make a lavender-fragranced ointment to rub on your pulse points like your wrists, temples, behind your ears etc., to inhale, so you will feel relaxed and start to feel sleepy. Oh, and I strongly recommend one of my beautiful handmade candles infused with more lavender to burn, creating a calming and serene atmosphere at nighttime. OK? OK. Then I'll prepare a special tonic to give you energy during the day."

"And what's in that, Doctor?"

"Belief, Cassie," laughed the doctor. "It's my own secret recipe but, trust me, it works. I will leave my forwarding address here with Mr. Slattery so you can contact me when you need more of it, or anything else. And finally, Cassie, because I am so humbled that you have opened your mind and accepted to begin a journey of wellbeing from the rewards of astrological medicine, I have a gift for you."

He gave her a small midnight-blue velvet pouch. Cassie untied it and pulled out a sapphire gem stone.

"It's your birthstone for Virgo."

Imitation though this gemstone was, Cassie was nonetheless captivated by her unique consultation and Doctor Asclepius. She bought the tonic, two jars of the ointment, the chamomile tea and the lavender candle.

Babs was next to see the doctor and she hoped she would get on as well as Cassie who was beaming when she passed her by in the hallway.

After an exchange of formalities and a concise introduction of the nature of the doctor's practice, they started off with her date of birth too, being the 1st of June 1912.

"So 1 plus 6 plus 1 plus 9 plus 1 plus 2 equals 20. 2 plus 0 equals 2. Your lucky number is 2, Mrs. Wheatley!"

"When am I supposed to use that?"

"Do a raffle, sweepstake, go to bingo."

"I don't feel like going anywhere at the moment, I am coughing and spluttering so much."

"Ah yes, the third house of Gemini is responsible for the respiratory system and Gemini is your star sign. I am charting your natal origin and your journey beyond and, yes, you are destined to suffer with your sinuses. But, fear not. Your chart also holds the key to unlocking your aliments and there is a good window for you now, Babs, because the sun is shifting into Gemini. A make-or-break opportunity to meet this bout of sinuses head on. Some cures are strong at the moment so you need to start a course of treatment straight away. I will prepare a concoction of honey and garlic mixed with shea butter. Rub this on your temples when you have a headache. I will also give you eucalyptus oil. Put a few drops in a bowl of boiling water. Cover your head with a towel and inhale this steam. This will decongest your nasal passages and kill any germs. If you don't like the inconvenience of that I will give you some oregano oil. Put a few drops of it directly on your tongue. Some people don't like the taste of it so that is why you might prefer to use the eucalyptus. Many find ginger tea beneficial too and, like the steam, it helps to unblock the congestion and it has other healing properties. I have a beautiful candle here infused with lavender oil which will help you relax when you feel frustrated with your symptoms or I can make up my special tonic to give you a bit of energy. Finally, Babs, because I am so humbled that you have opened your mind and accepted to begin a journey of wellbeing from the rewards of astrological medicine, I have a gift for you."

He gave Babs a pearl which is the birthstone for Gemini. Babs bought the eucalyptus and oregano oils but she declined his tonic and "exotic" ginger tea and told him that her husband had a grocery business so they had more than enough candles already. She thanked the doctor and left. Her prescription was nothing she had not heard of before, albeit a variation in one form or another. The jury was out as far as she was concerned and, with regards to her prognosis, only time would tell.

Nate attended the clinic in the evening. After listening to Babs recount to him both hers and Cassie's experiences, a stalwart Nate remained indifferent and approached his appointment in a neutral state of mind – besides, it would be a bit of craic to tell everyone the next day.

Immediately Nate was struck by the professional, if a bit flash, appearance of the doctor and as much as said so by the perplexed expression on his face.

"You're the doctor?"

"Yes, I am, Mr. Wheatley. I am not what you were expecting, no? You thought I was going to walk out from behind a jingling curtain wearing a turban on my head and dangly earrings?"

Both men laughed at the thought.

"I thought you would be using a crystal ball instead of a stethoscope."

"Anything else?"

"Maybe wearing eyeliner, rings and a floor-length gown," added Nate humorously, but also wondering if he was taking it a bit too far.

"You are not here to get your fortune read. You need a Physic Sonia or a Mystic Mary for that."

"But you are a real doctor?" asked Nate daringly.

"Of course. I am a qualified medical doctor who after years of practising conventional Western medicine started to research alternative cures and found astrological medicine in particular fascinating. My belief and passion for it overturned my original practice."

"I never heard of it before. But sometimes, I suppose, it takes a stranger to our shores to show us something new. Where do you come from yourself?"

"I am originally from Greece, the beautiful Island of Skepelos, but I studied and worked in London and then went to America for years. After some time I missed the close sense of community of my own island so I came to yours for a look and I have been here since. Now, Nate, it is I who should be asking the questions and not the other way round. Tell me about your occupation and what is wrong with you and we will begin."

After calculating that Nate's lucky number was 7, he told him his star sign was Leo, the star sign represented by the Lion, which pleased Nate.

"The fifth house, yours, is responsible for the spine, spinal cord and back and that is why you suffer as you do."

"Is there a cure for my back pain?"

"Sure, get a new job," said the doctor, smiling. "But I don't think you will want to do that. What would all your customers do without you and the wonderful service you provide for them? The best thing we can do is alleviate and control the flare-ups as they occur. First of all, Nate, you must be mindful of how you lift things. Bend those knees. Have you ever considered doing yoga?"

"No. Isn't that what women go to with a rug under their arm? I used to see them in England going to it."

"Nate, you make it sound like they were joining King Solomon and his flying carpet! Yoga has been practised all over the world for centuries by both women *and* men. It's a non-evasive and gentle way of stretching the body which greatly achieves lasting agility and flexibility. I think you need to open your chakras."

"Open my what?"

"We all have seven chakras. They are energy points in the body and you need to concentrate on the 6th one – the sacral chakra which is located in your back. But that is for a yoga master to teach you about and not me. Now, where were we? Oh yes, use a wheelbarrow or a trolley to lift heavy things but, most of all, ask for help. That is the greatest strength of all."

"I'm asking you, aren't I?"

"Yes, and the good news is, looking at your emerging chart I see that Mercury is about to go retrograde so you will feel tension in your back. I am going to prescribe the following natural plant-based medications for you that are seasonally at their prime right now due to the constellation and alignment of your stars and planets. Firstly, I am going to give you a small jar of turmeric powder. Add this to your dinners in meat stocks, stew and soups. It is a natural anti-inflammatory. In case you do not like the taste of that, I will also give you a bottle of willow-bark oil. This is to be rubbed on the affected area but not to be used at all if you are on any blood-thinning medication. You could get someone to massage it into your back. That would be nice, yes? Perhaps your wife? And what better way to enhance a romantic atmosphere than with one of my beautiful scented rose candles?"

Nate blushed and said nothing. The doctor sensed his discomfort and moved on quickly with another remedy.

"Another good warm rub is with ginger. Mix it with a drop of water into a paste. Leave on your back for a while and then wash off. Lastly, I can offer you my own tonic with a special pick-me-up recipe to give you a bit of pip when you need it. Now, before you go, Nate, I am so humbled that you have opened your mind ..." and the doctor finished with his usual platitudes of gratitude. He presented Nate with the gem that represented his birthstone. It was a peridot.

Nate definitely fell under the influence of the Zodiac, or something. By the time the consultation was over, whatever about opening his chakras he certainly had opened his wallet. He bought the turmeric powder, the ginger powder, the willow-bark oil and two scented candles. He thanked the doctor and hoped they would meet again.

"Next time I'll hum a Tibetan mantra for you, burn incense and maybe have a black cat too," said the doctor.

Nate laughed at his self-deprecating humour.

Both men were simultaneously thinking what a nice guy the other was.

Sammy was the most cynical patient of all about Dr. Asclepius and his alternative bandwagon of concoctions, but all of his friends had been for a consultation so he decided to go too just so he could give a further opinion from his already made-up mind.

He met Pa Leonard in Doctor Asclepius's waiting room a few days later. He was delighted to hear that Molly had taken like a duck to water with the camera.

"Already gone through two rolls of film. She has my heart broke. She saw a photography competition in the paper called 'From Dusk till Dawn' and wants to enter it. I'll have to get up and out at daybreak with her to take these photographs."

"You won't be wanting sleeping tablets so," slagged Sammy, nodding in the direction of the doctor who was beckoning Pa forward for his consultation.

Pa didn't care for the pomp and ceremony of his horoscope or the Zodiac reading. He wanted relief for his rheumatoid arthritis which he had suffered from seriously during the latter part of his life. His lifetime occupation as a farmer was a vocation of physical hardship and frequent exposure to the elements of very harsh Irish weather. His hands were deformed and crooked, giving him limited mobility and loss of power. He also experienced a similar lack of sensation in his hips and knees which had progressively burdened him with a limp in his right leg. He was bemused by the calculation of his lucky number, thinking it was childish but would be fun to do with the grandkids when he went home. Capricorn was his Zodiac sign and what it represented regarding his health went way over his head. This was acknowledged by the doctor who had sympathy for Pa so they focused on the medicinal treatments instead. He too was prescribed willow-bark oil to be massaged into his sore joints and muscles. A jar of turmeric spice was recommended to be added to his dinners and soups. Finally he was given a bottle of the doctor's tonic to give him some energy when the pain was overbearing.

At the end of the consultation the doctor presented Pa with his birthstone which was a garnet gem. Pa thanked him but he knew he would give the jewel to Molly as soon as he went home.

"4 plus 2 plus 1 plus 9 plus 1 plus 6 equals 23. 2 plus 3 is 5."

Sammy immediately had the horns out. "So what does that mean – what am I supposed to do with it?"

"Well, anytime you have to pick a number make sure it is number 5 and it will be lucky for you."

"But what has that to do with my health? I suffer from Reynaud's condition. My own G.P. diagnosed it."

"Yes, Aquarians are linked to the 11th house of the zodiac and they do indeed suffer from circulatory problems such as yours," replied the doctor calmly.

"And you think reading my horoscope is going to fix that?" challenged Sammy.

The doctor gave his usual brief introduction about his practical beliefs, astrology and its effects on plants.

"I am detecting some hesitancy here, Sammy, which is unfortunate as you really need to give it a chance for it to work."

"How is reading star signs going to heal anybody?"

"Faith, belief and trust. Are you a religious man?"

"Yes, I go to Mass every week and believe in God."

"Well, let me retest your catechism and ask you who created the world?"

"God did."

"So does that not mean that God created the sun, moon and stars too?"

Sammy was saying yes in his head.

"And tell me, Sammy, have you ever thought to yourself that there must be a full moon on witnessing the erratic behaviour of someone?"

"Loads of times," smirked Sammy.

"I know it sounds rather flippant but scientifically a full moon creates a gravitational pull on the water fluids in our bodies which results in us acting more het-up or out of character temporarily. Let me ask you something else. Do you think any two people are the same?"

"No."

"OK – so why treat them exactly the same way? I mean giving two people exactly the same medicine when the composition of their bodies is not similar due to their gender, weight, age, lifestyle etc. Doesn't seem to make a lot of sense, does it?"

"I suppose not," said Sammy, beginning to doubt himself.

"Tell me what happens to you and causes you discomfort."

"My hands and feet go so numb with the cold, even when it is not that cold. They go pure white just like a corpse. I have no feeling in them. I have burned myself a few times trying to warm them up again."

While the doctor was listening to Sammy he sketched up his natal chart.

"I can see what you have described emerging in your path. There is a malefic planetary combination. I suspect you have suffered from this from early adulthood?"

"I have," replied Sammy, thinking he got that right.

"Your astrological journey of health unfortunately shows that you will continue to suffer from this but the good news is we can treat and control it so its presence should not impact your life too much in the future. Luckily the sun and moon are in Aquarius right now so there is great impetus on the natural herbs and plants we will use as a result of this great stellar force."

"I'm lost."

"OK," said the doctor, laughing. "Let's focus on the physical remedies. I am going to prescribe a cayenne-pepper lotion for you. I will mix it with a base of shea butter infused with eucalyptus and peppermint oils so it will be very pleasant to apply, but the properties of this pepper will physically warm the muscles. Use it liberally before you go out in cold weather. Anytime you lose circulation don't plunge your hands into hot water or use a hot-water bottle for your feet because that only gives you chilblains which is another side effect of your condition. Besides, as you say, you could seriously burn yourself. Finally I will give you a bottle of my tonic to put pep in your step."

The doctor felt he had won Sammy over until he gave him his rendition of platitude by gifting him his birthstone gem which was an amethyst. Sammy then reverted to his Doubting Thomas attitude.

Eager to mend bridges, the doctor began to make small talk with him about the attractions of Ballantur and Sammy mentioned the hobby close to his heart – fishing. The doctor genuinely proclaimed that this was one his passions too. After a few minutes discussing this, he accepted Sammy's kind offer to take him out on the river the following evening, resulting in the doctor netting a fan after all.

Sammy and Mutey were waiting for Doctor Asclepius at the sandy lay-by at the brink of the river. This is where the local anglers tethered their boats to wooden stakes on the bank.

"Ahoy there, Captain!" said the doctor warmly as he greeted them.

"Good evening to you, sir," returned Sammy. "Let me introduce our skipper to you. Mutey, meet Dr. Asclepius. He can't speak, doctor, he's mute."

"Very pleased to meet you," said the doctor who immediately was aware that Mutey might be dumb but he was not deaf. "I find that frequently people who talk too much rarely have anything interesting to say."

Mutely smiled and nodded respectfully.

"In fact, it is Mutey who is taking us out on his boat," said Sammy. "Come on!"

The doctor stopped walking at the third boat lined up and looked at it.

"No, not that one. The *Titanic* lasted longer than that."

"Sorry, it reminds me of our beloved kaiki boats. That is the traditional fishing boats we have at home in Greece. It must be all the colours."

"Well, that one has not seen a shoal of fish in a long time. Don't even know who owns it, it's been left there so long."

The three fishermen set sail. The conditions were favourable. The weather was dull, humid and heavy, a perfect aperitif for the biting fish.

Doctor Asclepius got hooked straight away on the scenery surrounding them on the slow, meandering river. He was focused on every nook and cranny of its shady bends.

"It's so beautiful here, so peaceful," said the doctor.

"That's why Mutey and I like it so much. You wouldn't see a sinner out here."

"And what about the fishing, what do you catch?"

"Peace of mind, without a prescription. No offence."

"None taken. I can see why."

"We have beautiful trout, salmon, perch, pike and slippery eels."

"Oh yes – they are the ones you cannot kill."

"That's right. My father caught one years ago and put it on the frying pan with two rashers beside it one morning. He went outside for a bucket of turf and when he came back in the eel had the two rashers eaten."

"Sammy, I know you're pulling my leg but it's a funny story," said the doctor, laughing. "We have our stories too in Greece. My father had only three fingers on his left hand. He went out fishing one night for swordfish because that is the time when they like to feed. These fish can be monstrous and are capable of growing up to ten feet. One of them took the bait of squid at the end of my father's fishing rod. Because it was so dark he could not see how big this bad boy was, but he was getting a sense of how heavy it was. For some stupid reason, I suppose for a better grip, he wrapped some of the line around his hand. His opponent was not going to give up without a fight. The huge fish leaped out of the water with such ferocity the line ripped the fingers clean off my father's hand and the fish swam away victorious."

"Jesus, is that where the first fish fingers came from?" asked Sammy, not being able to help himself.

All three men burst out laughing and exchanged many fishing stories during the remainder of their expedition.

When the talk ran out, individually but comfortably they tuned into their own sense of peace. The sound of the trickling currents and the sight of two peaceful swans on the water's edge brought them serenity. Then this was all literally blown out of the water when suddenly Mutey was the first to hook a fish. Almost simultaneously, so did the doctor, which created a very unstable boat with both men trying their best to wrestle with their prizes. Several more fishes were caught that evening but their mutual catalogues of fishing stories had yielded the greatest pleasure of all.

The following Sunday night saw Nate, Pa and Sammy gathered around the bar in Slattery's. Sammy brought them up to speed about the enjoyable boat trip he shared with Doctor Asclepius and Mutey. They discussed the medicine the doctor had prescribed for each of them. Nate and Sammy had abstained from the tonic which Pa had nearly drunk already. He said Cassie was a big fan of it too and how he had seen her this evening up on a ladder washing the windows outside her shop.

Eventually but naturally, Nate changed the subject by regurgitating a joke he had heard from one of the customers on his rounds.

"A schoolteacher was giving her first-class students a lesson in geography," he said. "To make the lesson more interesting and fun, she decided to associate food with different places from around the world. 'For example,' she started, 'the Mississippi Mud Pie comes from the State of Mississippi in America and is made of chocolate. The Danish Pastry is from Denmark – it's a dough that is rolled around itself – it has cinnamon and raisins in it and it's usually sweet and sticky on the outside. The Cornish Pasty is from Cornwall in the South of England – it's a flaky pastry full of meat and vegetables.' Then one small boy spoke up. 'That sounds yucky to me, miss,' he said, 'but where do pigs in blankets come from?' A little girl raised her hand. 'What about a hotdog, miss?' she asked. 'I don't know about them,' said the teacher. 'Let's stick with ones we do know – now where was I?' Suddenly the teacher got a very dry throat and started coughing. After a sip of water and recovering her voice, she said 'Sorry about that. God, what is worse than a frog in the throat?' And little Jimmy, who was the cheeky class clown and never one to miss an opportunity to misbehave, shouted out: 'A toad in the hole!'"

The three men laughed loudly, especially Pa who nearly choked on his pint.

"Ease up on the jokes, Nate, you're nearly after giving Pa a heart attack," said Sammy.

At that, Pa suddenly turned the colour of ash, grabbed his chest and groaned. The pint glass fell out of his hand and he slowly slid off the high stool and onto his knees on the floor.

"Oh my God, I think he *is* having a heart attack. *Dennis, get Doctor Asclepius!*" Nate shouted to the barman.

"He's gone out. I'll telephone for an ambulance."

"No, it will take too long. I'll drive him to the hospital."

"You can't, Nate, you've been drinking. I'll drive him. Someone else tell Mrs. Leonard and bring her to the hospital," ordered Dennis.

Nate and Sammy went with Pa and Dennis. They were very worried about their old friend after seeing the frightening state he was in.

They stayed at the hospital with Mrs. Leonard until the doctors assured them that Pa had stabilized and was comfortable. They said they would run some tests in the morning to assess his condition and that was all they could do for the moment. The concerned visitors were advised to go home.

On their way they discussed Pa among themselves. Elsie said he was in fine fettle apart from the usual aches and pains. Nate and Sammy commented on how well he had been all evening with nothing to suggest otherwise.

Nate spread the news of Pa's hospitalisation to his customers the next day and all were genuinely sorry to hear it. They had a lot of affection for him. Good wishes were expressed by all and those sentiments were taken to Pa when Nate and Sammy went to visit him in the hospital that evening.

Pa was sitting up in bed with Elsie by his side.

"Well, *'the dead arose and appeared to many'*?" jested Nate who was delighted to see his friend making a visibly good recovery. "You gave us quite a fright last night. Good to see you sitting up. How are you feeling?"

"I'm alright," responded Pa timidly.

"Alright?" questioned Elsie. "He nearly had another heart attack this afternoon and so did I!"

"What do you mean?" asked Sammy.

Elsie continued, sparing Pa the stress of the revelation of the news the doctors had delivered in the morning. "They did tests on Pa, blood tests, and guess what showed up in them?"

Nate and Sammy stood and blinked.

"Drugs. Cocaine. That wretched thing you read about in the newspapers destroying people's lives and their communities."

"OK, calm down, I'm still here," Pa said.

"But where the hell did you come across that, Pa?" asked Nate in disbelief.

"Doctor Kyros Asclepius, that's where!" said Sammy in a slow drawn-out tone with no audible element of surprise. "I knew he was a bloody charlatan. What did he give you?"

"Willow-bark Oil to rub into my joints for the aches and pains."

"And he should not have been given that," butted in Elsie. "The doctor said it is not to be used if you are on blood-thinning medication which Pa is."

"Oh, yes, Asclepius mentioned that to me," said Nate.

"Well, he didn't mention it to Pa," said Babs. "And then, of course, he was drinking last night. No wonder he had a heart attack."

"Calm down, will you?" pleaded Pa again, getting frustrated with her condemnations.

"What else did he give you?" Nate asked.

"Only an energy tonic, that's all."

"I got that tonic from him too," said Sammy. "Do you know, I thought my heart palpitated a bit there during the week now that I think about it. Nate, did you get it?"

"No, Babs and I don't like taking something when we don't know what's in it," he replied innocently without trying to make the others feel foolish. "Do ye know anyone else who took it?"

"Yes, I told you, Cassie Quirke," said Pa.

"No wonder she was up a bloody ladder cleaning windows," said Sammy.

"Is that what they mean by 'getting high'?" said Nate, laughing out loud.

"It's not funny, Nate," said Sammy. "It might have killed Pa."

"Steady on, Sammy – it might only be a bunch of herbs in that tonic," said Nate.

"Well, there was cocaine in something! Let's find out then. Pa, do you still have it?"

"No, I drank it all."

"Drank it all? Already! The whole bottle? No wonder you had a heart attack!" said Nate.

"Come on, Nate," said Sammy. "I still have some at home and Cassie might have some too. Pa, mind yourself and we'll see you again tomorrow."

Nate stopped at Sammy's house first and they collected his tonic before driving to Cassie Quirke's. After telling her what happened to Pa and of their suspicions about the tonic, Cassie handed over her bottle to them immediately. They poured a drop each of hers and Sammy's into two tumblers and placed them on her shop counter.

Stooping to glass level, the three of them stared and surmised about the tonic.

"Same colour and texture to me," remarked Sammy.

"Smells the same to me," said Cassie.

Nate took a sip from each glass. "Tastes the same to me. Well, if it looks like a duck and walks like a duck ..."

"It's definitely goosed," said Sammy, cutting Nate off. "But it smells and tastes like red wine."

"It probably is red wine but it's what has been added to it, that's what we need to find out," said Nate. "Why don't we give one bottle to the gardaí and the other to the doctors in the hospital to test. Cocaine is an illegal drug so this could be very serious."

Sammy agreed and took one bottle to the Garda station immediately while Nate drove back into the hospital with the other. But neither man roused any urgency with their theory. The nurse told Nate she would be of the opinion that the lab technicians would have reported any untoward findings in Pa's blood tests to the gardaí already, while Sammy had an equally futile reaction from the new Garda Seán Tully.

"I'll tell Sergeant Lamb when he's back on duty in the morning. It's a big allegation, Mr. Joyce. It will have to be sent away for analysis."

"But it could have killed Pa, Cassie, or me, or anyone else taking it. You have to get the word out to stop taking it straight away."

"I understand your concern, Mr. Joyce, but like I said I will bring it to the attention of Sergeant Lamb in the morning."

"This phoney doctor only stays in one place for a week before he moves on so you need to get a move on!"

"Yes, Mr. Joyce, we'll look in to it."

"*Fuck sake!*" Sammy said under his breath as he stomped out of the station.

He called into Slattery's for a pint and met Nate there. Both of them decided to spread the word themselves on their own rounds, about Doctor Asclepius and the danger of taking his unauthorised medications.

Dennis told them the doctor had already left Ballantur for his next clinic.

The following day after work Nate and Sammy dutifully visited Pa again in hospital. They told him they had handed over one bottle of the tonic to Sergeant Lamb for drug-testing and other to the doctors. Sammy had dropped into the Garda station that morning. Sergeant Lamb told him that if the contents came back positive for cocaine, Pa and the State might have a case to prosecute Doctor Asclepius for a list of convictions such as possible manslaughter, possession of illegal drugs, fraud, breach of due care and diligence and how inevitably he would be struck off the Medical Register. That's if they could find him.

Dennis Slattery had told them that his next clinic was going to be in Enniscrone, County Sligo, and how he had left a forwarding address so his patients could get in touch to renew their prescriptions. Sergeant Lamb had requested the gardaí in Enniscrone to confirm his arrival there but, suspiciously, he didn't turn up. He'd obviously heard about Pa's sudden illness and had gone to ground.

A silent mood of unfortunate circumstances hung in the air of the ward momentarily until a cheerful Molly and Tadgh came in the door to visit their granddad. Molly had her photos developed for the photography competition and couldn't wait to show them to Pa and the others.

"And these ones are from the sandy lay-by, Grandad. Do you remember? Now you have to see if you can spot the difference between the two photos."

Pa did his best, but other than the sun going down and the sun coming up he didn't notice anything else, but remembered how tired he was getting up that early with Molly.

"No, silly, don't you see?" said Molly. "Grandad, in the dusk one the old boat is gone and in the dawn one it's back."

"We'll have to look somewhere else," said Sammy distantly.

"For the boat?" asked Nate.

"No, stupid, for Doctor Asclepius."

"But where would you even begin, Sam?" said Nate, trying to reason with him. "He's lying low for now and we don't know where the rest of his clinics were planned for. They could be anywhere in the country."

To say Sammy was passionate in general was an understatement. In this case, he was like a dog with a bone – he just wouldn't drop it. He tossed and turned so much that night when he went to bed that the sheets ended up like a rope beneath his back. The lack of sleep really frustrated him because he was due to get up even earlier the next morning as his postmistress was taking the day off.

Over a solitary cup of tea and a Jersey Cream, he sorted out his post for delivery. He thought he was feeling the negative effects of insomnia because he had to look twice when he came across a letter addressed to Doctor Asclepius, C/O Slattery's Guesthouse. He put down the cup of tea and the biscuit and looked at the envelope. If there was no clue going forward maybe there was one going back? Never in his profession had he ever crossed the unethical line of opening someone else's post, but this was about Pa, his good neighbour, his friend and in a lot of ways a father figure. He decided he was going to open it. He didn't care about the envelope. He would address a new one – no one would ever know.

The note was brief. It was from a lady who lived Strokestown, County Roscommon. She had been to his clinic there recently and wanted more of his tonic and asked how she could go about it. No surprise there, Sammy thought to himself. The birth of another addict, thanks to Doctor Evil. But maybe someone in Strokestown might know his itinerary going forward.

The bone was still firmly in Sammy's mouth and he purposely crossed paths with Nate later that day and convinced him to drive them both to Strokestown that evening.

"That's funny, "said Nate with a laugh as he turned his truck into the wide Main Street. "Poor Pa is after having a heart attack and here we are trying to help him by driving to 'Strokes-town'."

"You're hilarious," replied Sammy sarcastically.

"Sammy, would you lighten up? This could be an absolute wild goose chase. I know you are convinced that Doctor Asclepius caused Pa's turn but the gardaí have told us that without him or any hard evidence there is very little that can be done right now. The main thing is that Pa is going to be alright."

Both of them walked into Mahon's Bar on the Main Street, hoping to retrieve some information regarding the elusive doctor. They ordered two pints. It would be rude not to.

A young man was serving behind the bar but he was not very talkative.

"He's not going to make a good barman," whispered Nate to Sammy, stating the obvious.

Nonetheless, he did manage to tell them that "some doctor had a clinic going there alright" in Hegarty's Hotel not too long ago. Realising this was all the gold that they were going to dig out of this juvenile, they swiftly drank their pints and left.

Re-enacting their performance at the next establishment, being Hegarty's, they walked into the bar and ordered two pints. It would be rude not to. If they were perturbed by the minor running the former bar they were even more disappointed by the appearance of the octogenarian running this one. Though very hard of hearing, she did her best to comprehend the plight and enquiry of her two new customers.

"Carrick on Shannon," she announced finally after some silent thought.

"Are you sure? How do you know he'll be there," asked Nate loudly.

"I might be deaf as a dodo but I have the memory of an elephant. Strokestown, Ballantur, Enniscrone, Carrick on Shannon, that's what he told me."

"He didn't go to Enniscrone and that might mean he won't turn up in Carrick on Shannon either," said Sammy doubtfully to Nate.

"Oh, he'll be there alright," said the bar lady. "He goes there a lot, you know. Sure he's mad into the fishing."

And that was one thing that Sammy was certain about.

"One for the road?" he said to Nate.

"Sure it would be rude not to!" Nate winked back.

Despite both men been riled up at the realisation they were in a gasp of catching the fugitive doctor, it was Nate who regained reality first and spent a good ten minutes trying to talk Sammy around. They were sitting in the truck, still parked on the main street of Strokestown with Sammy feeling gung-ho and wanting to go straight to Carrick on Shannon there and then. Nate told him they would do more harm than good.

"There is no point in us confronting him. What would that do? Only scare him away altogether and then we will never see him again. The best thing to do is let Sergeant Lamb know he frequently goes to Carrick on Shannon and they will pick him up there when he returns. Besides, it's practically too late now to be going anywhere other than home."

Sammy bowed to Nate's better sense and agreed to share this new information with the gardaí.

A few days later Sergeant Lamb met Nate on the road. He told him that the doctor had turned up alright in Carrick on Shannon. His colleagues there had arrested him and detained him for questioning.

"The only thing he admitted to was the fact that he did not make up the tonic himself, even though he had been telling everyone that he did," said Sergeant Lamb. "He said it was better known as 'Vino Mariani' from the Continent and he gets it imported over to him from Greece. He said he was sorry to hear that Pa Leonard had taken ill but had no idea his tonic had contributed to it and he was not aware of any drugs used in its production. The gardaí searched where he was staying as indeed we did here in Ballantur. Mind you, Dennis Slattery had the room already cleaned out when we went over but Dennis said the doctor had left it as clean as a whistle anyway and there were no signs of anything to indicate he was mixing the stuff there in the room. The gardaí in Carrick on Shannon checked his car too but there was nothing in it either. Vino Mariani is a fortified red wine and on occasion, more so in the past, it has been mixed with cocaine and marketed as a tonic. Possession is a very serious crime to be convicted of but I'm sorry, Nate, Doctor Asclepius was released and no charges are to be brought against him. There is just no evidence to hold him directly responsible."

Nate thanked the Sergeant for the disappointing update. If Sergeant Lamb is sorry, wait till Sammy hears this, he thought.

And sure enough, Sammy was fit to be tied. He was livid.

"You mean that shyster is going to get away with it after what he did to Pa, never mind the trail of potential drug addicts he has left behind around the country, with them all becoming hooked on cocaine? Is it any wonder they were looking for more? Can the gardaí not see that he was lying through his teeth?"

"I know, Sammy, but what more can we do? Do you expect the gardaí to go from Carrick to Crete to track down the source of this wine?"

"He was from Skepelos," Sammy said.

"OK, Poirot, that's enough. You have let this get way too much under your skin. Pa is fine. Let it go," said Nate, fed up with Sammy's pointless obsession.

Sammy felt betrayed. He admitted to himself that when he met the doctor first he was sceptical but he abandoned his doubt and trusted him. He thought they had got on great on their fishing trip and that now he could consider him to be a friend. But he couldn't understand how the gardaí were accepting his lies. They needed evidence, they said.

Later that evening, he stood in front of the mirror in his bathroom and asked his reflection, "What am I missing? Where is the evidence? What if ... You don't think? I bet you a pound to a penny."

He grabbed his jacket and ran out of the house. He cycled as fast as he could to the sandy lay-by at the river, remembering Molly's "Dusk till Dawn" photographs and the old boat that had gone missing. Like a lot of people and things, you don't notice them until they're gone. The doctor knew no one owned it, so he also knew that no one would be looking for it. Sammy untied Mutey's boat and pushed it out onto the water. Then he looked as hard as he could at the contours of the river like he never had seen them before. A part of its current was known as *Poll na Bia*. The water was deep there and shaded by thick vegetation on the river bank, a noted good spot for fishing. Sammy noticed the bushes and ground looked like they had recently been disturbed. He rowed into the bank and decided to investigate further.

After alighting from the boat and conducting a quick rummage through the bushes, he found, wrapped in an old woollen blanket, two saucepans, a funnel, a sieve, an empty wine bottle and a small box with remnants of white powder. The doctor is in the house, Sammy thought, smiling to himself. He didn't touch a thing and immediately left the scene.

He told Sergeant Lamb straight away where they could find the precious evidence.

The items recovered were tested for fingerprints which were matched with those of Doctor Asclepius taken at Carrick on Shannon Garda Station when he was detained there. The recovery of the cocaine was significant and led to a plethora of charges against him. He was arrested in Carrick on Shannon for a second time and on this occasion he was sent back to Ballantur, the jurisdiction of his original charges.

Nate and Sammy were waiting for him outside the station.

Frieda Huber stepped off a bus coming from Castlebar and joined them to see what was going on. She had been away for a few days so Nate and Sammy filled her in. She started laughing.

"Doctor Asclepius? Seriously? You fell at the first hurdle. Did you not think there was anything suspicious even about his name? It's no wonder he pulled the wool over your eyes. Asclepius is the Greek God of Medicine!"

Sammy didn't laugh. Sometimes he hated that Mrs. Huber was smarter than he was.

When the gardaí marched the doctor into the station, Sammy couldn't help himself. "You've got the catch of the day there, Sergeant. You let the evidence through the net after all, Doc."

"You are to blame for this? I should have known. You had it in for me since the start," the doctor hissed back at him. "You have ruined my career, my livelihood. You will pay for this!"

"That's hilarious, Doctor Destiny," Nate butted in. "Did you not read your own horoscope? Sergeant Lamb, the doctor will see you now!"

And with that he was led away, leaving both Nate and Sammy with the satisfaction that justice had finally been done.

"Pint? Detective Wheatley?"

"Yes, I think so, Inspector Joyce. Wait till we tell the others – they won't believe it!"

CHAPTER 14

Loss

Caitlín arrived for duty. She had brought in her lunch and carefully placed it on the table. She looked at it, knowing it was probably the only bit of organisation she would achieve today, seeing how the last couple of days had gone. She didn't even manage to get her coat off before the phone started ringing. And we're off, she said to herself.

"Good morning, Ballantur Garda Station."

"Good morning, this is Superintendent Ruane from Pearse Street, Dublin. May I speak to Sergeant Lamb, please?"

Caitlín froze. It was the same Superintendent who had witnessed the illegal booze fiasco the day she started.

"Hello? Is there someone there?"

"Yes, yes, hold the line please, sir, I'll get him for you."

Caitlín knocked on Sergeant Lamb's door before entering.

"Good morning, sir. Superintendent Ruane from Pearse Street is on the line for you."

Caitlín could see her own terror reflected in Sergeant Lamb on hearing the name. He said nothing and picked up the line on hold. The quietness of the station meant that Caitlín could hear most of Sergeant Lamb's interrogation.

"Superintendent, how are you? ... Yes, the town folk are shocked, no doubt about it ... He was a lovely fellow, wouldn't hurt a fly, had an eye for the ladies though ... Yeah, we are still questioning the jealous husband ... Oh, I know that ... We'll have to charge him or release him ... His alibi is weak ... No, no other definite leads so far ... Yes, searched the house, nothing ... We have one more lined up for questioning ... The removal is this evening and burial tomorrow so our hands will be tied out of a mark of respect ... Oh, don't worry, we have plenty to be going on with here ... No, that won't be necessary, we have a great team here who are very dedicated and committed ... I know that, sir ... I understand. Give us another few days and if we feel we need more manpower from Dublin I'll let you know ... Thank you, sir. Goodbye."

God give me strength, Sergeant Lamb said to himself as he walked out of his office and collided with Detective Cullen who had just arrived into the station.

"*Whoa!* And good morning to you too," said Detective Cullen.

"I just had that bollox on the blower from Dublin – Ruane – sticking his oar in to see how we were getting on and threatening to send a team from Dublin '*to help*'– more like to take over."

"Don't mind him, Frank, sure they wouldn't know their arse from their elbow down here."

The phone rang again and Caitlín was only too glad to answer it to keep away from the wrath of Sergeant Lamb. It was Nancy Coyle who was ringing to see if she could get a suit for Sammy from his house.

"No problem, Mrs. Coyle. I'll meet you there in an hour."

And so she did, with Ralph and Nancy taking a slow unsteady step into Sammy's unfamiliar home.

"You've never been here before?" asked Caitlín.

"No, never," they replied, standing in the middle of the sitting room, looking around them.

"Oh, do you mind?" asked Nancy as she walked over, drew back the closed curtains and opened the window.

Caitlín started to sniff around her.

"No, it's not because of a smell – it's to let his spirit escape. Ralph, hand me down that clock hanging on the wall. What time did he die, Garda?"

"We're not sure exactly but we think about half seven or eight."

"OK, we'll set it to a quarter to eight," said Nancy, winding the hands around and then stopping at this particular time.

Then she went to the kitchen and came back immediately with towels she had removed from the clothes horse. She hung one over the mirror in the sitting room.

"Are there any more mirrors?" she asked.

"Maybe, I guess so." Caitlín didn't know what to make of this strange ritual.

"Oh, I'm sorry, love," said Nancy sympathetically. "I know this looks odd but just because we're not bringing him home to wake him doesn't mean we shouldn't show him the same level of respect as any other deceased person." She picked up the other towels and left the room.

"She's a traditional woman," said Ralph. "Means no harm – she just wants a proper send-off for him."

"Of course, that's fine, but I can't leave the window of a vacant house open."

"Oh, that's grand. Sure we have to close it again anyway so the spirit doesn't come back in."

"Right." Caitlín nodded slowly, wondering if these people were crazy.

Back at the station, she told Tully about it

"No, *ha*, *ha*, they are not crazy. Jeez, Cat, do you have any traditions at all at home?" scolded Tully. "Loads of people do that stuff when a body is being waked in a house – did you not hear of that before?"

"There must be a full moon or something – everyone is acting so strangely!"

"*What the hell are ye chit-chatting about?*" shouted Sergeant Lamb at them. "*Tully, get back on that phone and call the police in London. Kennedy! Get out there and do not return without Mrs. Huber for questioning.*"

Caitlín jumped in the car and then realised she did not know where Mrs. Huber lived. If anyone would know, it would be Nate but she decided it would not be appropriate to ask him under the circumstances and she daren't go back into the station anyway. So she did the next best thing – she drove to Pa Leonard's house and asked him instead.

Pa told her where but pointed out that he had not seen Mrs. Huber for a few days. Nevertheless, Caitlín drove to her house which was located in a remote place.

The car would only fit so far up the small boreen so she walked the remainder of the way between tall fir trees up to the house. If I wanted to hide and never be seen again this where I would live, she thought to herself. She struggled to shove the wooden gate open and continued up to the house. Her footsteps in the mossy grass sounded loud, such was the stillness around her. It was all beginning to make her feel a bit uneasy. She knocked on the door and waited. No answer. She knocked again, louder. No answer. She waited patiently for a minute before knocking a third time and calling out "*Mrs. Huber!*"

She started to get concerned and wondered if something had happened to the woman. She walked around to the back of house and down towards the sheds. The outbuildings showed no sign of use. She went back and knocked on the back door of the house. No answer. She then started to look in through the windows. The contents of the small rooms were simple and tidy and there was no sign of any current usage.

She tried the front door once more.

She gave up. So what now? Her stomach answered that question, groaning loudly. She decided she would have a think about it over lunch. "Lunch! Damn it!" She'd left it at the station and she could not go back there or Sergeant Lamb would eat her instead. She would have to settle for soup and sandwiches in Slattery's.

While she did not hold much hope for its culinary delights, she found the soup satisfying, but still had room for a cup of tea. While Dennis set about making it, Cassie Quirke came in, ordered the non-option soup and sandwich, and sat down near Caitlín.

Caitlín still hadn't decided if she liked this woman or not.

They exchanged pleasantries, then Cassie became brazen and started asking Caitlín all sorts about the investigation. Caitlin eventually had to close her down. Cassie had some neck to be so impertinent about such a sensitive matter. But then, turning the tables, she decided she should stick her own neck out a bit more and asked Cassie what she knew of Mrs. Huber.

"Frieda, the mysterious German woman?"

"Is she mysterious?" Caitlín asked coyly.

"People are only afraid of what they don't know, but I know Frieda well and I don't think there is anything wrong with her at all. I've known her since she arrived here in 1946, a young married woman with ten children in tow."

"Ten kids? At that age? Now that I don't believe!" Caitlín said, laughing.

"No, you dope, they weren't her own. How could they be? Did you never hear of Save the German Children Society?"

"No," replied Caitlín, not impressed with Cassie's tone. Had she forgotten she was speaking to a garda, she fumed to herself. Now she definitely didn't like her.

"You young people, you have no sense of history at all. The Second World War, did you ever hear of that?"

"*Excuse me?*"

"Germany was bombed by the allies, and Berlin, that's the capital of Germany, and other cities were obliterated – families separated, killed, maimed and missing. There were thousands of orphan children left and some of these unfortunate souls were sent here to Ireland to recover mentally and physically with temporary foster families. Frieda and her brood arrived here in Ballantur. The Church organised a house for them to live in, there at the top of the street. You know it. It's the hairdresser's now, Rapunzel's. Anyway, the woman was a saint. She was a mother, nurse, teacher and guardian to those kids. If you held any grudge against the Germans because of their reign of terror during the war, you should have seen these poor wee things. They would melt your heart. You couldn't but feel sorry for them. They were completely emaciated. Frieda said she couldn't even feed them anything sweet for months because their digestive systems were so weak it would only sicken them. Even the likes of an orange would make them throw up. They all had shaved heads, including the little girls, from lice infestations and the like. But it was the fear and sadness in their eyes that was the most harrowing. You couldn't imagine what they had seen and what they had been through."

"No doubt. So how did they get on?" Caitlín asked with genuine interest.

"Well, honest to God, like ducks to water. In no time at all they blossomed. We were told not to bother with them at the beginning, to go about our daily lives as normal, just so we would not be seen as a threat to them, you know. And it seemed to work. After a while they got more brave and curious. They started coming down to the square to watch our own kids playing football. They were testing the water to feel their freedom again and when the local kids started to pass the ball to them as an invitation to play, well, their joy and laughter was heartlifting. I suppose to live in a town that was not demolished into ruins under their bare feet, or where everything that was familiar was so cruelly taken away, must have restored a great sense of hope in them. Frieda got them settled into the local school here and spoke English and German to them. They really embraced the language and our way of life here, especially the boys who loved the football. If they had stuck around I'm sure some of them would have made the Mayo County Team! But seriously, I really hope they all have lived happily ever after because they deserved it."

"So the kids moved on, but Frieda didn't?"

"Yes, more or less. It took a long time to get suitable foster families for some of them, but she managed it. Some of those children never returned to Germany at all, such was the contentment they found in Ireland. Why would they want to return to family, relatives and a country they did not recognise? Frieda did not return either. Her homeland had too many bad memories to bear."

"Did she lose some of her family?"

"She did and her biggest loss of all was her new husband of six weeks. She said they were childhood sweethearts. Germany was being pulverised so they knew time was of the essence and they got married even though Frieda had already undertaken the resettlement of the children in Ireland.

He was a soldier and was supposed to join her here but – he didn't make it."

"Oh, that's so sad, but what has she been doing since?"

"She is a qualified teacher and does some substitute teaching but because she does not speak Irish she cannot get a full-time job. She also does a lot of translation work for the German Embassy. And she gets her widow's pension from Germany so all in all she's not doing too badly."

"Why did she move up to that old house she lives in now?"

"In many ways the children protected her as much as she guarded them. Once the last one left, that low life, Waxy Carolan, had a right go at her on the street, poor thing. He called her everything under the sun, because of her nationality and the sins of her fathers! I swear to God, if any of the local idiots who think they are 'real hard men' spent one day in the jaws of hell like those poor creatures had, they wouldn't be long clutching their mother's apron strings again. You know the type, rural men with their small rural minds that have been nowhere nor seen anything. If they even go to Dublin for a day they're talking about it for the week. Anyway, she moved into that house shortly after that because she probably felt ashamed following that public humiliation and became a bit of recluse. Apart from coming into my shop, of course. She always spoke to me." Cassie looked smug at that.

"And she was speaking to Sammy Joyce, I believe?"

"Oh, more than speaking. They had been seeing each other since the summer, I think."

"I was up at her house but there was no sign of her. Do you know where I might find her?"

"*Ha!* Good luck with that. Have you a passport? She's gone home to Germany for Christmas. She still has a brother living in Bernau. Or maybe she has fled the country after murdering her lover who was caught having an illicit affair with a married woman?"

"I'll go with the first theory," said Caitlín with a laugh. "Thanks for your help."

Well, at least she didn't have to worry about going back to the station now. There was nothing she could do about it if the woman wasn't even in the country. But a thought niggled at her. Despite dismissing Cassie Quirke's allegation, she couldn't help thinking that Mrs. Huber's sudden departure perhaps made her a stronger suspect than they had originally thought.

When Caitlín returned to the station Sergeant Lamb was coming out of the kitchen.

"Where is Mrs. Huber?"

"She is not here."

"Did I not tell you not to come back unless she was with you?"

"Well, unless I can borrow your lederhosen costume and get a passport to go to Germany it's not going to happen, because she is gone home for Christmas," Cassie said sharply.

Everyone started at Caitlín's ascending indignation. It was by the grace of God that Sergeant Lamb's ignorance of German culture caused her sarcasm to go over his head.

"The pathologist's report is in," Tully interjected.

Sergeant Lamb did not react to that. "When did she leave?"

"I don't know."

"After Sammy was killed, well, how convenient! Sweet Jesus, this is a nightmare. Get on that phone to the German Embassy and see if they can locate her. Do you know where she went over there?"

"Yes, sir, Bernau. I think it's outside Berlin."

"Right, get on it. I want everyone in the incident room in ten minutes and we will go through the pathologist's report."

Tully came over to Caitlín. "Jesus, Caitlín, you are skating on thin ice there with Lamb. What were you thinking? You're not even here a week."

"I'm just sick of him taking out his bad mood on everyone."

"There's no point locking horns with him – it will get you nowhere. Just let it go."

With cups of tea in hand they reconvened in the incident room which incidentally was lacking much incident.

"OK, Tully – London Police, what have you?" said Detective Cullen.

"Nothing yet, I'm afraid. I'm getting the merry-go-round from them. I still have not been able to speak to the leading officer over the case." He deflected his gaze. "But don't worry – I will keep on their backs until I get some answers."

"And you, Kennedy? What did the German Embassy say?"

"Very little for now. They took my details and said they would contact the police in Bernau, but other than confirming she is there I don't think they have the power to do much more for us."

Sergeant Lamb let out a sigh. "OK. Tully, what did the pathologist's report have to say?"

"Traces of alcohol were found in his blood but not a significant amount, so probably a little bit still there from the night before. The vehicle clearly came from behind due to the angle of an injury to the back of the head. Several bones in the back and neck were broken also. He had severe bruising consistent with the motion of the vehicle. There were no defensive wounds on the body, no indications of any struggle with another individual."

"Is that all? Is there anything else that we don't know?" said Sergeant Lamb.

Tully continued. "The contents of the deceased's stomach were liquid cocoa consumed earlier on the morning of his death and lamb chops, onions and potatoes consumed approximately twelve hours pre-mortem."

Caitlín had to bite her lip to stop herself from laughing out loud at the trivia of his consumption.

"So we are ruling out Waxy Carolan and Mrs. Babs Wheatley as suspects, right?" said Detective Cullen, getting to his feet and addressing the team. "Mrs. Wheatley can't even drive and unfortunately Waxy has an alibi, albeit a questionable one, which can be confirmed by his trusty friends. Mrs. Huber has just got through our net – do we know if she can drive, Caitlin?"

"I've been to her house and there is no evidence of any vehicle having been around it. In fact, the boreen is so narrow you can't drive a car up to the house anyway."

"Maybe she learned to drive before she came to Ireland," suggested Tully.

"Yeah, but where did she source a truck and how did she get rid of it so quickly after the murder before she left the country?" said Caitlín. "Though she wouldn't necessarily have to drive it herself – maybe she hired an accomplice to do the hit and run for her. She had a motive – being jealous about her lover's infidelity."

"But not enough time to organise a hit and run between Sammy's indiscretion the night before and half seven the next morning," said Tully. "This was pre-meditated. She probably doesn't even know he has been killed."

"OK, lads, we are only speculating now," said Detective Cullen, trying to stick to the facts. "Nevertheless, we will have to question Mrs. Huber about her relationship with Sammy and what she had come to know of his character, his contacts, his lifestyle and if she was aware of any enemies he might have had or anyone he had crossed. So for now the finger is pointing back at Nate Wheatley. No alibi, a threat made by him on Sammy's life with a motivation of a raging jealously compounded by public humiliation. So, what do you think, Frank?"

"We'll have to charge him."

Caitlín and Tully returned to their desks. They could plainly hear and feel the seriousness of the charge being delivered at the cell by Sergeant Lamb and Detective Cullen.

"Ignatius Wheatley, I am charging you with the murder of Sammy Joyce."

"*No, no – I didn't do it.*"

"You are not obliged to say anything unless you wish to do so –"

"*I didn't kill Sammy.*"

"But anything you say will be taken down in writing and may be given in evidence."

"*I swear, Frank, I didn't do it!*"

"Your arraignment will be scheduled for tomorrow at Castlebar District Court."

All was quiet at the station for a period of time following that development. Where is the job satisfaction now, thought Caitlín to herself. Her stomach felt sick.

Everyone was absorbing this uncomfortable feeling in their own way until a shrill ring of the telephone broke their cowering.

It was Castlebar Garda Station.

"That's grand, John, I'll tell them," said Tully. "While you are on the phone, can we schedule an arraignment for tomorrow?"

When he finished the call he told the others that Sammy's remains were leaving the morgue in the hospital and should be in Ballantur in about ten minutes.

All the staff left the station and headed outside.

The hearse slowed down on its arrival to the outskirts of Ballantur. Some cars had followed it from the morgue and formed an entourage behind it. As they drove up the Main Street towards the chapel, mourners who had gathered outside and lined the street on both sides started walking after the hearse too. The respectful quietness was moving. It was accompanied only by the sound of their footsteps and the ringing of the church bell. These elements were a show of solidarity with Sammy, a reassurance that he was not going alone.

A large crowd of people attended at the church and joined in the prayers to console the reposing soul that lay there overnight until the burial the following morning.

—ℓℓ—

While Sammy rested in plentiful attributes and mindfulness, poor Nate tossed and turned on his bed in his cell, knowing that he was facing a judgment day of his own tomorrow.

"God, that was a big turnout," remarked Caitlín to Seán as they walked back to the station.

"Yeah, not bad. Do you not have big attendances in Ennis?"

"Of course we do. Where are you from anyway, Seán?"

"Ballymoe."

"Never heard of it'"

"Ballymoe in County Roscommon."

"Is it not Ballymore?"

"No, it's Bally*moe*.'

"Why did ye leave out the R?"

"Less is more. Do you have a boyfriend that you pick on for all his shortcomings?"

"No. Do you have a long-suffering girlfriend that has to put with you, full stop?"

"No, I'm married to the job and you'll only be married to it until you get hitched and have kids and then you'll have to give it up."

"Excuse me, I am a modern career-driven woman. Before you know it, you'll be the one fetching the sticky buns and calling me 'sarge'."

"You might want to lay off the sticky buns," Seán teased back.

"Hey, how dare you!"

"I'm only joking – you have a good figure – I mean, you're slim – but not too slim ..." Seán realised he was saying more than he meant to.

"Thanks," said Caitlín, turning her head to look the other way so he wouldn't see her blushing.

She liked Seán. Things were easy with him. You could have random silly chats with him which was much-needed relief at a time like this.

The bells rang out at five minutes to ten the next morning and the locals turned up in their droves to attend the funeral, even though many of them would have been there the evening before too. They walked up to the top of the aisle, genuflected at the altar and paused at Sammy's coffin to say a quiet few prayers. The bonds between the locals and Sammy were strong, familiar and cherished but they still one by one filed by the top bench and sympathised openly and generously with Ralph and Nancy Coyle out of respect. They may have been the only blood relatives Sammy had but

Ralph lacked the memories of the laughs, the chats and the sportsmanship the community had shared with Sammy, whom if they did not know him by blood they definitely knew him by heart.

Father Morrissey in his eulogy recalled the first time he met Sammy many years before.

"I asked him for directions to where the parochial house was. He told me I was within a dog's whistle of it. None the wiser, I asked him to show me so he sat into the car beside me and he directed a left and a left again and we arrived only for me to realise I had now pulled up outside the back door of the house I had pulled into in the first place!"

The congregation laughed, knowing that was Sammy alright.

"Oh, he was a trickster alright," continued Father Morrissey. "I remember I was called out to read the last rites to poor old Skipper Carolan who suffered a severe and fatal fall after coming home from the pub. Sammy raised the alarm and he was waiting for me at Skipper's house when I arrived there. I, for a change, was trying to be the smart alec and I said to Sammy, 'Is he sober?' But Sammy was a smarter alec and replied, '*Only between sips*'."

Again the congregation laughed heartily. Collectively they savoured Sammy's good humour and even more his good intentions in helping people.

The priest spoke about Sammy's hobbies and how fishing was a great love of his. "He and Mutey would regularly go casting their nets together and Sammy used to say Mutey would never frighten the fish because he couldn't talk!" Mutey, who was present, smiled like everyone else at the endearment that it was.

The priest then said that Sammy also sang in the church choir from time to time. Usually at Saturday evening Mass. He said Sammy called it "penance before pints" or "Mass before mayhem".

The priest finished by saying that Sammy was on his final delivery now to heaven and the best thing he was bringing with him was his sweet singing voice and there could be no doubt that his presence there would be as cherished as it was here.

The choir preformed during the funeral Mass but it was strange for them. They normally sang for other people's funerals but now they were singing for one of their own. However, an unfamiliar voice gave a spine-tingling rendition of "Amazing Grace". The attendance strained their necks to see who had this young voice of an angel, and there she was, little eight-year-old Molly Leonard, singing as if her own life depended on it. Her frail mother watched proudly. She thought it was fitting they were able to give something back, seeing all the times Sammy entertained Molly for her when she wasn't able.

Six local pallbearers carried the coffin from the church to the nearby graveyard. Some prayers and a decade of the rosary were recited. The atmosphere was very sombre as the community watched their dearly departed friend leave them in such an incomprehensible way. Leaving the cemetery they knew this sad day would stay in the memory of their town forever.

Later that day, a prison van from Castlebar arrived at Ballantur Garda Station to take Nate to his arraignment.

Detective Cullen and Sergeant Lamb attended the hearing. It was short but not sweet.

The judge informed the defendant of the charge brought against him and the maximum penalties involved in such a crime. He asked Nate how he would like to plea and Nate replied, "Not guilty".

Castlebar was a District Court so, once the charge was handed down, Nate was not offered the opportunity of bail and was further detained in custody. A Book of Evidence would be prepared for Director of Public Prosecutions.

Nate was exhausted and emotionally numbed by the ongoing ordeal that was turning more on him as time went by. Sergeant Lamb allowed a compassionate visit to Nate by his wife, although he was unsure whether Nate wanted to see her or not.

Babs, on the other hand, was grateful and relieved to get this opportunity because they had not spoken since his arrest. But Nate was unresponsive. He didn't have the energy or the will to engage with her when she joined him. Notwithstanding, Babs told him how sorry she was for what she did to him, sorry for what happened to Sammy, sorry for all of it and hoped he would forgive her and how she would do everything she could to help him.

Nate said nothing, He looked like he had accepted a fate of defeat.

After the funeral the locals gathered at Slattery's. The hot soup and sandwiches were scooped up immediately to rekindle the heat in limp fingers and lead toes that had seized up due to the exposure outside in the cold morning. Some of the hard men compensated and went straight for the pints of stout and "a half one", to restart the circulation. A few of the ladies spoiled themselves with a hot toddy but the real indulgence was in the spread laid on by Mrs. Coyle. She had Christmas cakes, queen cakes, mince pies and apple pies. Hardly a crumb for the birds was left over. They complimented her for all the trouble she had gone to and expressed their gratitude to herself and Ralph for all their efforts in this very difficult situation, especially when they did not even know Sammy very well. They assured them their endeavours would be blessed and that Sammy himself would have been delighted with the ceremony and the afters. They told them that if this was someone else's funeral he would be talking highly of it on his rounds.

The locals spent the rest of the afternoon relating their own stories about Sammy and the mark he had left on them, not to mention the loss and the sorrow. Finally, they all agreed that the two most responsive people to an occasion such as this were not there: Sammy and Nate.

Despite all efforts to keep the situation neutral and unbiased, being the day that was in it, their loosening tongues could not help themselves and when they heard the news about Nate's arraignment it wasn't long before the conspiracies started to crank up again.

CHAPTER 15

Chinese Whispers

The following night was Bridge night and the local committed card players attended the Community Hall for their weekly dealing.

One of the tables seated Cassie Quirke, Father Morrissery, Dennis Slattery and Pa Leonard. They all agreed that Sammy had a lovely funeral but they were bemused by all the exasperating stories that had been circulating about his death, which seemed to tarnish his send-off.

"That's Chinese Whispers for you," said Father Morrissey. "You know, when something is whispered around between a circle of people to see if it ends up the same way as it started. It's nothing more than gossip, which is open season on the assassination of character without ownership of the trigger, if you ask me."

"Absolutely," agreed Cassie, who loved to gossip more than anyone. "It's like a boomerang – sure, it will hit the target but eventually it will come back to you."

"It's similar to a wildfire that can spread far and wide," Father Morrissey continued to preach. "Of course the worst thing about a wildfire is how hard it is to put out and it's impossible to know how it started in the first place. Look, we all like to partake in a bit of gossip, that's normal and healthy. Having a rant about someone else makes us feel better about ourselves. Hearing someone else's miseries can make our own problems seem not so bad after all. There is a satisfaction there that creates a level playing field, especially when the begrudgers believe the bereft have 'notions' about themselves. It affirms that no one is untouchable to bad circumstances."

"Yeah, but then there are those that take gossip to another level," interjected Dennis Slattery. "It can be allergic to control, a force hard to master."

"You're so right, Dennis," agreed Cassie, speaking from experience. "A successful gossiper can promote their status in a social circle. Everyone wants to know what they know. It's a strong person who can forego gossip and say to someone's face what everyone is saying behind their back."

"You know that kind of judgement is cowardly because it always passes in the person's absence when they are not there to defend themselves," said Pa empathically. "Frequently, something simple like being hard of hearing or just a simple misunderstanding can distort the truth and the most peculiar thing about it is that sometimes it's what is not said, or who is not mentioned, that results in the greatest noise of all."

The "practice what you preach" sermon on gossip and its consequences shared by the card players soon evaporated into thin air, with Dennis the first of them to fold to its addiction.

"And a prime example of tattle-tale was well exercised during the summer. Did ye hear all the shenanigans that were meant to have happened between Babs Wheatley and Frieda?"

"No," replied Father Morrissey, sticking his neck out.

"Ah here, wait till you hear this, it was knives out," said Dennis, rubbing his hands in glee. "A few women in the town gathered together at the school gate and started talking about the weather as a rite of passage before getting on to the more serious stuff – the goss. Some of them believed that

Sammy's affair with Babs started last April at the annual spring fair after one heard Cassie say she saw them *'holding hands'*."

Cassie threw her eyes to heaven.

"Several other sightings were also reported. One woman said she saw them sitting on the wall outside the church chatting for ages. Another said they saw them in a coffee shop in Castlebar having tea together. They were also seen going for walks along the river and spotted driving around Westport. While all of these chance meetings looked innocent at the time, now they were incriminating both of them as adulterers. The gossip got juicier after an alleged bitchy confrontation at the market one Saturday afternoon between Frieda and Babs. Frieda must have been suspicious of Babs having an alleged affair with Sammy and could not resist a public humiliation at Babs' expense – according to the tale ...""

Babs was looking through the men's clothes at one of the stalls, oblivious to Frieda standing behind her as she engaged with the stall owner.

"Anything I can help you with, ma'am?"

"Yes, I need a birthday gift for the man in my life."

"Which one?" asked Frieda coldly but not quietly.

The other shoppers paused their purchases to listen to this in surprise.

"*Excuse me?*" said Babs.

"Is it your husband's birthday or your bit on the side?"

"I don't know what you are going on about," tutted Babs, turning back to the rack of ties in front of her.

"How about the blue tie there for Sammy, to match his blue eyes? I hear you have been gazing into them a lot these days."

"Frieda, I don't like what you are implying here. I thought you and he were an item? If he is getting tired of you, don't presume he is looking at me instead."

"Ha! You are no Elizabeth Taylor and as for Maureen O'Hara, well, she's getting a bit more like me every day, so it might be more in your interest to reconsider who you think is looking lethargic."

The people around them sniggered at the dig.

"Look, Frieda," said Babs crossly. "I don't know what rumours you are basing this on but you are way out of line. I'm a married woman."

"Well, why don't go back to the husband who doesn't want you and stay away from Sammy Joyce?" ended Frieda, quickly walking off.

"But Babs wasn't long getting back at Frieda," said Pa. "I heard of another squabble between the two women that was meant to have happened the time they went to County Clare. Both ladies were members of the Country Women's Association (CWA). This autumn the annual trip was organised by their local branch which included an overnight stay at the Summer Hill Hotel in Ennis."

This excursion was centred around a team-building module of self-esteem and confidence. After their arrival to the hotel that afternoon, a sequence of speakers encouraged self-belief and self-worth. All the ladies were asked to write a rhyme about the lady sitting opposite them to represent the virtues that other people see in them but not necessarily what they see in themselves. Thankfully Babs and Frieda were sitting at polar ends of the table. Once the ditty had been penned, they were told to roll them up and place them in front of their intended recipients. However, before they were read out it was time for another tea break which was served in the hotel lobby.

After their unsatisfactory "teabag" tea and much-applauded but controversial "carrot" cake, they returned to their seats. Their instructor then asked each to them to read out what the other person had written about them.

Sentiments ensued such as:

"When we need someone to lean on,

Your strength is always there,

Despite your own troubles,

You always show you care."

These sickly proclamations continued until it came to Babs who unfolded her piece of paper and read aloud her appraisal, which came from her friend, Helen.

"Even though I am married,

My loyalty doesn't carry,

If your handsome fella's single,

Then I am ready to mingle."

Babs had read it out before she realised what she had just said.

A howl of laugher rang out from the other women.

"What?" That's not what I wrote, I swear," squirmed Helen, who was sitting opposite Babs.

One glance at Frieda and Babs knew exactly who was responsible.

Over a few vodkas and Cokes and three bags of Tayto at the hotel bar later that evening, Babs discussed her disgrace with her two friends and what she was going to do about it. She felt this defamation was getting out of hand and her reputation was being ruined publically. The more she thought about it, the angrier she got. "Fight fire with fire" was the general consensus of the Vodka & Coke Company.

The following morning at breakfast the cackling voices of the ladies reverberated loudly under the high ceiling of the dining room. Babs made sure she and her two friends were sitting at a table close to where Frieda had already sat down. Suddenly, as if on cue the entrance door was opened roughly by a man struggling to carry a huge bouquet of fresh flowers. All eyes in the room followed the red roses, white gypsophila and green fern which were presented to Babs. Bashfully she accepted and, egged on by the excited ladies beside her, she opened the attached card and read it out loud.

"*Roses are red,*

Your corset is blue,

I don't want another,

If I can't have you."

"*Whoooo!*" said the others. "Who knew Nate was such a romantic?"

"They're not from Nate," said Babs, trying to sound surprised, and in an added staggered tone she read loudly: "*From your secret admirer.*" Then, looking directly at Frieda she declared: "Looks like I can turn a few heads after all."

She could tell Frieda was jealous, it was written all over her face. Babs then winked at her two friends with satisfaction. Mission accomplished.

These audacious acts were the talk of the weekend. Nothing this salacious had happened on a CWA trip before. The branch leader was so distraught she considered resigning from her position.

The flowers proved to be inspiring and were used again as a weapon of choice shortly after that. A popular initiative to make the branch town look more appealing was driven by the CWA. An area at the crossroads at the top of the street in Ballantur was landscaped so the group could plant it with flowers.

Babs was very happy with her contribution, sowing white alyssum and blue lobelia accordingly around the edge. But, to her horror, she was told the next day that her arrangement had been destroyed overnight and her plants had been replaced with nettles. Inspecting this interference, Babs found a small white note weighted down by a stone which read: "*If you don't want to get stung, don't play with a scorpion.*"

The Bridge game was halted entirely at this stage because the scandal had wielded a stronger hand.

"And it was myself who avoided their handbags colliding at dawn and instead banged their heads together when the two enemies arrived into my shop coincidentally," said Cassie." Babs confronted Frieda first. And it went like this ..."

"Is there someone or something in here you want to interfere with too?" Babs said. "I know it was you who dug up my flowers."

"I don't know what you're going on about!" Frieda replied indignantly.

"Well, let me simplify it for you. You have some nerve to be going on about the righteousness of others. I heard it was you who invited that plank, Doctor Celsius, to do a clinic in this town in the first place because you believe in all that mumbo-jumbo. Well, poor Pa Leonard nearly died and yet you continue to try and hurt someone else now – me!"

"Oh, take your two-trick pony of pettiness and hoof it out of here, will you?" replied Frieda.

"I'd had enough," said Cassie, "so I rang the shop bell on the counter. *Ding, ding, ding!* 'Time out, ladies,' I told them. 'I don't know what is going on between you two,' a blatant lie, 'and I don't care what is going on,' another blatant lie, 'but ye're fighting each other and letting the real enemy get away. What about lover-boy, eh? I think he is accountable for his actions too, don't ye? He's the one ye need to straighten out, not each other.' The two women looked at one another, knowing that I was right. Then I ushered the two of them into my back kitchen and made a pot of tea for them. 'Now don't come out again until you have resolved the matter and made peace,' I said, leaving them at it. And they did. They agreed that he was making a fool out of them both so together they decided they would form an alliance and deal with him!"

"That's a load of rubbish!" said a woman at the local knitting group after the theory that Babs and Frieda together killed Sammy Joyce was presented. "Babs can't even drive and Frieda wasn't even in the country."

"That's why it was genius," said the relay storyteller who had heard at Bridge the night before how Babs and Frieda had put their heads together and planned the murder of Sammy. "They got someone else to drive the truck."

"Who?"

"Dr. Kyros Asclepius, of course."

This speculation was carried to another part of town and debated at the petrol pumps where someone confirmed Dr. Asclepius threatened Sammy outside the Garda Station for destroying his life following his arrest on suspicion of poisoning Pa Leonard.

"But he went back to Detroit. It was in the paper. There was an article all about his arrest. No, no, that fellow didn't do it, he was far too refined for something like that."

"Yeah, but he lost everything because of someone else. That can change a man's priorities. Something like that can draw out a darkness in a person."

"He's right. I heard he was seen around the area here again the time Sammy died. He was scheming with Babs and Frieda. The women of course had perfect alibis. Babs can't drive and Frieda had gone back to Germany. No one would have expected the doctor to be that brazen and come back. It would be far too risky and that is why he hid, only coming out that morning to run down Sammy."

"Hid? Hid where? Sure he must have got some help from someone else?"

"He did, think about it. Who else had it in for Sammy?"

"Nate."

"No, Waxy Carolan."

"I'm lost. Why did Babs kiss Sammy in the hot-press if she hated him so much?"

"To frame someone else."

"Her own husband?"

"Well, I don't think there was any love lost there. Listen to this. One evening Waxy arrived up to Nate's truck to buy stuff. Nate was parked at the crossroads between Tullybeg and Tullymor. Nate was having the craic with Pa Leonard and a few neighbours. And it went like this . . ."

～ell～

"Hello, Mr. Carolan, I'm honoured for your rare custom. Are you not going to your fancy supermarket in Castlebar?"

"It's too late to drive there so you will have to do."

"Charming," responded a slighted Nate.

"Give me a Swissroll, a packet of Goldgrain biscuits, a bag of Barley Sugars and a bar of Fruit and Nut – oh, and a bottle of red lemonade."

"Jeez, are you having a children's party?" Nate asked, laughing.

"A party for one, I'm afraid. I'll have to find a woman to do a bit of cooking for me."

"Luckily the rest of them have escaped so far," said Nate.

"Charming!" returned Waxy who grabbed his box of treats and headed off.

After the rest of the chin-wagging and shopping was finished, Pa on his way home noticed Waxy had left his box on the wall outside the old forge. He looked inside and it was empty.

"Better again," he said, put the box under his arm and continued on.

"So why did Waxy leave the box there?" asked one of the listeners at the petrol pump.

"Because he wasn't bringing that stuff home at all, Numpty. And it gets better. A few days later I heard that Waxy came into Gillespie's butcher's and took a bit of a wobble. Initially those in the shop thought he was drunk but there again it was only midday so they gave him the benefit of the doubt. They sat him down on a chair and the staff got him a glass of water. They asked him if he was alright. Waxy told them he was feeling lightheaded because he had not taken his medication for his diabetes."

"He's a diabetic? God, I never knew that."

"Neither did I but that explains everything. There is no way Waxy would have eaten all that sugary stuff he bought from Nate. He was buying it for you know who, because it was cheap and handy."

"And he was hiding in the old forge?"

"Well, it is derelict. I don't think anyone uses it. Maybe we should go there and see if he left any wrappers behind."

"No, you need to tell the gardaí. They could test those wrappers for fingerprints and look for footprints too. So don't go near the place."

"Did anyone see him?"

"Cassie Quirke said someone stole her milk. She gets a daily delivery for the shop at first light. When she went outside the front door one morning two bottles were missing from her order in the crate. She didn't think it was kids, it never happened before. Besides, she said someone must be really hard up if they have to lie in wait for a bottle of milk that early in the morning. And Mrs. Leonard said she thought someone was knocking around their house at night."

"Oh, now I'm getting the chills. Why, what happened?"

"She said she went outside the house the next morning and the tap in the yard was dripping."

"Dripping?" replied the unenthused individual.

"Yes, you know, every house has their nuisances. Like our front door that shudders every time it's opened because it is warped, or a drawer that you have to push in before you can pull it out. Anyway, only she and Pa knows that the washer in the tap is well worn and you have to squeeze it really tight to turn it off properly. Kyros is a doctor and he would know better than to drink that dirty water from the river so he must have been taking water from the tap."

"He could have used Cassie's empty milk bottles."

Another punter butted in, "That's neither here nor there – what about the little matter of the truck? Where did he get that? Eh?"

"If the price was right, Waxy would have sorted that out for him too. He has a way and means of getting anything. We all know that."

—ℓℓℓ—

This tale was regaled again in Cassie Quirke's shop later that day but some of the customers just didn't buy it.

"I don't believe any of that. The doctor didn't do it. The only one with a vendetta against Sammy with more ability and a bad nature to do it is Waxy himself. There was plenty of bad blood between them. Sammy was becoming a real thorn in Waxy's side. He was his moral compass in a way. Waxy couldn't handle it anymore. I mean only a day before Sammy died they got into a fight over Waxy being abusive to Mutey. Then, remember the time of the hurricane? Sammy roughed him up below in the square because he didn't cover the well after him and little Molly Leonard fell into it. He humiliated him in front of everyone. Sammy had some temper on him."

"No, he hadn't. He was conscientious and just wanted to stand up for people who could not stand up for themselves, especially from a bully like Waxy."

"And the big red flag of course was the art theft up at the Big House. Nate Wheatley said it was Sammy who tipped the gardaí off that time, you know. Waxy served three years in prison for that."

"But Waxy wouldn't have known that it was Sammy who told them."

"Nate said it was in the paper. How the tip-off was believed to have come from disclosed postal correspondence between the convict and a prominent art dealer in Dublin. Three years of his life that he won't get back. That would leave a sour taste in anyone's mouth. And still Sammy continued to turn the screw on him."

"I suppose it was a ripe occasion to kill him alright. The consequences of Sammy's actions from the night before led to the finger being pointed at a lot of suspects that took the heat off Waxy."

"No. That was not an opportunistic murder. It was premeditated. Waxy is a good driver and I heard he had got the lend of the truck from a fellow in Claremorris. This guy works in Conneely's bar there. The pair of them did their best to cover their tracks and would have done if it wasn't for one shrewd customer drinking there at the time. This regular noticed straight away that Waxy was a stranger when he walked into the pub and started talking to the barman. By all accounts the barman was cut from the same cloth as Waxy, in that he was perceived as being dodgy, shady and sneaky. They were a pair of smooth operators who brazenly went about their business in front of everyone else, but in a code. Firstly, they pretended they did not even know one another and no one was taking much notice anyway apart from the independent observer. Waxy asked for a bit of change for the phone box and slid a pound note across the counter. 'No problem at all,' said the barman, rattling through his cash box, picking out coins. 'Did you come up through the town? We have a car boot sale taking place on the green.' Waxy said. 'Oh, have you? Sounds good, I'll have a look there now. God knows what you would pick up.' This casual conversation went unnoticed to everyone else but not to our spectator. His suspicion was aroused by the fact that not only did the barman give Waxy his coins but he also slid his pound note back to him. He continued to watch Waxy through the window when he left. Standing in the street, Waxy pulled the money out of his pocket and looked at the pound note in particular before walking away. He didn't use the phone box."

This perplexed the listeners in Quirke's.

"What was that all about?" asked one of them.

"My informer believes that the barman left the truck for Waxy parked at the car boot sale."

"But the car boot sale would have been full of vans and lorries. How would Waxy know which one was for him? Why didn't the barman just tell him?"

"He did tell him. I bet he wrote the registration of it on the back of pound note before giving it back to Waxy."

"But what about a key?"

"Probably left it in the ignition. It was hardly going to be the truck of the year, more like the banger of the month so I don't think anyone would steal it. The less remarkable the better. With so many lorries and vans pulling in and out no one would have noticed Waxy driving away with it."

Another listener thought this was plausible and they continued on with the speculation.

"And you know he probably slept in it for the night, lying in wait. He was a neighbour of Sammy so of course he knew around what time Sammy used to set off on his route in the mornings and which way he would go. He also knew with it being that early in the morning and very frosty, hardly anyone else would have been on the roads. It provided a quick and easy way for him to carry out his terrible deed before dropping the truck off somewhere again."

"You know Sammy's postbag went missing too?"

"Yes. No doubt Waxy had a good rifle through the post. He wasn't reading the letters looking for news, he was looking for money. Loads of people send cash home to their families this time of the year. Not only did he take Sammy's life but he got a nice Christmas bonus for it too."

"*Shhhh ...*"

The customers suddenly stopped talking when Garda Kennedy came into the shop to get some provisions for the station.

"Garda Kennedy, just the woman I wanted to see," said Cassie.

Caitlín replied sharply. "Look, if this is more conjectures about who killed Sammy Joyce, I would beg you to make a formal statement in the station on the condition that you have evidence to back it up. Our resources are stretched enough without responding to wild goose chases."

"No, not at all. We were just going to tell you about the fantastic Christmas Concert we are holding in the town hall and, with you being new here, it would be a nice way for you to meet members of the community. The school gets involved, we have local music and dance groups, drama groups. The local GAA club usually pull something out of the bag too. There will be a big turnout, it's very popular and has gone from strength to strength every year."

She shoved a flyer into Caitlín's hand with all the performance details on it.

Caitlín felt embarrassed for giving out to them and was glad they were talking to her about something different for a change.

"Thanks for invite. It sounds like a great night but I think I'm working. Don't worry. I'll tell the others. Now I'd better get the Sergeant his order or I'll get a performance from him."

The story of Waxy and his procurement of the truck travelled all the way to the sidelines of the football pitch while a match was in play.

"That's a load of bollix. I know Waxy is as crooked as a ram's horn but he is not a killer. They charged the right man if you ask me."

"Poor old Nate?"

"Yes, I heard when he went to England he was 'let go' from his first job – driving a truck. Then he got a new job driving a boat, strange for someone who never grew up near water. Anyway, there is a rumour of some sort of accident. The boat he was driving hit a boy. That's why he had to hightail it to America. He's no angel."

By this stage the locals were of the opinion that Nate, Waxy, Babs, Frieda and Dr. Asclepius were all worthy suspects. The suspicions and speculation went into overdrive. Rumours were growing legs and tales were gaining more meat on the bone when really they were nothing more than a carcass of lies. Sammy's death was one of biggest and shocking tragedies ever to harm the area and everyone had a theory on it. The national pastime of gossiping had never been so indulged. Even the most loyal and moral found it difficult not to partake in the exaggerations.

Unfortunately, one group who were not getting any reprieve from the incessant talk of the town were the local gardaí. Each member was approached by the locals who were eager to tell them who and why they should be looking for even when they were not on duty.

It all came to a head one night when a brick was thrown through Cassie Quirke's shop window in retaliation for allegedly tipping off Dr. Asclepius about Pa Leonard's collapse which gave the doctor a chance to leave town immediately and not answer for the consequences of his actions.

Cassie was livid and chewed the ear off Sergeant Lamb about it the next morning.

When she left the station he called all the staff together and declared, "Enough is enough. I'm sick and tired of everyone, short of the dogs in the street, telling us how to do our jobs with this obsessive drivel spewing out of them. We have charged someone for God's sake! What's the matter with them? Now they are resorting to vandalism by throwing rocks through windows over these daft stories. I wish I could tell the whole lot of them to cop themselves on!"

"Maybe you can," said Caitlín.

"What do you mean, Kennedy? Spit it out."

"How about you make a public announcement at the Christmas concert in the town hall? I hear there's going to be a big local crowd and anyone who is not there won't be long hearing about it, judging by how fast news travels around here, quick as a hiccup. Look, the community is still reeling from the shock of the murder. Maybe if everyone was brought up to date on how the investigation is going, they might feel more reassured. A lot of them believe the killer is still out there. I think there is a nervousness that is causing all of these irrational theories. Perhaps a gentle reminder to convince them that using all of our resources chasing up tittle-tattle is wasting our time and unless someone has substantial evidence to prove their hunches about who they think killed Sammy then they should all calm down and stop this propaganda about each other."

"Great idea, Kennedy. Set it up. Type it up. Then I'll have a look at it before you tell them."

"*Me?*"

Sergeant Lamb didn't answer her. He walked back into his office and closed the door.

"See what happens when you pitch an idea in this office, Caitlín?" said Tully. "You get hung with it. So the next time you have a brainwave keep your mouth shut and you'll get the same thanks as everyone else."

Caitlín could see his point but on this occasion the problem was bigger than the pettiness of office politics. She knew it was a good idea and, if she could pull this off, it could soothe the rash of gossip that was spreading in the district.

Later that evening at least one piece of affirmation came through. Finally an officer from the London Metropolitan Police returned Garda Tully's phone calls and he was briefed on Nate's involvement in the drowning of Hilary Rogers. A witness by the name of Akoni Dacosta (otherwise Eddie) had eventually come forward and gave a statement to say that he saw Simon Thomas driving the boat when the collision occurred and not Ignatius Wheatley. He said he saw Ignatius going to the toilet at the time of the accident. Simon Thomas went on the run during the investigation and it is only recently that he had been tracked down and arrested. He had the misfortune of becoming an alcoholic leading to a life of destitute homelessness. He has confessed to the charges of careless driving and manslaughter. After the charge sheet had been read out to him he said that at least in jail he would have a roof over his head and three meals a day.

So a silver lining had brought a divisive sense of comfort to Simon Thomas but could the same be said for Nate? Is there much relief in knowing you are not been charged with one murder but are helplessly being charged with another? What is the point of coming up for air when you are being circled by a shark?

CHAPTER 16

The Final Curtain

Elise Leonard got the bucket and mop to wash the vinyl-covered kitchen floor as she often did when she got the house to herself. The grandchildren were not due again until tomorrow and Pa was gone to the pub, so the less footfall around the better, she thought. As usual, with a tight squeeze she shoved the plastic bucket into the kitchen sink and ran the mixer tap into it. She gave the floor a quick sweep of the brush while it was filling. The bucket was nearly full when she returned to turn off the tap but it would not turn. She squeezed it as hard as she could but it would not budge. Now the bucket was overflowing and filling up the sink. Its tight fit blocked the overfill grill so there was no escape for the water other than over the kitchen counter and down onto the floor. Elise was working herself into a helpless state and didn't know what to do. She paced over and back then grabbed a towel that was drying by the range to give her more of a grip on the tap. But she didn't make it back to the sink. Instead she skidded on the wet floor and fell down. She cried out in pain and wished that someone was in the house with her now. She tried to get up but her ankle was too sore when she manoeuvred to put any weight on it. She would have to lie there with the cold swirling water circulating around her until Pa came home.

Meanwhile her bonny spouse was enjoying his ritual of three pints of beer and a half one in the pub.

"That's a hard night's frost outside. Don't you be walking home tonight, Pa. I'll run you up in the car," offered Dennis as he collected empty glasses off the vacated tables in his bar.

When Dennis pulled up outside the Leonards' house he got out of the car and guided Pa around to the back of the cottage with the aid of his flash lamp. Their chit-chat suddenly stopped when they saw a flood of water seeping from the back door.

Dennis opened the door and rushed inside. Elise was lying on the floor.

Pa read the situation with the tap and walked straight over and turned it off.

"Pa, how did you do that? I couldn't turn it off at all," said Elise after Dennis had managed to pull her up and put her sitting on a chair.

"You were trying to turn off the wrong tap. It was the other one you had left running," said Pa, who appeared be detached. "I'll get a yard brush in the shed."

Dennis could tell something was wrong other than the obvious so he followed Pa outside.

"Is everything alright? What happened?"

Pa signed heavily. "Ah, she's done it before – tried to turn off the wrong tap. She's getting more forgetful every day. I don't know what to do. It's hard enough looking after the grandkids when we have them, but now I feel I am watching her too."

"I'm sorry to hear that, Pa. You have a lot on your plate. Pass me out that brush and I'll sweep out the water for you. She can swivel her ankle, so I don't think she has broken anything – maybe give her a painkiller if you have one. I'll go up to the surgery first thing in the morning and tell the doctor to come and see her as soon as possible. Make sure you tell the Doc the whole story though. You can't look after everyone."

Babs organised a visit to see Nate in prison while he was remanded in custody. She was relieved when he accepted her request because she didn't know if he would ever want to see her again. She still felt like this was all her fault and was so ashamed of her actions. She had barely left the house since it happened. She took a pound of grapes and biscuits with her, like you would when going to a hospital. She didn't know what to take to a prison or if she would be allowed to take anything in at all. The looming prison building had an air of despair about it which made her more nervous than she was in the first place. She was shown into the visiting room with all the other women.

Once Nate, who was already seated behind a table, smiled at her she felt a lot better.

After a weak hello to one another and then an awkward silence, Babs spoke.

"Nate, I don't know where to begin."

"I do. What the hell got into you, Babs? Look at the trouble all that playacting with Sammy caused."

"I know. I'm sorry, Nate. I suppose I was looking for a bit of attention that you weren't giving me anymore."

"I don't know what you mean by that."

"That's the thing, Nate. You don't know, like you don't know I'm not there until your dinner is not on the table or a clean shirt is not left out for you on the bed. You have the life of Reilly, Nate. You head off on your rounds everyday chatting and having the craic and then go to the pub at the weekend and do it all over again while I'm left at home just ... existing. It's like you don't care."

"Don't care? I'm locked up in jail for an act of passion. I'm accused of murder over you!" Nate was getting angry. He brought his voice down to a whisper when he realised all the other people were in room could hear him and were staring at them. "I'm accused of murder over you – what more proof of me caring for you do you want?"

Babs sighed and put her head in her hands, disheartened that Nate still wasn't getting her point of view.

"I'll pack my stuff when I get home," she said, "I'll be gone when you come back."

"I might never be back if I am found guilty and given a life sentence."

"It won't come to that. They won't have enough evidence at your trial, you'll see. Besides, with all the stories that are going around everyone is a suspect. I've been accused along with Frieda, Waxy and Dr. Asclepius. The gardaí are getting fed up with all the people going to them with their mad stories about who did it. There is a lot of support for you, Nate. They know you are a good man and didn't harm Sammy."

Babs started to adjust her headscarf and got ready to leave.

The words of encouragement and faith in him meant the world to Nate. Suddenly he could not imagine her not being there for him.

"No, Babs, don't go anywhere. I can't see my life without you in it."

"Then make mine matter."

"How? What do you want me to do?"

"I want to get a job. You are gone all day long and I have nothing to do."

"There is no need, Babs. I make enough money for the two of us."

"God, there you go again! You're not listening!" She picked up her bag.

"OK, OK, it's not for the money. It is for you. What kind of job were you thinking of?"

"I could go back to waitressing, preferably part-time, plenty of places in Castlebar are hiring."

"With respect," said Nate, treading carefully, "how will you go in and out to work if I have already left in the mornings?"

"I want to get a car and learn how to drive. Then I could spend my spare time doing what and going where I like."

"Well, you did what you liked before and look where that got us," sniped Nate, unable to help himself.

"Forget it. I knew it was a mistake coming here maybe I am better off without you." She got up to leave.

Nate caught her arm. "I'm sorry. I certainly wouldn't be better off without you. I'm still angry, Babs. You both betrayed me and publically humiliated me. Sammy was meant to be my friend. We knew each other since childhood."

Babs sat down again. She couldn't argue with that.

Nate continued. "But look, I am responsible for my own actions too and lashing out at Sammy that night is a consequence that I have to pay for, not you. Can we call a truce and start again?"

Babs was so relieved. She loved Nate. She loved the house they lived in, the town and its people. Where would she go anyway? She knew she was not old but her nerve to start afresh had diminished. She didn't want pastures new, she just needed a bit of support to make small changes for a big improvement. She had read that in a women's magazine.

"OK, as long as you show me a bit more consideration and give me the chance to pursue a few goals of my own."

"Sure," replied Nate eagerly, still not sure what she was going on about but he felt now was the time to smooth out the tension. "Get yourself some driving lessons and then you can come and pick me up from here, *eh*?"

"Are you mad? Sure by the time you get out of here I'll be too old to drive," teased Babs.

They both laughed and it felt good. They purposely did not discuss the inevitability of things not going Nate's way at the trial. Instead Babs told him all the wild stories that were circulating at home and before they knew it the bell had rung and visiting time was over.

It was freezing outside the prison while Babs waited for her bus home. She could not wait to start driving and imagined all the advantages such liberty would bring her. She knew she could not blame Nate for all her own shortcomings and despite what was coming down the line she saw this as an opportunity to start over on so many levels and how invaluable they might come to be.

Caitlín could see her breath as she exhaled when she ran into the cold town hall on the morning of the day the Christmas concert was going to be held. She pulled two tables and a few chairs to the centre of the stage for the delivery of her announcement to the audience. Sergeant Lamb had looked over her notes but he didn't change anything because he knew he wouldn't be able to do a better job than Caitlín had done anyway. She didn't feel nervous about doing it, she just felt bad doing it on an occasion that was meant to be festive and cheery. But this was the only way to get word out to everyone at the same time and, at least, doing it before the concert commenced would ensure that this "order of business" would not leave an air of negativity at the end of the night instead.

Around her, she could see people setting up for the night. Fresh evergreens with red bows made a worthy garland that was strung across the front edge of the stage. A large Christmas tree decorated in handcrafted baubles made by the schoolchildren stood at the edge of the stage. They had also made a massive banner in silver tinfoil which hung high up at the back to say "Merry Christmas". Santa's Grotto was erected down the back so the children could visit the great man himself. This was a bit worrying for the parents because they really hoped the children would not change their minds now or poor Santa might not have the resources to get different toys at this stage, as was strongly pointed out at the Christmas Concert Committee meeting some weeks ago.

The concert itself was hosting a series of comedy sketches influenced by events such as the inauguration of John F. Kennedy and his Irish ancestors. The global space race was also getting a spot and the costume department impressively produced a large cardboard space rocket and several astronaut suits. Local céilí bands and singers were going to do a few sets for the music slot. And of course Christmas is never without a bit of magic, so a magician would be depending on a volunteer from the audience to help them wave their magic wand and make something disappear. A raffle would predictably be held at the interval. Prizes included a turkey, a ham, a box of oranges, a bottle of whiskey, a teddy bear and a curling tongs which the ladies already had their eye on. Finally, the show was going to close with a beautiful recital from the Castlebar Choral Society performing a selection of Christmas carols, when everyone would be asked to join in to end the show on a peaceful and heart-warming note.

At this point the noisy stagehands were not the only ones who were flat out busy. Cassie Quirke was setting up a stall selling Christmas cards, candles and cakes, as well as tins of biscuits, sweets and minerals. She was in direct competition with Dennis Slattery who was also setting up a stall of refreshments to sell to the audience.

"*Whooo,* it's cold!" said Cassie, rubbing her two cold hands together. "It's forecast to snow tonight, Garda Kennedy, did you hear that?" Cassie didn't care much about her weather report. It was just her way to break the ice so she could ask Caitlín what she was doing here.

Caitlín still didn't care much for Cassie, but she knew there was no harm telling her that An Garda Síochána were giving an update tonight in relation to the investigation of Sammy Joyce's murder. She knew Cassie would spread the word and the more people that came to hear it, the better.

"Right," said Cassie slowly, taking in that surprising and unusual development. "Good timing, because Sammy's cousin and his wife from Claremorris are coming tonight too. What's his name again? Ralph?"

"Ralph Coyle."

"Yes, there will be a minute's silence for Sammy and I think there is talk of donating a park bench, plaque, tree or something in his memory."

"That's thoughtful," replied Caitlín, turning on her heel and heading back to the station as quick as she could because she could not feel her feet anymore and she hoped to God it would be a lot warmer when she returned to the hall later on.

Dennis Slattery delivered on his earlier promise. There was a knock on the Leonards' door bright and early. The doctor examined Elise and strapped her sprained ankle up and told her to rest it. Pa walked the doctor out because he could sense the doctor had a fear of the dogs but more importantly he wanted to tell him about Elise becoming progressively forgetful, or senile, or something, all of which were out of character.

The doctor advised him to wait until she was literally back on her feet and to bring her in to see him in his surgery in the New Year under the guise of a follow-up examination of her ankle injury. He would do some cognitive tests on her and if that raised any concerns he could refer her to a consultant. Seeing the worry on Pa's face, he went on to reassure him that he thought that Elise was in great form and they should all enjoy the Christmas and not to be worrying beyond that.

Indeed, there was no need to be anxious at all, for word got out about her fall and with the reoccurring ailing health of their daughter, the kindness of their friends and neighbours began to flourish.

Cassie sent up a box of provisions containing tea, sugar, butter and bread along with a tin of biscuits and a Christmas cake. Dennis called for a visit with half a dozen of stout and a naggin of whiskey, but this was more for Pa. The hairdresser called in and offered to do Elise's hair for her at the house for Christmas some evening next week. The most generous of all surprisingly came from the Big House. Mrs. Wentworth came down with a small carpet which was more than adequate to replace the sodden one in Leonard's small sitting room. The water had spread there too and ruined their existing one. But, as well as that much-appreciated gift, she presented them with a striking nativity set in which all the figures were carved out of wood and beautifully hand-painted. Tadgh and Molly were delighted when they saw it and immediately ran over to set it up as soon as they arrived. Pa shouted at them to be careful, reminding them that the figures were not toys.

In the afternoon Garda Tully and Garda Kennedy called on them to see if they could assist in any way. Caitlin had brought colouring books and crayons for the kids and was glad she had brought something when she saw the generosity of everyone else.

"The greatest gift you can give anyone is your time," said Elise, "so thank you for coming."

"Well, you're spoilt for choice with all the visitors you've been having," said Tully, accepting a nice cup of hot tea from Pa.

Meanwhile the kids were busy showing Caitlín the nativity set.

"There're all made out of wood," they told her.

"I always knew that young fella was a bit thick," joked Garda Tully, pointing at Baby Jesus.

"Tully!" said Caitlín. "God forgive you!"

"Kids, come away here and let Garda Kennedy have her tea," Pa ordered.

Over the welcome brew and Cassie's biscuits, Elise recounted how she sprained her ankle. "I have a head like a sieve," she said, laughing.

Molly appeared from her room with photographs she had taken when she first got her camera. She had individual pictures of herself, Tadhg and Pa. She wrote their names on the back of each one.

"Here, Granny, now you won't forget who we are."

"They're lovely. But have you none of me?"

"We'll always remember who you are, Granny," replied Molly, giving her grandmother a big hug.

"Why don't you take one of her now?" encouraged Caitlín.

"Yes, and we'll get in it too," said Tully. "It will look like the day she got arrested!"

"I don't think that will work – I'm laughing too much," said Elise.

"Hang on, can I use this?" asked Tully, taking up the empty cardboard box the nativity set came in.

"Yes," said Molly.

"Throw us over those crayons, Caitlin."

After a few minutes Tully had cut the side of the box into a picture frame with the words 'WANTED' written underneath. They had great fun taking photographs with Elise and they all pulled silly faces within the WANTED frame.

"Are you looking forward to the concert tonight, Elise? Caitlín can't wait," said Tully, winking at his colleague.

"Oh, I don't think I'll be going. I am too much hassle for everyone right now."

Caitlín saw disappointment on the children's faces.

"Nonsense. Tully here will give you a lift. Won't you, Seán?" she suggested, getting her own back on him by creating some inconvenience for him tonight too.

"No problem at all," he genuinely replied. "How about a Garda Escort for the lot of you and a seat in the front row due to the crutches? Everyone will think you are all V.I.P.'s arriving."

"Promise you won't put the siren on," said Elise, taking him seriously.

"*Promise you will!*" squealed Tadgh in delight.

The two gardaí were still laughing when they sat into their car.

"I hope Sergeant Lamb never sees those photos or we'll be sacked on the spot," said Tully.

"You're such a big kid, Seán, but you know the Leonards have been through so much and they're such a nice family, it's great to put a smile on their faces and the good news is there is no paperwork to go with it! Seriously, though, did you see all the stuff they got and all the visitors that have already been to see them? This is a caring community when push comes to shove and yet they are tearing strips off each over with all the malicious stories about the murder."

"Christmas brings out the best in everyone so maybe you should remind them of their compassion towards one another in your speech tonight. I'll be there – with my camera."

"Shut up, Tully."

The hardy pupils from the 6th class of the local National School could be heard singing "Silent Night" outside the town hall as the crowd began to arrive in conjunction with the first snowflakes of the year. At least the snow took the poor children's minds off the harshness of the night and they began to daydream of tobogganing down hills, building snowmen and having snowball fights the next morning.

Until the begrudgers started: "Oh, we'll get in alright but we might not be able to get home," one said.

"You'll be grand. It won't stick, the ground is too wet," another replied.

Caitlín was literally waiting in the wings of the stage, watching the hall fill up. She could see the bashful and beaming Leonard family sitting in the front row beside Sammy's cousin, Ralph Coyle and his wife Nancy.

At 7 o'clock sharp she gave the nod to Sergeant Lamb to indicate it was show time.

Garda Martin had joined them to make up numbers as Tully had been dispatched to the train station in Castlebar to pick up the results of an overdue forensic test in relation to the murder investigation. The three gardaí sat behind the desk at the front of the stage.

After the stage manager hustled to get a bit of hush within the crowd, Caitlín started her address straight away. She felt if she thought about it any longer she would bottle it.

"*Ahem* ... Ladies and Gentlemen, I know you are all very much looking forward to the concert so we will not keep you long, I promise, and we certainly don't mean to subdue the lovely Christmas atmosphere that is circulating here tonight. I know the boys and girls are dying to get on stage as much as you are excited about seeing them."

"Get on with it, Kennedy," nudged Sergeant Lamb.

"Yes ... well. We would like to bring you up to date with our investigations into the murder of Sammy Joyce." She paused, realising this was harder than she thought with all the still faces looking up at her. "*Em,* we don't have an update really because we have already arrested someone, Nate Wheatley, and a Book of Evidence is currently being prepared for trial."

"Do you want me to do it?" nudged Sergeant Lamb again.

"No. Sorry. Mr. Wheatley is as much respected in this town as the late Mr. Joyce was. It is not long since it happened and I know the town is still grieving over this horrific event and emotions are running high. In fact, our station has been inundated really with yourselves coming forward with opinions of who you think was responsible for his death. The problem is, without any hard evidence, it is very difficult to investigate your allegations. And, to be honest, a lot of what you are telling us is based on hearsay, unfortunately at the expense of each other. A vicious allegation resulted in a brick being thrown through Cassie Quirke's shop window. This is a criminal offence and comes under the Unlawful Damage to Property Act. So is slander and this comes under the Defamation Act. We are appealing to you all to be mindful about who you are talking about and what you are saying. You may not realise how much damage you are doing or the fact that you are breaking the law yourselves. These are your friends and neighbours. You should be pulling together now, not throwing bricks through windows. We are also here tonight to remember Sammy. Is falling out with one another the memories you want to have? This gossiping has to end *now*."

The whole audience sat silently like reprimanded school kids who were staring back at Caitlín with blinking eyes.

"Well, she's the one that started it," said a woman, suddenly jumping out of her chair and pointing at Cassie Quirke. "She said Babs and Sammy were having an affair for ages."

"*No, I did not!*" replied Cassie.

"You did. You told us you saw them holding hands at the spring fair."

"I did not! I said they were *holding hams* at the spring fair. You know, high up in the air, for the raffle, so people could see what the prizes were."

"Whatever, then you said they were seen driving around Westport together."

"I never said that. Everyone knows neither of them can drive, you twit!"

"You said the jealousy got so bad between Babs and Frieda Huber that they had no option but to join forces and murder Sammy for all the pain he had caused them."

"I told them to cop themselves on and get Sammy to account for his actions, not kill him! Anyway, how could Babs and Frieda carry out such an atrocity? Frieda isn't even here, she is in Germany."

The woman backed off and sat down again, realising she had got the wrong end of the stick. But then, another man in the audience stood up.

"That's why I heard they got someone else to do it," he said. "The doctor, what was his name again? The weird one, doing the horoscopes and the herbs, Dr. Clippitus. Pa Leonard was reading about him in the paper. At the time of his arrest the doctor was heard to threaten Sammy for ruining his life and how he would pay for it. That's why he came back and murdered Sammy."

Another man butted in. "It can't be that doctor – were you not listening to Pa when he was reading it out? He said the doctor had returned to America, back to Detroit."

"Oh for God's sake!" interjected Pa who was now standing up too in vexation. "Obviously neither of you was listening to me. I did not read he was gone back to Detroit. I read he had a lump in the back of *the throat*! And if ye had hung around you would have heard me reading out further that he was currently in the Mater Hospital in Dublin receiving treatment for a terminal illness. So it was hardly him that did it, now was it?"

"Did he not see that coming himself?" said Waxy Carolan out loud. "He should have taken a bit more of his own medicine!"

The humour was a slight relief but the incriminations continued when another woman stood up and started attacking Waxy.

"I don't know what you are laughing about! How dare you come in here and walk among us as bold as brass? You should be locked up. Everyone knows it was *you* who killed Sammy."

An audible murmur swept through the hall.

Waxy ever so coolly took it on the chin and decided to enjoy the attention.

"Would you like to tell the court there, missus, how you came to that conclusion?"

"The dogs in the street knew you and Sammy hated each other or should I rephrase that? You hated Sammy. Sammy hadn't a bad bone in his body. He had goodwill for everyone. We had seen him call you out on numerous occasions for a lot of your misdemeanours. Like, little Molly Leonard's accident, that art robbery up at the Wentworths' house and bullying Mutey. Will I go on?"

"Yes, please do. I wasn't sure about him ratting on me on the art theft but thanks for confirming that for me. While you are at it, what proof have you to show that I had anything to do with his murder?"

"We know where you got the truck to run him down."

"Well, that's more than *we* know," said Caitlín to Sergeant Lamb.

"Jesus, this really is turning into a pantomime. I'm enjoying this. Let them at it," the Sergeant said, chuckling.

The woman continued her crusade. "You got it at the dog pound in Claremorris."

"What dog pound? Is there even a dog pound in Claremorris?" asked Waxy who was loving this fabrication.

"We heard you found the truck at the pound," she repeated.

"No, we didn't," said another man. "You're barking up the wrong tree altogether, woman, with your dog pound. We heard the location of truck was *written down* on a pound. A *pound note!*"

Everyone started laughing at this twisted tale.

"I don't think you should be applying for your Private Investigator's Licence there yet, love," said Waxy to the lady who had turned scarlet and sat back down into the hole in the ground that she wished was there. "They have arrested and charged Nate Wheatley for his murder so I don't know why you are still coming after me. You can go to hell, the lot of ye!"

"Nate Wheatley is an innocent man," said a voice from the back.

"Yeah, but do we know the real Nate Wheatley?" said a man from the side of the hall. "Sure we all know Nate was a great man for the gossip himself. No better man for carrying tales from one house to the next and adding a bit on if he felt like it. He didn't care at whose expense either, as long as he got a laugh or a boost of popularity out of it. Well, now he's caught the hot end of the poker for a change." The man was getting quite agitated about it.

"That's not fair!" shouted up a Nate supporter.

"Nate wasn't all sweetness and light, you know," the angry man continued. "I bet you all didn't know he killed a boy when he was working in England?"

Another murmur swept through the crowd.

Raised eyebrows were visible at the Garda table.

"Oh, this will be good," sniggered Sergeant Lamb.

Garda Tully arrived and pulled up a chair beside Caitlín.

"You're just in time. There's great entertainment at this concert," she whispered to him. "You wouldn't believe the allegations the crowd are flinging at each other over the murder."

"Well, I hope you find this equally entertaining because I'm at a loss," said Tully, handing over the results of the delayed forensic report to Caitlín.

Its findings were in relation to the depository residue that was lodged between the tracks of the tyres and transferred onto the fibres of Sammy's coat during the impact of the truck used in the hit and run. The fibres showed that the tyres had a very high percentage of sand and seaweed. It flummoxed Caitlín. She could feel the blood rushing to her face. Had they got it all wrong? Had they charged the wrong man? They were miles from the sea here. There was nothing significant in the results when they tested Nate's tyres other than the natural vegetation in accordance with the area the truck travelled in. She got a bad feeling and realised something was very amiss here.

Meanwhile, the carnage of character assassinations went on to its third act.

"Oh, Nate had form alright. He killed that boy in England and absconded to America and went on the run until he came home again.

Imagine, a murderer living among us all that time and now he's managed to kill someone for a second time."

"*That's way out of line!*"

"*That's not true!*"

"It most definitely is not true," agreed a gentleman, standing up. "I was the one who told you he had hit a 'boy' and damaged a fancy boat belonging to his employer and that is why he fled to the States. But it was a B.U.O.Y not a B.O.Y, you pleb! I have no idea where you heard the rest of that rubbish. Knowing you, you probably made the whole thing up. It would not be the first time you lit white smoke, mister!"

"I'll blow it up your arse if you don't take that back, you self-righteous prick! And I still think he's guilty, so there!"

"He is not. He is a good man."

The hall was beginning to divide into anti and pro Nate supporters. The tone was changing all for the worst with numerous snide remarks being exchanged to the point where no one could hear each other anymore. The comedic element was over for Sergeant Lamb and this arguing was getting on his nerves. He walked to the back of the stage and picked up a wooden lath. Returning to the table he struck the lath as hard as he could on top of it. The loud smack made some people jump with fright and it definitely brought everyone to heel.

"What is wrong with ye?" he asked loudly. "Have we just not pleaded with you to stop all of this torrid abuse of one another? All this stuff is figments of your imaginations. I mean, Jesus, is there anyone out there who can honestly tell me who killed Sammy and have the evidence to prove it?"

A mutual silence of shame settled on the audience.

Then, slowly, a hand was raised towards the back of the hall.

"Who is that?" said Sergeant Lamb. "I can't see. Can you shine the light down there?"

A spotlight shone on Mutey who was beginning to stand up.

"Sweet suffering Jesus," muttered Sergeant Lamb. "The only person who can tell us is the only one that can't speak. You couldn't make this stuff up."

Caitlín could sense Mutey's trepidation and beckoned him to come forward.

When he had walked up the isle to the front row, she asked him gently if he knew who had killed Sammy.

He nodded back at her.

"Is that person here?"

Mutey nodded again.

A whir of excitement charged through the crowd.

"Can you point the person out to us?" asked Sergeant Lamb.

Mutey raised his hand and pointed his finger at the front row on his left-hand side and, in particular, at Ralph Coyle.

"*What! That's outrageous!*" protested Ralph, his eyes popping.

"Have you anything to prove this, Mutey?" Caitlín asked him, seriously hoping he was above the hysteria of the others.

He pulled a letter out from his inside coat pocket.

"What is that?"

He handed it to her and started to gesture a fishing motion.

"What are you trying to say, Mutey?"

"At the river!" shouted up Pa Leonard who was familiar with Mutey's ways of communication.

Mutey pulled out the pen and notebook he carried and quickly scribbled down: *"Stuck in broken branch under bridge."*

This explained why it wasn't wet. Caitlin could see the letter was addressed to Sammy. It was dated the Friday before he was killed and it was from a solicitor's office in Castlebar.

"When did you find this, Mutey?" she asked.

Mutey made a pointing-down action with his finger.

"Today, he means today," explained Pa.

Mutey showed his watch to Caitlín and pointed at three o'clock.

Caitlín looked at the front of the envelope which was addressed to Sammy Joyce. She turned it over and could see the gum had perished since it had been exposed out in the open air so she could presume that Mutey had seen the letter already. She read the contents to herself.

Main Street

Castlebar

Co. Mayo

8th December 1961

Mr. Samuel Joyce

Station Road

Ballantur

Co. Mayo

Private & Confidential

Re: In the Estate of Margaret Gray, deceased.
Late of No. 240 Riverside Boulevard, Lincoln Square,
Manhattan, New York, U.S.A.

Dear Mr. Joyce,
We refer to the above entitled matter and we are satisfied to inform you that your cousin, Mr. Ralph Coyle, is no longer in a

position to pursue a claim on the Estate of your late aunt Margaret Gray.

His change of circumstances is due to a lack of evidence to show that he and your aunt endured any natural love and affection or any kind of a communicative relationship. Fortunately, your letters to and from your aunt over a substantial period of time proved you had a very meaningful and mutual relationship.

We therefore are making arrangements with Bank of America to wire the monetary balance of her Estate to us on your behalf in the sum of $100,000.00.

May we take this opportunity to wish you a very happy Christmas and a peaceful and indeed prosperous New Year.

Yours sincerely,

William R. Silke

W.R. Silke & Co. Solicitors

"Ralph Coyle, I am arresting you on suspicion of the murder of Sammy Joyce," said Caitlín, springing to her feet.

"*Kennedy, what the hell are you doing?*" demanded Sergeant Lamb.

"You can't arrest me over a letter," said Ralph.

"Oh, I think we can," she replied. "I've got it," she said, turning to her colleagues.

"Kennedy, you better be damn sure," threatened Lamb.

"I am. I just need to question Mrs. Coyle first."

"Do we need to get Detective Cullen?" asked Tully.

"I don't think so."

ell

Both Mr. and Mrs. Coyle were cautioned and brought directly to the Garda Station.

Caitlín led the line of questioning in the company of Sergeant Lamb and Garda Tully.

Nancy Coyle was brought in first.

Sitting across from her, Caitlín got straight to it.

"Can you confirm where you were the morning Sammy was killed?"

"I was still in bed, I suppose."

"Is there anyone who can confirm this? What about your husband?"

"The kids can confirm it. Ralph had left early that morning."

"Mrs. Coyle, I know this arrest is a shock but any information you can give us is very important, OK? It was brought to our attention that you are a proficient gardener, especially when it comes to growing roses. In fact, you have won prizes for them, is that correct?"

"Yes, I have won a few. But what has any of this to do with arresting us?"

"I know you may have a secret to your success, Mrs. Coyle, but you will have to share that with us now. I recall on the two occasions when I came to your house there was a pungent smell which I suspect may have been a natural fertilizer eroding in your garden. Do you use fertilizer in your garden?"

"Yes, we do."

"How often do you use it?"

"*Em*, a few times a year, maybe autumn, winter and again in spring."

"What type do you use?"

"Horse manure. Then we top that up with seaweed, not only on the roses but on the other plants and fruit trees too."

This was exactly what Caitlín was hoping to hear.

"Tell me, Mrs. Coyle, where do get the seaweed?"

"Ralph gets it in Westport. Why are you asking me about seaweed?" Nancy was clearly bewildered.

"Just bear with me, Mrs. Coyle. How exactly do you transport the seaweed to your garden?"

"Well, this year the man who Ralph gets it from gave him the loan of his truck. There was already a load on it so he told him to take the truck himself and use as much of it as we needed."

"Do you know when you did this last?"

"Yes, it was the day before Sammy died. Why, what's wrong with that?"

"When did Ralph return the truck?"

"First thing the next morning. The man wanted it back before he started his own job at nine o'clock." She paused, her eyes wide. "Oh my God, are you thinking Ralph hit Sammy? You are! Oh God ... if he did, it was an accident. Maybe he panicked, or maybe he didn't even see him."

"Take a deep breath, Mrs. Coyle. We'll move on. Can we talk about Sammy and Ralph's late aunt, Margaret Gray? We have information that Sammy was to benefit from an inheritance from her Estate, whereas perhaps Ralph was not. Do you know anything about that situation?"

"Ralph told me that his mother and this aunt who lived in America fell out years ago but Sammy's mother was in contact with her, until she died, and then Sammy himself kept in contact with her over the years. I believe her husband predeceased her and they had no children. Ralph said she was very well off. So when she died well, yeah, he was disappointed not to be a benefactor. So he tried to contest the Will but because he couldn't prove having any kind of relationship with her while she was alive, unlike Sammy, we were told his claim was not valid."

"And how did you feel about this?"

"Me? I was indifferent. You don't miss what you haven't got," she shrugged.

"And how did Ralph feel about it?"

"Ah, you know, he was disappointed, naturally. I mean it wasn't his fault that his mother and aunt fell out and yet he felt he was paying for that, while Sammy was going to do alright out of it. But, in fairness to him, he put it behind him. He just said the other day, 'If something is for you it will not pass you by'."

"Thank you, Mrs. Coyle. You have been very helpful."

Nancy Coyle was released without any charges and taken home.

Exhalations were released in the interview room. A mutual relief that the real killer with a real motive had been caught.

Ralph Coyle confessed to the murder once they put everything to him that Mrs. Coyle had confirmed. It was futile for him to deny it. He admitted that if Sammy was not in the picture anymore it would be he who would inherit the substantial legacy from his rich deceased aunt.

"Fair play to you, Kennedy! Well done," praised Sergeant Lamb. "How were you so sure Ralph had done it?"

"I was as baffled as everyone else when a seaweed deposit showed up in the forensic report. I couldn't stop thinking about how this was implicated in the hit and run. Then after reading the solicitor's letter I got a flashback to that pungent smell I got at Coyles' house each time we went there and then simultaneously I had another flashback to my summer holidays at my aunt's house in Lahinch, County Clare. She had a house near the beach and depending on which way the wind was blowing sometimes the smell of rotting seaweed would knock you out. So I knew then the truck and the seaweed were connected to the Coyles and that is why I wanted to speak to Mrs. Coyle first so I could join the dots together as to where the truck came from, who drove it, the timeline etc., before Ralph got a chance to put a different spin on it."

"Again, good job, Kennedy. We have a new bloodhound in the pack," said Sergeant Lamb.

"What about the letter though?" asked Tully. "Ralph said he knew nothing about it when we interviewed him. Isn't it a wonder Sammy didn't have it on himself, like in his coat? I mean, as it was a personal letter."

"He could have put in a separate compartment of his bag and then it fell out with all the others and blew away," said Caitlín. "Ralph admitted only taking the bag to make it look like Sammy had been killed for something that was in it. And he was in a way. 'If it's not for you it won't pass you by.' Well, Ralph Coyle certainly wasn't going to let that inheritance pass him by, that's for sure."

"It didn't pass Mutey either though," said Tully.

"Poor old Mutey. Not a bit of heed paid to him and yet he was the shrewdest of the lot," agreed Sergeant Lamb.

"No flies on him, that's for sure. They should donate another park bench to Mutey right beside Sammy's," Tully said, laughing.

"Right. I think we all deserve a reward of our own tonight," said Sergeant Lamb, rubbing his hands together. "Come on, grab your coats, we'll make it to Slattery's before closing."

Nate Wheatley was released from custody first thing the next morning. The gardaí dropped him home. Babs cooked up a big fry for him. He said it was the nicest he had ever eaten.

The town and its hinterland were covered in a sheet of snow. A fall of this nature appears to have a magic spell that puts a coat of serenity and stillness on the landscape. The town enjoyed a very peaceful and restful Christmas.

CHAPTER 17

Redemption

January generally is a quiet month due to spirits and purse-strings being a bit tired after the Christmas period, with nothing on the horizon to look forward to either. For Nate, this kind of normal was heavenly and he was enjoying being back on the road with his shop, meeting the regulars and getting on with routine. Today, however, would turn out to be a very special day for him. A rewarding affirmation of the good honest person he was.

The new postman dropped a package through the letterbox which Nate carefully opened. He read the accompanying letter of the enclosure first.

Pearl Bay
Honolulu
Oahu
U.S.A.

6th January 1962

Dear Nate,

I hope this letter finds you well, in fact, I just hope it finds you. I will never forget the night we had in 'Havana', even if I could not remember much of it the next day!

On my return home to Hawaii I hitched a ride with a cattle dealer. Unfortunately, his truck overturned somewhere outside of Tulsa in Oklahoma and I ended smashed up in hospital for 8 weeks. I heard you came looking for me. Hank and Betty told me how good old Mauna Loa ran you out of town.

I'm still with the magazine and sincere apologies for the delay in bringing the enclosed to fruition after all this time, but they are doing another feature on the expansion of the country and, wouldn't you know, the Irish are still in the thick of it. So here it is, long overdue and it couldn't happen to a more deserving guy.

Kindest regards,

Max Grundig

Nate turned over the enclosed magazine and there he was, pictured on the front cover of *Globe International*, standing covered head to toe in dirt, holding his shovel like a Samurai, with the words printed along the top: ***THE HANDS THAT BUILT AMERICA.***

"Oh my God! Babs ... Babs, come here quick and look at this! Wait till I tell everyone!"

THE END